# THE
# INVISIBLE
# THREAD

# GRAHAM ELIOT NOVELS

*The Well of the Soul*
*Among the Ashes*
*The Place of Descent*
*The Invisible Thread*

A GRAHAM ELIOT NOVEL

# THE
# INVISIBLE
# THREAD

## DOUG POWELL

**BRENTWOOD**
PRESS

# THE INVISIBLE THREAD

First Edition: 2023 White Fire Press
Second Edition: 2025 Brentwood Press, LLC
P.O. Box 132
Arrington, TN 37014
BrentwoodPress.net

ISBN: 979-8-89689-003-4 (print)
979-8-89689-007-2 (digital)

"Eye in the Sky" by Eric Norman Woolfson and Alan Parsons. Published by Universal Music - Careers on behalf of itself and Woolfsongs Ltd. and Multisongs on behalf of itself and Parsonics Tunes.

10 9 8 7 6 5 4 3 2 1

# ONE

For the first time in his life Graham Eliot stood in a library where he didn't recognize the title of a single volume. Three oak bookcases built into the walls blocked his way after entering the only door to the small room, leaving him in the company of strangers named—according to their spines—Erdnase, Hugard, Dunninger, Annemann, Tarbell. Many seemed to be limited editions published by small specialty houses, or self-published, but none were ancient manuscripts.

Unusually heavy traffic slowed the drive from his home near Disneyland to the Hollywood mansion a block away from the Chinese Theater, leaving him no time to examine the books. He located the gilded owl perched on one of the shelves, leaned forward, and spoke to it, hoping he didn't look as foolish as he felt.

"Open sesame."

The owl's eyes blinked red, and the middle bookcase retracted the wall, revealing an opulent salon filled with people in formal suits and gowns. He stepped through the secret passage and scanned the room, looking for a priest's collar among the black ties, having no other way to identify the man who invited him here, given that they had never met.

An ornately appointed bar spanned the opposite wall, elegant arches framing its shelves of spirits. Art glass, carved wooden beasts, and architectural findings festooned the room in a surprisingly eclectic coherence. His gaze landed on a pair of red velvet settees facing each other along the wall on his left. He watched a man ask a woman to pick a card as several people looked on. After she committed it to memory, she put it back.

The man cut the deck and flipped one of the packs over before shuffling the faceup half into the facedown stack. He cut randomly into the deck several times to show the stack was truly messed up. But when he spread the cards, only one was faceup—the selected card.

"Triumph!"

Graham turned, following the voice over his right shoulder to find a man in a black suit and tie smiling modestly at the woman's delighted shock. His short, black hair and wire-frame glasses gave him a practical, orderly appearance.

"It is one of the famous tricks of the professor," the man said through a thick Spanish accent.

Graham pinched his brow in a question.

The man pointed his chin toward the settees. "The professor, Dai Vernon. That is where he would entertain. But forgive me. You are the professor, too. You are Dr. Eliot?"

"And you're Father Arturo?" Graham asked, offering his hand.

"In Spain, it is Don, not Father. Don Arturo Negrón."

"And where in Spain did you say you were from?"

"Oviedo. In the mountains along the northern coast. I am the dean of the Cathedral of San Salvador." Don Arturo turned, gesturing to the staircase. "Let us talk on the way to the theater."

They passed between griffins guarding the bottom steps, overseen by an eleven-foot-tall grandfather clock on the landing. "Why are we meeting at the Magic Castle?"

"I have something to discuss that requires we see the performance tonight. Afterward, we will dine, and I will explain."

"But this is a private club for magicians. How did you get us in?"

Don Arturo smiled before answering. "The cousin of my mother is Juan Tamariz. He is a member here."

"I'm sorry," Graham said, "I don't know who that is."

"He is the greatest magician in Spain. Some say the world." Don Arturo punctuated the claim with a shrug.

To the right of the stairway, another bar filled the space, strangely decorated with dozens of owls. Don Arturo led the way to the left, threading through a dining room beneath a dome of kaleidoscopic art glass. They entered a long hallway filled with posters and playbills of magicians, some of whom were famous enough for Graham to recognize.

The hall ended at another lounge with yet another elaborate bar. Decorative tin panels covered the ceiling, and the walls, displaying more vintage posters, including several advertising someone named Chung Ling Soo. The lounge served as the lobby to a theater with a sign reading Palace of Mystery.

"This place is way bigger than it looks from outside," Graham said.

Don Arturo nodded, smiling appreciatively. "There is another, smaller theater on the other side of this one. The Parlour of Prestidigitation. And there is a room for close-up magic, as well as one in the basement. But we need to find our seats. The performance is about to begin."

An usher had saved a spot for them on the second row, and they were the last to be seated. Graham quickly took in the mahogany paneled theater as he made his way down the row, estimating over a hundred people filled the steep seats. The usher who had shown them in stepped onto the small stage as the lights dimmed and addressed the audience.

"Ladies and gentlemen, welcome to the Magic Castle's Palace of Mystery! Our featured performer tonight has won many awards including the FISM Grand Prix, Magic Circle's David Devant Award, and has been named Magician of the Year two times by the Academy of Magical Arts. He's lectured at universities including Harvard, Oxford, and the University of Chicago. He's performed in over fifty countries, and tonight he is here. Please welcome Christopher King!"

Graham couldn't recall hearing the name before, and he didn't know whether to expect a tuxedoed stereotype or someone who looked like a reject from a heavy metal band. Instead, a man Graham guessed was in his early fifties stepped into the center of the small, empty stage dressed in a black tailored suit, sky blue shirt, and matching silk tie. A salt-and-pepper goatee complimented hair swept back from his face, completing a look that was more corporate than Mephistophelian.

"Tonight, you will witness wonders that make you question the very nature of reality. You will be confronted with phenomena outside your experience, beyond the reach of your ability to explain them. Not so long ago, what you are about to see would have been considered miraculous. But even in our more enlightened world, the most scientific minds will be confounded. This is the Palace of Mystery, after all." King paused for polite laughter. "Let me be clear: I make no claim to supernatural abilities. And yet when you leave, that admission will be the most difficult thing for you to believe."

Over the next forty-five minutes, King made good on his promise. He asked for a birthday, a time of day, and a ZIP code, each from a different audience member, and added them to two randomly chosen three-digit numbers. The resulting number was 1,017,732.

When King reminded the audience it was October 17, 7:32 p.m., a collective gasp left a moment of stunned silence before the applause began.

After shuffling a deck of cards and placing them on a

small table, he threw a foam rubber ball blindly into the audience. He asked the person who caught it to throw it randomly to someone else, then asked the next person to do the same, making the third person to catch it a completely random selection. He invited that person to the stage, asked them to call anyone they wanted, and put it on speakerphone.

When the person answered, King introduced himself and asked that person to name a card. Then King asked the audience member to pick up the deck of cards that had been sitting untouched on the table the entire time and spell the name of the person he had called, dealing one card off the top for each letter in the name. The final card in the name was the same card that person had chosen.

The entire performance was surprisingly minimalistic, using only a few simple props. Other than the phone trick, there were no card tricks.

Aside from a brief infatuation with Doug Henning as a kid in the 70s, Graham had never been into magic, dismissing it as frivolous. His only real exposure to magic was through his former graduate student, Alexander Pearl, who had paid his way through school working as a restaurant magician. Alexander was engaging and entertaining, but King's performance was on an entirely different plane. It was mysterious, evoking a sense of awe and wonder—a response only enhanced by King's denial of the supernatural. Graham was so engrossed in the performance that he forgot he had been invited there for a reason until King introduced the final trick.

"Why do we believe what we believe?" King asked the audience. "Philosophers have asked this question for thousands of years. And there have been many answers: we believe because of our experience, because of a trusted authority, or through critical thinking and reasoning. But in our most honest moments of reflection, we confess that sometimes we simply wish to believe. We want something to be true that has no support whatsoever.

"For example, several years ago, eBay hosted an auction for a piece of toast featuring a pattern that resembled the face of Jesus. And someone actually bought it. And this isn't uncommon. People have claimed to see the face of Jesus in stains made by leaky water pipes or in the grain of a piece of wood. To quote Charles Fort, what they 'call knowledge is ignorance surrounded by laughter.' Our laughter.

"There is no greater example of this than the Shroud of Turin, the purported burial cloth of Jesus Christ that bears the full-body image of a man. Exactly how the image was made on the linen cloth is not known with certainty, though pigment on the cloth indicates it was painted. But there are several plausible explanations, none of which require a miracle. Its advocates include not only the gullible and simple-minded, but many intelligent and otherwise rational people, despite being conclusively, scientifically proven to be a medieval creation.

"I, myself, have seen it with my own eyes during the last exhibition. What impressed me most was how the sincerity of the pilgrims in the church around me created a profoundly reverent atmosphere. And yet the object of their faith is a lie.

"Despite being—according to its defenders—the most studied artifact in history, to my knowledge it has never been examined by an expert trained in deception and the techniques of forgery with a knowledge of artistic techniques. In other words, it has not been examined by a magician. To that end, I have offered my expertise to the Roman Catholic Church to examine the cloth at no cost to them. Pro bono. Not surprisingly, I have not heard back." King held a sardonic smile, allowing a few chuckles. "What are they afraid of? Perhaps it is this."

King turned to reach into the wings of the stage and retrieved an 11-by-17-inch frame with a built-in base.

"I have taken a piece of linen and mounted it in a frame. As you can see, there is nothing on it." King descended the steps from the stage, into the audience, and handed it to several spectators to examine. Each held it freely, turning it to study the frame for hidden mechanisms or to discern any discreet marks on the cloth. "Is everyone satisfied that there is nothing on the linen? Yes? And no secret trapdoors or anything on the stand? Excellent!"

After returning to the stage, he set the frame on the small table, then stepped forward, to one side, keeping the frame in full view. "Ladies and gentlemen, what you are about to see is not a product of the modern age. You will witness a phenomenon that could have been seen long before the industrial revolution and science harnessed the forces of nature, before electric power, before photography. Voltaire said, 'In the beginning God created man in His own image, and man has been trying to repay the favor ever since.' And so I answer Voltaire by using the Hebrew phrase that means I create by speaking. Abracadabra!"

King flicked his fingers, splaying them toward the frame. Several seconds passed, building anticipation. Then the cloth began to mottle, discolored spots spreading and connecting. Parts of the stain became fixed, waiting for others still blooming. When all the stains came to a rest, a familiar face stared from the frame. The face from the Shroud of Turin.

# TWO

For the first time in his life Graham Eliot stood in a library where he didn't recognize the title of a single volume. Three oak bookcases built into the walls blocked his way after entering the only door to the small room, leaving him in the company of strangers named—according to their spines—Erdnase, Hugard, Dunninger, Annemann, Tarbell. Many seemed to be limited editions published by small specialty houses, or self-published, but none were ancient manuscripts.

Unusually heavy traffic slowed the drive from his home near Disneyland to the Hollywood mansion a block away from the Chinese Theater, leaving him no time to examine the books. He located the gilded owl perched on one of the shelves, leaned forward, and spoke to it, hoping he didn't look as foolish as he felt.

"Open sesame."

The owl's eyes blinked red, and the middle bookcase retracted the wall, revealing an opulent salon filled with people in formal suits and gowns. He stepped through the secret passage and scanned the room, looking for a priest's collar among the black ties, having no other way to identify the man who invited him here, given that they had never met.

An ornately appointed bar spanned the opposite wall, elegant arches framing its shelves of spirits. Art glass, carved wooden beasts, and architectural findings festooned the room in a surprisingly eclectic coherence. His gaze landed on a pair of red velvet settees facing each other along the wall on his left. He watched a man ask a woman to pick a card as several people looked on. After she committed it to memory, she put it back.

The man cut the deck and flipped one of the packs over before shuffling the faceup half into the facedown stack. He cut randomly into the deck several times to show the stack was truly messed up. But when he spread the cards, only one was faceup—the selected card.

"Triumph!"

Graham turned, following the voice over his right shoulder to find a man in a black suit and tie smiling modestly at the woman's delighted shock. His short, black hair and wireframe glasses gave him a practical, orderly appearance.

"It is one of the famous tricks of the professor," the man said through a thick Spanish accent.

Graham pinched his brow in a question.

The man pointed his chin toward the settees. "The professor, Dai Vernon. That is where he would entertain. But forgive me. You are the professor, too. You are Dr. Eliot?"

"And you're Father Arturo?" Graham asked, offering his hand.

"In Spain, it is Don, not Father. Don Arturo Negrón."

"And where in Spain did you say you were from?"

"Oviedo. In the mountains along the northern coast. I am the dean of the Cathedral of San Salvador." Don Arturo turned, gesturing to the staircase. "Let us talk on the way to the theater."

They passed between griffins guarding the bottom steps, overseen by an eleven-foot-tall grandfather clock on the landing. "Why are we meeting at the Magic Castle?"

"I have something to discuss that requires we see the performance tonight. Afterward, we will dine, and I will explain."

"But this is a private club for magicians. How did you get us in?"

Don Arturo smiled before answering. "The cousin of my mother is Juan Tamariz. He is a member here."

"I'm sorry," Graham said, "I don't know who that is."

"He is the greatest magician in Spain. Some say the world." Don Arturo punctuated the claim with a shrug.

To the right of the stairway, another bar filled the space, strangely decorated with dozens of owls. Don Arturo led the way to the left, threading through a dining room beneath a dome of kaleidoscopic art glass. They entered a long hallway filled with posters and playbills of magicians, some of whom were famous enough for Graham to recognize.

The hall ended at another lounge with yet another elaborate bar. Decorative tin panels covered the ceiling, and the walls, displaying more vintage posters, including several advertising someone named Chung Ling Soo. The lounge served as the lobby to a theater with a sign reading Palace of Mystery.

"This place is way bigger than it looks from outside," Graham said.

Don Arturo nodded, smiling appreciatively. "There is another, smaller theater on the other side of this one. The Parlour of Prestidigitation. And there is a room for close-up magic, as well as one in the basement. But we need to find our seats. The performance is about to begin."

An usher had saved a spot for them on the second row, and they were the last to be seated. Graham quickly took in the mahogany paneled theater as he made his way down the row, estimating over a hundred people filled the steep seats. The usher who had shown them in stepped onto the small stage as the lights dimmed and addressed the audience.

"Ladies and gentlemen, welcome to the Magic Castle's Palace of Mystery! Our featured performer tonight has won many awards including the FISM Grand Prix, Magic Circle's David Devant Award, and has been named Magician of the Year two times by the Academy of Magical Arts. He's lectured at universities including Harvard, Oxford, and the University of Chicago. He's performed in over fifty countries, and tonight he is here. Please welcome Christopher King!"

Graham couldn't recall hearing the name before, and he didn't know whether to expect a tuxedoed stereotype or someone who looked like a reject from a heavy metal band. Instead, a man Graham guessed was in his early fifties stepped into the center of the small, empty stage dressed in a black tailored suit, sky blue shirt, and matching silk tie. A salt-and-pepper goatee complimented hair swept back from his face, completing a look that was more corporate than Mephistophelian.

"Tonight, you will witness wonders that make you question the very nature of reality. You will be confronted with phenomena outside your experience, beyond the reach of your ability to explain them. Not so long ago, what you are about to see would have been considered miraculous. But even in our more enlightened world, the most scientific minds will be confounded. This is the Palace of Mystery, after all." King paused for polite laughter. "Let me be clear: I make no claim to supernatural abilities. And yet when you leave, that admission will be the most difficult thing for you to believe."

Over the next forty-five minutes, King made good on his promise. He asked for a birthday, a time of day, and a ZIP code, each from a different audience member, and added them to two randomly chosen three-digit numbers. The resulting number was 1,017,732.

When King reminded the audience it was October 17, 7:32 p.m., a collective gasp left a moment of stunned silence before the applause began.

After shuffling a deck of cards and placing them on a

small table, he threw a foam rubber ball blindly into the audience. He asked the person who caught it to throw it randomly to someone else, then asked the next person to do the same, making the third person to catch it a completely random selection. He invited that person to the stage, asked them to call anyone they wanted, and put it on speakerphone.

When the person answered, King introduced himself and asked that person to name a card. Then King asked the audience member to pick up the deck of cards that had been sitting untouched on the table the entire time and spell the name of the person he had called, dealing one card off the top for each letter in the name. The final card in the name was the same card that person had chosen.

The entire performance was surprisingly minimalistic, using only a few simple props. Other than the phone trick, there were no card tricks.

Aside from a brief infatuation with Doug Henning as a kid in the 70s, Graham had never been into magic, dismissing it as frivolous. His only real exposure to magic was through his former graduate student, Alexander Pearl, who had paid his way through school working as a restaurant magician. Alexander was engaging and entertaining, but King's performance was on an entirely different plane. It was mysterious, evoking a sense of awe and wonder—a response only enhanced by King's denial of the supernatural. Graham was so engrossed in the performance that he forgot he had been invited there for a reason until King introduced the final trick.

"Why do we believe what we believe?" King asked the audience. "Philosophers have asked this question for thousands of years. And there have been many answers: we believe because of our experience, because of a trusted authority, or through critical thinking and reasoning. But in our most honest moments of reflection, we confess that sometimes we simply wish to believe. We want something to be true that has no support whatsoever.

"For example, several years ago, eBay hosted an auction for a piece of toast featuring a pattern that resembled the face of Jesus. And someone actually bought it. And this isn't uncommon. People have claimed to see the face of Jesus in stains made by leaky water pipes or in the grain of a piece of wood. To quote Charles Fort, what they 'call knowledge is ignorance surrounded by laughter.' Our laughter.

"There is no greater example of this than the Shroud of Turin, the purported burial cloth of Jesus Christ that bears the full-body image of a man. Exactly how the image was made on the linen cloth is not known with certainty, though pigment on the cloth indicates it was painted. But there are several plausible explanations, none of which require a miracle. Its advocates include not only the gullible and simple-minded, but many intelligent and otherwise rational people, despite being conclusively, scientifically proven to be a medieval creation.

"I, myself, have seen it with my own eyes during the last exhibition. What impressed me most was how the sincerity of the pilgrims in the church around me created a profoundly reverent atmosphere. And yet the object of their faith is a lie.

"Despite being—according to its defenders—the most studied artifact in history, to my knowledge it has never been examined by an expert trained in deception and the techniques of forgery with a knowledge of artistic techniques. In other words, it has not been examined by a magician. To that end, I have offered my expertise to the Roman Catholic Church to examine the cloth at no cost to them. Pro bono. Not surprisingly, I have not heard back." King held a sardonic smile, allowing a few chuckles. "What are they afraid of? Perhaps it is this."

King turned to reach into the wings of the stage and retrieved an 11-by-17-inch frame with a built-in base.

"I have taken a piece of linen and mounted it in a frame. As you can see, there is nothing on it." King descended the steps from the stage, into the audience, and handed it to several spectators to examine. Each held it freely, turning it to study the frame for hidden mechanisms or to discern any discreet marks on the cloth. "Is everyone satisfied that there is nothing on the linen? Yes? And no secret trapdoors or anything on the stand? Excellent!"

After returning to the stage, he set the frame on the small table, then stepped forward, to one side, keeping the frame in full view. "Ladies and gentlemen, what you are about to see is not a product of the modern age. You will witness a phenomenon that could have been seen long before the industrial revolution and science harnessed the forces of nature, before electric power, before photography. Voltaire said, 'In the beginning God created man in His own image, and man has been trying to repay the favor ever since.' And so I answer Voltaire by using the Hebrew phrase that means I create by speaking. Abracadabra!"

King flicked his fingers, splaying them toward the frame. Several seconds passed, building anticipation. Then the cloth began to mottle, discolored spots spreading and connecting. Parts of the stain became fixed, waiting for others still blooming. When all the stains came to a rest, a familiar face stared from the frame. The face from the Shroud of Turin.

# THREE

Don Arturo rested his elbows on the table and folded a fist into a palm. "I learned of your work to photograph all existing biblical Greek manuscripts when you visited the Biblioteca Nacional de España last year."

Graham squinted, searching his memory. "A tenth-century minuscule manuscript. All four gospels with commentary. Beautiful book."

"Your work, together with your reputation as a scholar of the Ancient Near East with more than twenty years of experience in archaeology, makes you qualified uniquely for what I am proposing. Rather than digitize a manuscript, I would like you to digitize both the Sudarium of Oviedo and the Shroud of Turin in order to compare them to see if they correspond."

Graham cocked his head. "I don't understand. You already have excellent photographs of both cloths. You just told me they had been used to make the kind of comparison you're talking about."

"Yes and no," Don Arturo said, raising a finger. "The photographs were taken by different people with different equipment at different times. The best photographs of the Shroud were taken before high resolution digital photography. And when those images were taken, the ability to take advantage of multispectral lighting was very limited. That is one of the things that most impressed me about your work at the BNE. I believe I read you take twenty-four images of each page, using different light wavelengths?"

"That's right," Graham said. "It allows text that has been erased or overwritten or obscured in some way to be recovered."

"Exactly! In addition to testing for correspondence, think of what might be made visible with your technology."

"But critics can easily dismiss my images by saying they were manipulated in Photoshop to get the results we wanted."

"That is precisely the problem we are trying to address, Dr. Eliot. To have the work of a single photographer using an identical process with identical equipment would produce images that could not be as easily questioned. The scale would match, the colors would be calibrated. And with the additional information due to multispectral imaging, even more detail could be compared. It could reveal a correspondence in the cloths not apparent before. In that regard, your work has an advantage over bringing the two cloths together physically."

Graham steepled his fingers, bouncing them off his chin as he thought. "Why not use the photographer from the 1978 team? I'm sure they used the most advanced equipment available. They could do what I do, and they've already been trusted with the work."

"There were two photographers in 1978," Don Arturo said, "one of whom is still alive. Interestingly, he is a Jewish man, raised Orthodox. He is agnostic now, yet he is convinced the man on the Shroud is Jesus. But he does not have the additional credibility of being a biblical archaeologist as you do. What is needed is a new face." The priest raised one eyebrow comically. "Forgive the choice of words. But we have an opportunity to conduct a new test for the first time since the carbon-14 results overshadowed the good work done by STURP."

"What's STURP?"

"The Shroud of Turin Research Project," Don Arturo said. "STURP was how the investigation came to be known."

"Okay, that makes sense." Graham nodded. "But why now?"

"Because of the SIFT challenge. A publicity stunt about to be announced by the Skeptical Inquiry of Free Thinkers: SIFT for short."

"SIFT and STURP," Graham repeated, deciding not to interrupt with a joke about how they sounded like the criminal organizations in James Bond novels—SMERSH and SPECTRE.

"Do you remember when several of your so-called televangelists and faith healers in America were exposed as frauds?"

"Back in the 80s?" Graham asked. "I remember something about an earpiece a preacher wore. His wife read information to him off of prayer cards over the radio, and he acted like he was receiving a message from the Holy Spirit."

"Exactly," Don Arturo said. "SIFT detected the radio frequency and recorded the feed. Quite a shameful incident."

"I'm glad they did it," Graham said.

"Yes, some of their work has been beneficial." Don Arturo bowed his head in acknowledgement. "They also offered a million-dollar reward for proof of the supernatural or miracles. It is a standing offer, still available to claim. Anyone who passes the initial inquiry are invited to SIFT's annual conference to demonstrate their proof, but no one has collected the prize money yet.

"Several years ago, they did something similar. They encouraged people to post videos of themselves on YouTube committing blasphemy. Quite disturbing. And I have learned their next publicity campaign is a contest for replicas of the Shroud of Turin, proving it can be created through artistic means or natural processes. Christopher King, the magician tonight, is a fellow at SIFT."

"He's just an entertainer," Graham said. "He's an excellent magician, but why would anyone take him seriously as an authority on anything other than magic?"

"That, my friend, is the problem exactly. Because of his skills as an entertainer, he has a presence that is strong in the media. He makes good television and has many social media followers. He has celebrity, which is the same as credibility to young people. The STURP team published their findings in peer reviewed scientific journals only, Physics, chemistry, and microscopy journals. Sadly, the most trustworthy sources often are poor at getting information to the general public. STURP did almost no public relations.

"Not so for their critics. They had excellent media contacts and no peer review requirements. It is said this is the information age, but I believe it would be better to call it the age of perception. How you are perceived in the media is considered truth. An illusion, if you will. Whatever clever methods are used to create replicas of the Shroud of Turin for the SIFT challenge will not prove how the image was made. But the different methods will reinforce the belief that the Shroud is a forgery.

"Sindonologists have learned from the mistakes in 1978. Your photographs would provide new evidence at a perfect time to counter their criticisms. It may even persuade the archbishop of Turin to allow new tests to be done on the Shroud. After the carbon-14 dating, the church has not allowed more scientific examination. At this point, they are content merely with preservation of the Shroud."

Graham frowned. "I'm not sure I understand. Why did they okay this plan, then?"

Don Arturo smiled conspiratorially. "It is a secret project. There have been several examinations kept from the public until after they were completed. There were such projects in

1969, 1973, and 1982. In fact, 1982 included a secret carbon-14 test done on a single thread from the Shroud. One end was AD 200, the other AD 1000. What I am proposing is another such secret examination. If your results show what we are sure they will, then for once we will be prepared to counter any criticism in the media."

"And if they do not?" Graham asked, holding a shrug.

"Then nothing has changed," Don Arturo said, then looked up to the mural on the ceiling. "Which circle of Hell do you think Dante would assign those who attack the church? The sixth—heresy, or the ninth—treachery?"

Graham chuckled. "Let's hope we never find out."

# FOUR

The grunge groove of Peter Gabriel's "Digging in the Dirt" churned from Graham's phone, announcing a call. The ringtone was an archaeological joke that quickly turned stale, then grew so overdone it became humorously predictable.

"I was going to sing that song from the 70s, 'Magic,' but I have a cold. Can't hit the notes."

"Alexander the Great," Graham greeted, calling his former graduate assistant by the stage name he used as a child magician. "Can you remember who did that one?"

Graham had made a quick connection over a common love of classic rock within a week of Alexander becoming his graduate assistant. Several running jokes evolved, one of which was quoting lyrics in normal conversation. Another was answering the phone by singing a line from a song.

"I want to say ELO, the Electric Light Orchestra."

"Sounds like it, but no. It was Pilot. Scottish band. Here's some bonus trivia. It was produced by Alan Parsons. As in *Eye in the Sky, Dark Side of the Moon, Abbey Road.*"

"No way," Alexander said. "Got me on that one. So, what'd you think of the Castle? I told you open sesame wasn't a prank."

"I'd still be stuck in the lobby library if not for you."

"Did you see the owl bar?" Alexander asked.

"Is that a Harry Potter thing?"

"Now it's my turn to drop some arcane trivia on you," Alexander gloated. "Did you see the big white owl in the middle of the other owls? It belonged to a different Harry."

"Houdini?" Graham guessed.

"No. Kellar."

"I'm not familiar with Harry Kellar," Graham said. "Guess he didn't make any movies."

"Actually, he did, kinda," Alexander said, sounding as if Graham had taken the bait. "He's the Wizard of Oz. Apparently, that's who the original illustrator of the book used as a model. Kellar was as famous as Houdini back in the day. But enough of that. What was your mysterious meeting about?"

"Ever heard of the Sudarium of Oviedo?"

"Sounds like something from *The Lord of the Rings*. New manuscript discovery?"

"Not exactly. Oviedo's a city in Spain."

"Never heard of it."

"It's in the northern part of the country. The cathedral there has a linen cloth about the size of a pillowcase they believe covered the face of Jesus on the cross and was buried with Him."

"You mean like the Shroud of Turin?" Alexander asked.

"Exactly. Except no image. Just blood and dirt and some other stains. They call it the Sudarium. They asked me to do multispectral photography on it and the Shroud."

"You're going to photograph the Shroud of Turin?"

"It's all very hush-hush, so don't tweet about it or whatever it is you kids do these days."

"Are they trying to find similarities on the two cloths?"

"That's the idea," Graham said. "But it really is a secret project. Seriously."

"I thought the Shroud was supposed to be a fake."

"Me too. That's why I didn't keep up with it after the carbon-14 test said it was no older than the mid-thirteenth century."

"What changed your mind?"

"The priest I met shared several pieces of information that were the result of other scientific tests on the Sudarium. The blood type matches the Shroud, and the wounds on the man in the Shroud generally correspond to the wounds that made the stains on the Sudarium. If that's true, then the carbon-14 date of the Shroud is somehow flawed because the Sudarium hasn't left Oviedo since the 700s."

"Very interesting," Alexander said. "But why would someone from Spain fly all the way over here to have a meeting about a secret project with you at the Magic Castle?"

"Have you ever heard of SIFT, the Skeptical Inquiry of Free Thinkers?"

"Those guys?" Alexander said. "They sponsored some YouTube blasphemy thing a few years ago. It's like atheists have become evangelical. They're better at proselytizing than Christians these days."

"Too true, unfortunately." Graham laughed. "The priest, Don Arturo, wanted me to see Christopher King's performance."

"Did he do the one where he has an audience member call someone on the phone and name a card?"

"He did. Amazing. But the priest wanted me to see a trick where he shows a blank cloth in a frame—hands it out to the audience to examine and everything—and then makes the face from the Shroud of Turin appear on it."

"What?" Alexander asked.

"It just kind of faded in, like a Polaroid."

"Why did the priest want you to see that?"

"Because King is a fellow at SIFT, and they are about to announce some new campaign or contest for people to try to recreate the image on the Shroud."

"No way."

"They want to use my images to answer the doubts the contest might create."

"But what if the pictures don't show any connection?" Alexander asked.

"That's one of the reasons why it's secret," Graham said. "As long as no one knows I'm there, then if there is no correspondence it won't create any bad publicity."

"Okay, but that still doesn't explain how you got into the Castle."

"Turns out Don Arturo is somehow related to some famous magician from Spain. His mom's cousin or something."

"Juan Tamariz?" Alexander asked.

"You've heard of him?"

"He's one of the best in the world. In fact, he's the guy who came up with the phone trick, though King puts his own spin on it. Tamariz is a magician's magician. Very influential."

"I'm impressed you're so impressed," Graham said.

"Maybe if you get to Madrid, your priest friend could get you to a performance."

"I don't know about that, but I am going to Madrid. Don Arturo had a plan already in place to give me cover. Remember when we first started working together, I went to the national library in Madrid to digitize a manuscript?"

"Sure," Alexander said. "I didn't go, but I helped process the images."

"Don Arturo arranged a lecture for me there. And while in Spain, I'll go up to Oviedo."

"And you need an assistant to help lug equipment around and help with the work, right?" Alexander said. "I mean you're like fifty, practically antediluvian, so you need all the help you can get."

Graham laughed. "Wish I could, but I have to go solo. Secrecy and all that."

"After I told you the secret password to get into the Castle?" Alexander protested.

"Sorry, man. It's a fallen world, full of injustice."

# FIVE

Graham almost lost his train of thought as he spoke, distracted by the observation that the single aisle of hardwood bisecting the seats of the assembly hall of the Biblioteca Nacional de España resembled a bowling lane. The long, narrow auditorium seemed like an afterthought, repurposing a space intended for something else. A hundred people or so listened to his stock lecture, most of them through headphones providing a simultaneous translation.

After a demonstration, he positioned himself to one side of the copy stand flanked by a pair of lighting instruments. The mechanical cradle was designed to support a fragile codex so that it exposed a page without damaging the spine. Above it, a screen projected images as he wrapped up the talk.

"Most of my career has been focused on archaeology. Up until a couple of years ago, I would have been lecturing next door at the National Archaeological Museum. In fact, they have an item on display there that is a brick from Babylon with an inscription mentioning the name of Nebuchadnezzar II." Graham showed a picture he'd taken of the display earlier that morning. "That's the kind of thing I worked on. I didn't specialize in ancient manuscripts.

"The work I've demonstrated here today was pioneered by Dr. Andrew Singer. After his unexpected death three years ago, I took over his project. One of the first manuscripts I digitized was here, at the BNE." He changed slides to show a sample of the work he had done.

"Most of the time I travel to private libraries or monastery libraries. Before the internet, New Testament scholars either had to travel to these places themselves or relied on published images, which were often not very high quality because of how the books were printed. Dr. Singer's goal was to make high resolution images of all known original language New Testament manuscripts and early translations available for anyone interested in seeing them.

"But even now, it can be hard to get permission from the owners. And even after cultivating trust and receiving permission, it's still sometimes difficult to get access. I mean literally. I've visited monasteries where the only way in was by being hauled up by rope into a trapdoor thirty feet off the ground."

Graham advanced to the next slide in his presentation, a photo of himself in a rope basket, suspended in the air, halfway to the hatch. The image sparked an unexpected flashback of lowering himself into one of the cisterns beneath the Temple Mount, watching the hatch above grow smaller as he descended, just before he watched his friend Daniel Harel get murdered and he himself killed another man in self-defense. He shook the image from his mind, forcing himself present.

"Back in the 1840s when Constantin von Tischendorf started the first search for original language manuscripts, he traveled for a couple of weeks by camel to reach Saint Catherine's Monastery, at the foot of the traditional Mount Sinai. That's where he found the oldest known Bible in existence—a fourth-century manuscript now in the British Museum, though some pages are still at Saint Catherine's. And to enter the Monastery, he had to be hauled up just like this.

"At that time, there were about 1,500 known original language manuscripts of the New Testament. Because of his work and those who have followed his lead, that number is now over 5,800—far more than any other ancient book. Interestingly, none of the 4,000 additional manuscript discoveries have changed the Greek text we use for translations. The manuscripts confirm the text as it was known back then."

Graham left time to field some questions, relayed by a translator. The final question came from the translator herself, asking if he had been to Saint Catherine's.

He paused before answering, allowing another memory to flash through his mind. Two years ago, he had been working there when the librarian, Father Nikolaos, asked him to recover an ostracon. The letter written on a shard of pottery was one of over a dozen that had been recovered in the 1930s excavation of Lachish in Israel. But the archaeologist who had discovered it, James L. Starkey, had been murdered before he could deliver it to the Rockefeller Museum in Jerusalem. Starkey's driver secretly delivered it to the monastery for safekeeping, and the librarian at the time had taken it to the church's ecclesiastical embassy in Istanbul, where it had been lost.

"I've had the privilege of visiting Saint Catherine's a couple of times. Fortunately for me, these days they use a door. The library there is now a world-class, state-of-the-art facility. It's the oldest continuously operating library in the world. Fascinating place. I could spend a lifetime there."

After promising to make himself available for questions, he ended the talk and began to pack his gear as several people made their way to the front. A woman emerged from a side door and squeezed through the group, then addressed them in a husky voice. She spoke administratively with a quick burst of Spanish before turning to Graham.

"I'm your translator, Iris Elizondo."

Graham shook the hand she offered, processing her unexpectedly perfect English accent. As she conveyed each question, he noted different details in her eclectic appearance.

A red rose adorned a headband, blooming off-center from a thicket of long brown hair, streaked with blonde, collected in a wild, loose bun. Dark eyeliner and bright red lipstick accented green eyes, echoing colors from the flower pattern of her black blouse with billowed sleeves. A long black skirt completed a look as charming as it was unique.

After the last audience member thanked him, Iris added another question of her own.

"When you were at Saint Catherine's, did you see the Pantocrator icon?"

"They have a few," Graham said. "I saw some in the small museum they have, but I didn't study them."

"The one I'm talking about is the oldest Pantocrator icon," Iris said. "From about AD 550. Beautiful example of encaustic painting. I have no idea how anyone could paint with hot, colored wax like that."

"I think I know the one you're talking about," Graham said, remembering glancing at it when he studied the Ashtiname, the covenant made by Muhammad to protect the monastery, granting them the freedom to practice Christianity. "The colors are surprisingly vivid."

"Only after restoration," Iris said. "It was covered in yellow varnish when they discovered it at the monastery in 1962. Took them years to restore it."

"Are Pantocrator icons a special interest of yours?" Graham asked, nodding at her necklace.

"What do you mean?" Iris asked.

"Your necklace. It's an orb with a cross emerging from the top, like a regal orb in pantocrator images."

Iris flattened the necklace on her palm to study it, then made a throaty laugh. "No, no. That's a Vivienne Westwood. It's her logo."

"Who's Vivienne Westwood?"

"Patron saint of punk rock. She invented it. The look,

anyway. You know—the Sex Pistols and all that lot. Some of those guys even worked at her store. Her partner, Malcolm McLaren, was their manager. Chrissie Hynde from the Pretenders was one of her models early on."

Graham smiled, catching on. "I know who you're talking about. I remember reading about her. I love all that stuff. Never got into American punk, but the English bands were great. And they definitely had a distinct look."

"I was too young to appreciate it at the time. I discovered her while I was at art school. That's what I do here. I'm an art historian. But I work as an English translator when they need me. My special interest is mainly focused on Byzantine and medieval portraits of Christ."

"Interesting specialty," Graham said.

"I'm intrigued by your work, Dr. Eliot, because it made me think about trying to start a similar project to document and collect these portraits for the purpose of comparison."

"Do you have a specific goal in mind? Something you're trying to prove?"

Iris nodded emphatically. "There is a compelling case that after the mid-sixth century, the images of Christ seem to be using an exemplar. Not universally, but there is an overwhelming correspondence of over a dozen common stylistic features. The Sinai Pantocrator is the earliest example."

"That's a fascinating observation," Graham said, "but why is it important that so many works of art copied off the Sinai Pantocrator?"

"Oh, they didn't copy off the Sinai Pantocrator. The icon itself was created from an example."

"And you are hoping to track down the exemplar?" Graham asked.

"No, the exemplar is already known." Iris smiled. "It's the Shroud of Turin."

The mention of the Shroud caught Graham off guard, and

he was unable to control his expression. He felt exposed as Iris smiled knowingly, nodding.

"How can that be?" Graham asked, recomposing himself. "The Shroud is dated 700 years later than the Pantocrator icon. And the two don't look much alike to me."

Iris's smile remained unchanged, apparently anticipating the challenge. "Seven hundred since it was first displayed in Europe. The carbon-14 date is too problematic at this point to allow it to outweigh the other evidence."

"For example?" Graham asked.

"There are many lines of evidence, actually. The one I am focused on, as I said, is based on art history. What makes the Sinai Pantocrator so interesting to me is that when the face is overlaid on the image of the Shroud the match is startling. There are about 170 details that correspond directly. Points of congruence."

"Have comparisons been made between the Shroud and other paintings of Jesus? Or other photographic portraits compared to the icon?" Graham asked.

"No photos match the Pantocrator," Iris said, "but dozens of paintings match the Shroud. Almost all Byzantine. And not just paintings. The first known coin minted with an image of Jesus is from about 695 and matches as well. The overlay shows 145 points of congruence."

"Sounds more like the Shroud was copied from them," Graham said, playing devil's advocate not only to mask his mission, but also because he was curious where this was going.

"Not according to the monks at Saint Catherine's," Iris said, growing more enthusiastic and confident with each challenge. "They believe the icon was painted using the Shroud as the exemplar, not the other way round. Setting aside the fact that the image on the Shroud cannot be explained and was certainly not painted, it is theoretically possible the Shroud could be created using the Sinai Pantocrator as the model."

But that doesn't explain the sudden appearance of similar images after the Pantocrator was created. The Pantocrator is a beautiful work of art, but that doesn't mean it would suddenly become the standard way of depicting Jesus. Something made these painters believe their exemplar was the actual face of Christ."

"You're talking about six or seven hundred years after Jesus lived," Graham said. "That is more than enough time for a standardized depiction of Christ to develop."

"Again, theoretically you are right. But the facts say otherwise. Prior to AD 545, there were a variety of ways Jesus was portrayed. There was no standard. If you'd like, I can show you the research. Do you have time?"

"I have to be at the airport in a few hours," Graham said, checking his watch. "But I can talk now."

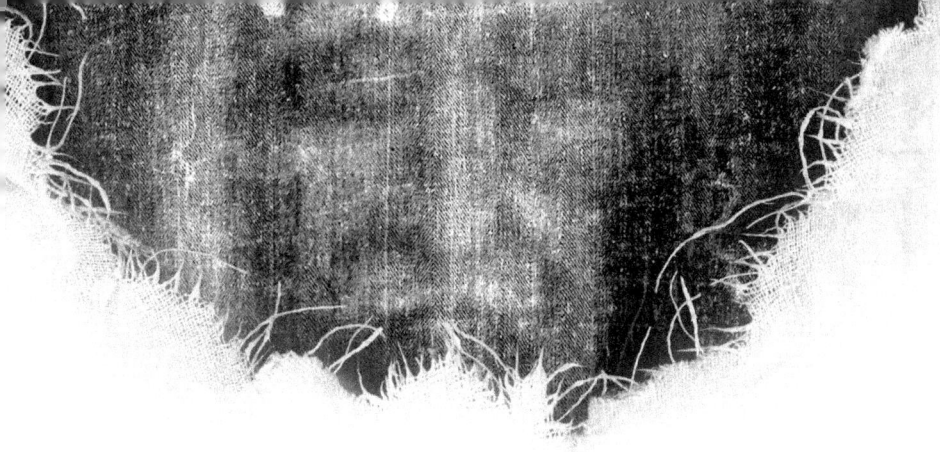

# SIX

As they walked across the street from the museum, Iris explained the Café Gijón had been a gathering place for writers, artists, and intellectuals for more than a hundred years—a taste of real Spanish culture rather than the sterile museum café. Red velvet upholstery covered the chairs and benches, matching the heavy drapes framing the picture windows against the street. Wood paneled walls held dozens of sketches Graham assumed had been made by the artists who frequented what looked like a set from a movie about expatriates between the World Wars.

She claimed a corner table, away from the window, big enough to share her laptop screen and leave room for tapas of eggplant sticks and cane honey. "Technically, the oldest image of Jesus is from the first century," Iris said, assembling a slideshow of images as she spoke. "But it doesn't really count because it's graffiti."

"Are you talking about the Alexamenos inscription?" Graham asked, picturing the crude stick figure of a crucified man with a donkey head.

"Uh huh." Iris nodded. "Alexamenos and his god. But it's obviously not trying to depict Jesus. The oldest image is from the second century, in the Callisto Catacomb in Rome." She angled the screen to display a painting on a whitewashed plaster wall. A figure stood gesturing to a second figure emerging from what looked like a guard shack, though most of the detail had been worn away by time. "It shows Jesus with short hair and no beard raising Lazarus. And look at His left hand—He has a magic wand."

Graham leaned forward, getting a better look at the line emitting from the fist of Jesus. "Funny. That scrape is in just the right place."

"It's not a scrape," Iris said. "It really is a wand—of sorts. Probably a shortened rod, like the staff Moses used in his miracles. It's actually not uncommon to show Jesus with a wand when He's performing a miracle. Here's another from the Callisto Catacomb," she said, changing the image. "Third century. Here, Jesus is shown as the Good Shepherd. See the sheep around His shoulders? Again, short hair, no beard. In this case, the artist recreated a 400-year-old image of a Greek god, putting Jesus in his place."

She advanced the slide to a similar image, though this time Jesus was shown in a toga. "This is another good shepherd image from the third century, from the Priscilla Catacomb in Rome. Yet again, short haired and beardless."

The next image was more crude, carved into a dirty wall. One figure pointed or waved an arm over a person lying on the ground. A third figure, to the side, carried a mat on his back.

"This was discovered on the wall of a house church in Syria. Jesus is healing a paralytic. Probably a wand right here." Iris traced a faint streak on the screen, then scrolled quickly through a couple of images. "Here's a fourth-century mosaic from a Roman floor in Dorset, England, that shows Jesus with short hair. And these are a couple more fourth-century images from Roman catacombs, one of Jesus healing the bleeding woman, and one between Peter and Paul. As you can see, Jesus has a beard in the second one."

Iris paused long enough to dip a spear of fried eggplant into honey and pop it in her mouth.

"In the fifth century, they start to differ even more." She stopped on each slide just long enough to make her point. "Yet another from a Roman catacomb with short hair. Here's a mosaic in Ravena, Italy, with medium length hair. And a mosaic from Santa Pudenziana in Rome with long hair and beard."

She stopped on a slide collecting the images in a mosaic. Iris took another spear of eggplant and used it as a pointer, waving it toward the screen. "Jesus is depicted in a number of ways. Good shepherd. Fisherman. Miracle worker. He's most often beardless with short hair. Clearly a recycled Roman or Greek god." She ate the tapas, giving time for Graham to absorb the information. "The point is that once Christians began depicting Jesus, there was great variety. Augustine, himself, even complained about it. He wrote—and I quote, 'For even the countenance of our Lord Himself in the flesh is variously fancied by the diversity of countless imaginations.'"

"Hard to argue with Augustine," Graham said, with a vaguely deferential gesture. "About almost anything."

"Yes, well, I'd love to see the look on Augustine's face if he could see what happened to the face of Jesus a hundred years after he said that. It wasn't until the 1930s that someone picked up on the dramatic change. A French biologist noticed it. Starting in the mid-sixth century there was suddenly a surprising uniformity."

Iris advanced the slides, showing several before continuing the narrative as she shuttled the images. The Sinai Pantocrator was followed by an image embossed on a silver vase, a coin, more catacomb images, icons, frescos, and mosaics.

"In the 1970s, historian Ian Wilson developed this observation further." She timed her comment to land on another slide presenting a batch of images as a mosaic. "There are at least fifteen features that consistently occur in images from the mid-sixth century onward that are strange details to include. And every single one of the details are found on the Shroud."

She tapped the spacebar, triggering an identical slide with the addition of the face of the Shroud of Turin in the middle of the screen. The Shroud image was shown in negative, revealing a positive image that could be compared to the images around it.

"See this V-shape at the bridge of the nose?" Again, she used a piece of eggplant to indicate the screen, then glanced at Graham, apparently wanting to see his reaction in lieu of Augustine. "It's in more than 80 percent of the icons." She pointed to the same spot on the forehead of several images. "There's a strange streak across the forehead in the Shroud. There's another running across Jesus's throat. Here they are in the icons, although the one across His throat is turned into the top of His clothes. See it?"

"Remarkable," Graham mumbled, entranced, already looking for other similarities.

"The right eyebrow is raised," Iris continued, no longer pausing between features. "And the eye itself is slightly larger. The hair is parted in the middle. They almost all have forked beards. See the connection?"

"Absolutely. Once you know what to look for, you can't miss it."

"Exactly. Now look at this."

The next slide placed the Sinai Pantocrator next to the negative image of the Shroud face.

"Earlier, back at the museum, you said you didn't see the resemblance between these two images."

"I still don't," Graham shrugged. "I see how they share the same odd details, but they don't look like each other to me."

"Right. Well, here is the Shroud by itself," she said, advancing the slide, displaying the image in the center of the screen. "And here is the Pantocrator by itself." The icon eclipsed the Shroud image. "Watch what happens when I blend them, overlaying one on the other."

The combined images appeared on the screen; the dark areas of the Shroud image subtracted to allow the icon to show through. The lighter parts of the Shroud image discolored the darker parts of the icon, as if it had been recolored.

"It's an exact match." Graham leaned closer to the screen. "The eyebrows, the pupils of the eyes, the beard. They fit together perfectly. It's like the icon colors in the Shroud image. The hairline is the same, the part and everything. And the blood stains from the Shroud map right onto the icon."

"The nose is the same size and shape," Iris added. "All the features register together."

Graham leaned back, keeping his eyes on the overlay. "I don't know what to say. I'm stunned."

Iris waved a hand near the screen. "Like I said, there are 170 points of congruence. And here's the coin I was talking about," she said, tapping the spacebar.

A gold coin replaced the image, featuring a portrait that vaguely resembled the Pantocrator. She tapped again, showing a close-up of the face.

"This was minted in 695 by Justinian, the first time Jesus appeared on a coin. Check out this overlay."

This time the highlights of the coin became highlights on the Shroud, giving the image dimension.

"Another perfect match," Graham said.

"With 145 points of congruence," Iris said.

"You've convinced me. The theory definitely has merit. What do people who doubt the authenticity of the Shroud say about this theory?"

"The same thing you said, actually. That the Shroud is the product of the development of a standard depiction. They say that what I just showed you is a process that led to the

Shroud. Basically, they dismiss the theory as advocates just seeing what they want to see, like seeing shapes in the clouds."

"I've looked at clouds from both sides now," Graham deadpanned, then smiled.

"Never liked that song," Iris said archly. "But I love Peter Gabriel."

Graham realized his phone was ringing and excused himself, still feeling Iris's smile as he stepped out to the sidewalk.

# SEVEN

A coughing fit greeted Graham as he answered the phone.

"Sorry about that." Alexander suppressed another cough. "I was trying to do 'Never Been to Spain.' But I have a tickle in my throat."

"Alexander the Great, you did not miss your calling as a singer," Graham said, stepping into the shade of the café's crimson awning.

"Hey, man, I haven't been to bed yet, so I deserve a little grace."

Graham calculated the nine-hour difference as he looked at his watch. "It's only two a.m. If you're pulling an all-nighter, you're going to need something more rockin' than Three Dog Night. Doing some research?"

"Yes, but not for school," Alexander said. "I was at the Magic Castle. After you told me about Christopher King's Shroud illusion, I had to go see it."

"Figure out how it's done?"

"I worked out possible methods for some of the others, but not that one. However, I did end up chatting with him."

"Tell him your owl trivia?" Graham asked.

"Ha! No, we were at the Hat and Hare. A British pub they have in the basement. I was sitting there showing the guy next to me a couple of tricks, and King took the seat on the other side of me. The Houdini Seance had just let out, and it was the only open seat."

"The Houdini Seance?"

"It's a special room you can book with a private chef. And after the meal, there's a seance to contact Houdini. That's what Houdini's wife did every year for ten years on the day of his death—Halloween."

"Wait a second," Graham said, "I thought you told me once that Houdini crusaded against Spiritualists. Why would his wife try to contact his spirit?"

"Houdini didn't rule out the possibility of the spiritual realm. What he was against was con men using magic techniques to prey on people and cheat them out of money. Magicians are honest liars. They know you know they don't have any powers and that the tricks aren't done as the magician says when he presents them. But everyone pretends otherwise for the show. It's entertainment. Like watching a movie. But Spiritualists weren't honest liars. They were just plain liars. That's what Houdini fought against."

"Still doesn't explain the seance, though," Graham said, signaling Iris through the window with a finger, asking for one more moment.

"So, while Houdini was dying, his wife came to his hospital bed and he told her, 'Rosabelle, believe.' Except his wife's name wasn't Rosabelle, it was Bess. They had an arrangement that when one of them died, the other would hold a seance, and if there really was a way for spirits to contact the living through a medium, they would have a way to prove it. Otherwise, they'd know the medium was a fraud."

"How could they prove that?" Graham asked.

"Rosabelle was the name of a code they used in a mind reading act they did early in his career. They could speak to each other in code that sounded like normal conversation. Bess would be blindfolded onstage while Houdini went into the audience. They would hand him items and he would ask Bess what he was holding, or what the year was on a borrowed coin.

"So anyway, 'Rosabelle, believe' meant that if Bess heard the medium use the code words to spell out the word believe, then she would know Houdini had made contact, and that the medium was legitimate. Bess held seances on the anniversary of his death for ten years."

"Did she hear it?" Graham asked.

"Once. But the guy was a fraud who probably got the code out of her when she was drunk. Or from a book published in England that revealed the secret. But Houdini fans still hold the seance every year. And it's a nightly occurrence at the Castle.

"Anyway, that's how Christopher King ended up next to me. I didn't know he was there at first. He watched me for a bit, then he gave me some suggestions, and we just started talking. I told him how much I enjoyed his show. I think I mentioned I was a student, but I didn't say where or what degree I was working on. Never came up.

"Then I remembered a couple of Gospel magic tricks that illustrate some miracles, and I told him about them. I told him it's interesting that the same trick can be used to illustrate a biblical truth in one magician's hands but debunk it in another. And that turned into this great discussion about religion. I didn't argue against him, just asked questions and let him make his case."

"Did you lose your religion?" Graham asked.

"That is not me in the spotlight," Alexander said, completing the REM reference. "But he did tell me about SIFT. And then he invited me to the SIFT convention, ThinkCon, they call it. You know like the Ancient Near East Society annual meeting you go to each year. He said this year's meeting is next week, in Nashville. He said if I can get myself out

45

there and find a place to stay, he'll comp me a pass, being a student and fellow magician."

"A spy in the house of love."

"Yeah, like Houdini. Except instead of going undercover to expose Spiritualists like he did, I'll be undercover with the skeptics. That must be where they're going to make an announcement and launch the PR campaign."

"I was thinking the same thing," Graham said. "How about I give you some frequent flier miles to get you there. I have a bunch of hotel points, too. It might be helpful knowing what's happening on the other end. I know it's short notice, but can you get someone to cover your classes?"

"Not a problem. I'd love to do it."

"If you learn anything undercover, we could use the Houdini code."

"Sounds like a plan," Alexander laughed. "How's Spain?"

"Just finished my lecture at the BNE. Leaving for Oviedo in a couple hours. Actually, I'm in the middle of talking to an art historian whose focus is on how the Shroud is the exemplar for early portraits of Jesus. She's got a compelling case."

"She?" Alexander exaggerated the question.

"Don't go there. She's also my translator. British expat."

"Well, this just gets more fascinating."

Graham pointedly ignored the comment. "Say hello to Music City for me."

# EIGHT

"Sorry for the interruption," Graham said, retaking his place. "You have a pretty convincing case that the images seem to be using an exemplar. But what I don't understand is why it suddenly happened in the mid-sixth century."

"The Image of Edessa." Iris froze in anticipation, searching for recognition in Graham's eyes before continuing. "That's when it was discovered, in AD 544. Walled up in a niche above the city gate. Except now Edessa is called Urfa."

"I've been there. Driven through it, at least." He considered recounting the all-night bus ride across southern Turkey to the U.S. consulate in Adana a year earlier but decided his escape from Kurdish freedom fighters in Cizre was too much of a distraction. Especially because it would mean explaining he had been there to investigate the real location of the mountains of Ararat, landing place of Noah's Ark—and it was two hundred miles south of the traditional Mount Ararat. "You're talking about the legend of the face of Christ on a cloth, right?" Graham asked, putting his thoughts on track.

"It's not a legend," Iris said. "Well, certainly some of the story is, but not all of it. There's too much historical evidence supporting it. Not enough to prove the cloth was authentic, but enough to be reasonably sure it was an actual object and an historical event."

"And you're telling me that the Image of Edessa is the

same thing as the Shroud of Turin? Pretty big leap in logic, isn't it? Why would the burial Shroud of Jesus be hidden in the wall of a city five hundred miles from Jerusalem?"

"You really don't know?" Iris tilted her head, studying him.

"I told you—I lost interest after the carbon dating. And I was never that into it in the first place."

Iris brushed a stray hair away from her face, composing herself to tell the story. "Right. The tradition goes like this. Abgar, king of Edessa, suffered from some kind of medical condition. Probably leprosy. He had heard about Jesus's healing miracles, so he sent an envoy with a letter asking Jesus to come. Jesus responded with a letter of His own that said—"

"Wait a sec," Graham interrupted. "Jesus wrote a letter?"

"Yes, according to Eusebius. It's in his *Ecclesiastical History*, so the story was widely known by 325 or so." She woke her laptop, quickly navigated to a highlighted passage in the PDF, and began to read:

> "Blessed art thou who hast believed in me without having seen me. For it is written concerning me, that they who have seen me will not believe in me, and that they who have not seen me will believe and be saved. But in regard to what thou hast written me, that I should come to thee, it is necessary for me to fulfill all things here for which I have been sent, and after I have fulfilled them thus to be taken up again to him that sent me. But after I have been taken up I will send to thee one of my disciples, that he may heal thy disease and give life to thee and thine."

Graham felt Iris watching him as he studied the text. "And you think the letter is authentic?"

"The people of Edessa thought it was. They treasured a

document they claimed was the original. And the text is copied in an ancient inscription in a tomb there. Egeria, the early Christian pilgrim, wrote about it in her *Travels* fifty years after Eusebius. She was even given a copy of it by the bishop. But I think the letter itself is apocryphal. That's the legend part. However, it does document an early conversion by King Abgar of Edessa. Jesus was crucified shortly after supposedly writing the letter. Following Jesus's ascension, the apostle Thomas sent Addai to Edessa. Addai was one of the seventy Jesus sent out during His ministry, also called Thaddeus. Addai healed Abgar, and the city embraced the faith."

"Okay," Graham said, reading the screen, "but I don't see any mention of the Shroud."

"That detail comes from a different *Ecclesiastical History*, by Evagrius in 590." Iris opened another PDF and scrolled to a highlighted section. "Evagrius called it 'the divinely wrought image, which the hands of men did not form, but Christ our God sent to Abgarus on his desiring to see Him.'"

"I'm still confused." Graham leaned back, folding his arms across his chest. "The first time any kind of image is mentioned is five-and-a-half centuries after the crucifixion. If Eusebius and Egeria knew about the letter, surely they also knew about the Shroud. So why didn't they mention it?"

Iris nodded in anticipation before Graham finished the question. "As I said, it was hidden until 544. When Abgar converted to the faith, he destroyed the statue of a Greek god standing at the city gate. Anyone who wanted to enter Edessa had to offer a prayer to it. He put what they called the acheiropoieta—the image not made with hands—in its place. He mounted it on a board and adorned it with gold so that everyone who passed through the gate could see it. Most likely, the cloth was folded in eighths and placed in a gold box with a window cut out of it, revealing the face.

"King Abgar's son shared his father's faith. But Abgar's

grandson reverted to paganism. The bishop was afraid the grandson would destroy the image, so he placed a tile on top of it and walled-in the niche that held it. By the time Egeria visited, it had been hidden for three hundred years."

"Even if the location was lost, surely they didn't lose the memory—if it really existed at all in the first place."

Iris shrugged. "All we know is that it was lost and not mentioned until the Persians besieged the city in 544. During the attack, the bishop was visited by an angel who told him to recover the image and use it as a palladium—a talisman of protection. The angel guided the bishop to the exact location of the Shroud. Not only was the Shroud preserved, but the tile that had been placed over it had a copy of the image. Somehow the image had been transferred to it.

"The angel told the bishop to carry the image through the city. This time the bishop was guided to a spot where copper pots started rattling. The Edessenes realized the shaking was caused by the Persians tunneling under the city wall. The people of Edessa dug down to the tunnel, poured oil into it, and lit a fire, killing the Persians and ending the siege."

"Another legend, of course," Graham said.

"Probably," Iris admitted, "but the siege is historical. And that was the point in time when an image was displayed. Even after the Muslims conquered the city a hundred years later. It remained in Edessa up until 943. That was when the emperor sent soldiers to retrieve the image and bring it to Constantinople. The Muslims discovered there were actually three images. Copies had been made by the Nestorian Church and the Monophysite Church. But the bishop sent by the emperor could tell the difference and took the authentic cloth back. The next year it was welcomed by Constantinople in a procession parading it around the city before being added to the relics in the Church of Blachernae. Fifty years later, the letter from Jesus was retrieved."

"And this is documented where?" Graham asked.

"*The Narratio de Edessa*, a history commissioned by the emperor when the image was recovered and put on display. A crusader by the name of Robert de Clari, wrote about it just before Constantinople was sacked in 1204 during the Fourth Crusade."

"A proud moment in church history." Graham shook his head.

"Christians attacking Christians," Iris said. "Brilliant. The letter from Jesus was destroyed. And that was when the Mandylion—as it had come to be known—disappeared."

"Not destroyed?"

"All we know for sure is that a hundred and fifty years later, the Shroud was displayed in Europe for the first time, in Lirey, France. It was owned by a French knight who did not explain how he had come into possession of it. Eventually, the king of Savoy acquired it and brought it to the capital, Turin, in 1578. There's more to it, of course, but that's the general itinerary. It's all in Ian Wilson's work. Very well documented."

"I'm not sure what to say," Graham stammered. "I'm completely overwhelmed with the sheer mass of documentation you've gathered. Quite impressive."

Iris made a curtsey bow as well as she could seated behind a table. "Well, thank you."

"What do you know about the Sudarium of Oviedo?"

"I'm not at all sure what you're talking about," she said, shaking her head.

"Not important," Graham said. "You have given me a great deal to think about and I wish we could talk more. But, unfortunately, I have to start heading for the airport."

Iris rummaged through her bag, pulling out a card and placing it in front of him. "If you have any questions or need a translator while you're in Spain, please don't hesitate to give me a call."

# NINE

Graham slid noise-canceling headphones over his ears and propped his iPad on his lap. He had downloaded a PDF of *Conquest of Constantinople*, an eyewitness account mentioning the Image of Edessa by Robert de Clari, the crusader cited by Iris. The hour-long flight to Oviedo would give him just enough time to look into it.

He typed Shroud into the search field but had no results. He entered Edessa, but again found nothing. He paused, considering possible terms to use, then searched relic. Several hits came back, listing two sequential page numbers, indicating the same passage. He clicked the first hit and began reading.

> *The palace of Boukoleon was very rich. Within this chapel were found many rich relics. One found there two pieces of the True Cross as large as the leg of a man and as long as half a toise, and one found there also the iron of the lance with which Our Lord had His side pierced and two of the nails which were driven through His hands and feet, and one found there in a crystal phial quite a little of His blood, and one found there the tunic which He wore and which was taken from Him when they led Him to the Mount of Calvary, and one found there*

*the blessed crown with which He was crowned,*
*which was made of reeds with thorns as sharp as*
*the points of daggers. And one found there a part*
*of the robe of Our Lady and the head of my lord*
*Saint John the Baptist and so many other rich*
*relics that I could not recount them to you or tell*
*you all the truth.*

Although he had only been there a handful of times, Graham still considered Istanbul one of his favorite cities to explore, and he pictured the ruins of the palace along the shore, between the Sea of Marmara and the Sultan Ahmed Mosque—the Blue Mosque. But it was the memory of his last visit that distracted him from the book.

He had honored Father Nikolaos's request to try to find Starkey's lost ostracon in the abandoned metochion, the church's ecclesiastical embassy near the Ecumenical Patriarchate. He had also visited the Topkapi Palace Museum, headquarters of the Ottoman Empire, and now archive of its history. He had gone there to tour the Chamber of Sacred Relics, hoping to view the original Ashtiname—the compact with Muhammad.

Instead, he was surprised to discover an exhibit of biblical relics. The staff of Moses, King David's sword, Abraham's cooking pot, Joseph's turban, and the hand of John the Baptizer were displayed without any caveats questioning their authenticity. Graham wondered if they were part of the same collection Robert de Clari had seen. He shrugged, then continued reading.

*Now there was still another relic in this chapel*
*which we had forgotten to tell you about. For*
*there were two rich vessels of gold hanging in the*
*midst of the chapel by two heavy silver chains.*
*In one of these vessels there was a tile and in the*

*other a cloth. And we shall tell you where these relics came from. There was once a holy man in Constantinople. It happened that this holy man was covering the house of a widow with tile for the love of God. And as he was covering it, Our Lord appeared to him and said to him (now this good man had a cloth wrapped about him): 'Give me that cloth,' said Our Lord. And the good man gave it to Him, and Our Lord enveloped His face with it so that His features were imprinted on it. And then He handed it back to him, and He told him to carry it with him and touch the sick with it, and whoever had faith in it would be healed of his sickness. And the good man took it and carried it away; but before he carried it away, after God had given him back his cloth, the good man took it and hid it under a tile until vespers. At vespers, when he went away, he took the cloth, and as he lifted up the tile, he saw the image imprinted on the tile just as it was on the cloth, and he carried the tile and the cloth away, and afterwards he cured many sick with them. And these relics were hanging in the midst of the chapel, as I have told you.*

Graham leaned back, evaluating what seemed to be a corruption of the Edessa story. Except the cloth wasn't purported to be the burial Shroud of Jesus. In fact, there was no mention of anything that could be taken as the Shroud of Turin. He reminded himself to ask Don Arturo what his take was on Robert de Clari. The thought of Don Arturo triggered the memory of how he had described himself as a sindonologist. *Sindon.* The Greek word for *Shroud.* Graham searched for the word and returned a hit.

*And among the rest, there was another of the
churches which they called My Lady Saint Mary
of Blachernae, where was kept the sindon in
which Our Lord had been wrapped, which stood
up straight every Friday so that the features of
Our Lord could be plainly seen there. And no
one, either Greek or French, ever knew what
became of this sindon after the city was taken.*

Graham planted his elbows on the armrests of the seat,
tenting his forearms and resting his chin on his fists as he
stared at the passage. Yet again, he was startled at the amount
of evidence indicating the Shroud was known in history prior
to the carbon-14 date.

Robert de Clari's account might not be conclusive evidence for the authenticity of the Shroud of Turin, but it was
another link in the chain of provenance. *If* it was authentic,
Graham reminded himself. The account didn't seem fanciful,
but de Clari could have seen a copy or a forgery. And what
did de Clari mean that it *stood up?* The only image Graham
could picture was of the Shroud of Turin displayed vertically.
But was he injecting an artifact that had yet to be created into
the scene, or was he recreating what de Clari saw?

The plane began the descent into Oviedo, and Graham
watched the city lights grow closer, rippled by hills between
the mountains of Asturias. He was surprised at its size, given
that he had never heard of it. Signs at the airport bragged it
was the hometown of the queen, but that was the extent of his
knowledge of it. The sack of Constantinople less than a year
after de Clari's account reminded him that Asturias was one
of the few regions in Spain not conquered by the Moors. The
claim that the Shroud was secreted to safety in Europe had
precedence in the Sudarium.

# TEN

The website for the Metropolitan Cathedral Basilica of the Holy Savior described its Gothic tower alternately as a finger pointing to heaven, a watchtower, and a stairway linking heaven and earth. Graham decided it was most like a location pin, visible above the terra cotta roofs between it and the hotel, enabling him to navigate there without a map.

He had arrived at the Gran Hotel España twelve hours earlier, exhausted, still acclimating to the time difference, leaving him no energy to explore the area. When he awoke before dawn, he was fully rested, unable to will himself back to sleep, and redeemed the time testing his equipment.

The Graz Traveller Conservation Copy Stand packed into a shell the size of a large suitcase. After placing it on the coffee table, he unfolded the lighting instruments and camera mount, then attached the power cable. He used the control unit to open the cradle to 105 degrees, its maximum angle, and placed the assembly instructions on the surface for a test image.

He mounted the fifty-megapixel camera, connected it to his laptop, used the laser to focus the image precisely, then shot the image. The 300-megabyte file saved, and he changed the lighting temperature and took another test image.

In his work with manuscripts, he would take twenty-four

different images of the same page, changing the lighting for each. He wondered what the same technique could possibly reveal on the Sudarium and Shroud.

He collapsed the equipment and packed it in less than ten minutes, using the remaining time to review what he had learned about the Sudarium.

Now, at 10:00 a.m., Oviedo still seemed to be waking up as he entered the cathedral plaza a block and a half from the hotel. Three elaborate arches—the central one larger than the others— formed a portico covering the entrance to the church, an iron gate spanning each of them. Inside, several tourists waiting for the doors to open to tourists looked toward Graham as the sound of the small dolly holding the camera stand case rattled across the flagstone pavement. He studied the facade of the cathedral on his left as he passed it, heading for the building directly ahead of him.

Three plain arches humbled by their neighbor opened into a small courtyard next to a bookstore for the diocese. He stepped through the door into a small waiting room with a reception desk. A middle-aged woman looked up, keeping a neutral expression on her face.

"Excuse me, I am here to see the dean."

Before she could respond, an elderly priest with a kind face entered the room, hands clasped across his stomach. "Welcome. You are Dr. Eliot? We have been expecting you. I am Don Gustavo. I am the dean."

"I am here to see Don Arturo," Graham said, feeling lost again.

"The bishop apologizes for the…" the priest hesitated, searching for the word, "inconvenience. Don Arturo is not dean anymore. I serve in his place temporarily."

"I'm sorry, I don't understand." Graham quickly scanned the room as if looking for an explanation. "I exchanged emails with him yesterday. Is he okay?"

Don Gustavo made a single, slow nod. "He is serving elsewhere. The bishop is aware of the arrangements you made, but your work is needed no longer. Again, the bishop apologizes."

"But I have all the equipment right here," Graham said, bobbing his head toward the case and backpack. "It only takes a few minutes to set up. I could be done in an hour."

"It is not the issue, Dr. Eliot. The bishop appreciates your willingness to serve the church, but he has chosen not to proceed with photography. At this time there is no service for you to perform."

"After I came all this way?" Graham tried to strain confrontation from the words while still registering protest. "I had to completely rearrange my schedule to accommodate this trip at such short notice. What's really going on here?"

Don Gustavo bowed in acknowledgment, his face a mask of impenetrable benevolence. "Your confusion is understandable. I know you are disappointed. Unfortunately, there is nothing to be done."

"You can't explain it to me?" Graham asked, affecting a tone that asked for mercy.

"But I have already." Don Gustavo added an apologetic arched brow to his otherwise unchanged expression.

Graham made a futile gesture, releasing a sigh as his hands dropped to his sides, as if pumping a bellows. He drifted in a fog of confusion out of the courtyard and stared up at the cathedral wondering what happened to Don Arturo. He stopped and pulled out his phone to call Don Arturo, but was interrupted by the sound of his own name.

"Dr. Eliot, why did they not let you see the Sudarium?"

He turned to see a tall, big-boned man holding a camera in front of his face, making the furry shotgun mic look like a unicorn horn. Long hair draped from beneath a loose beanie onto the shoulders of his hoodie.

"Why did they not let you see the Sudarium?" the man called again.

Graham squinted, stupefied, trying to figure out how the stranger knew his name and why he was there. And how could the man possibly know he had been turned away?

"What is the church hiding, Dr. Eliot?"

"I don't know," Graham stammered, unsure how to respond or if he should even try. The fact that the man asked the same questions he was asking himself both affirmed him and amplified his confusion. He decided the best course of action was to keep walking.

"What is your opinion of the Sudarium?" the cameraman asked, tracking alongside Graham. "Is it a fake?"

Graham stopped, surprised by the question, and looked at the man, dully repeating the word as if testing it. "Fake." He collected himself, focusing his attention. "Who are you?"

"I want the truth," the man said. "No hiding. No lies."

"I'm sorry, I can't help you." Graham turned from the camera, grabbed the case, and hurried away as quickly as he could, thankful the man didn't follow him to the hotel.

He pushed into his room, seeking sanctuary from any more surprises. But as he turned to lock the door, he realized he was standing on an envelope signed with the letter A. He tore it open, tapped out the folded paper, and read.

*Ermita de Santiago, Monsacro, as soon as you can come. Do not call. Don Arturo.*

Graham opened Google Maps, entered Ermita de Santiago, Monsacro, and found it fifteen miles south, in the hills outside of the city. He had no desire to leave, yet he needed to speak with Don Arturo to learn what was going on.

After the concierge arranged a taxi, he walked self-consciously through the lobby, expecting another ambush from the cameraman. He scanned the area from the safety of the taxi as it pulled away but saw no sign of the man.

The driver struggled to find the English words to explain there was no road to the Ermita de Santiago. It was only accessible by hiking. The closest he could get was the village of La Collada.

Graham nodded and gave the driver a thumbs-up, having no other choice, then opened his map again to confirm what he thought he understood. What he had interpreted as a road was apparently a hiking trail with the trailhead on the edge of the village.

It took thirty minutes winding through hills to reach La Collada, at the foot of a small mountain. Graham watched the taxi leave, feeling cut off from the world, then studied the trail map posted on the side of the road. The two-and-a-half-kilometer route zigzagged in switchbacks before straightening out to end at the meeting place.

The smooth line of the map didn't convey the rocky terrain he had to cross—the difference between plans and how they actually worked out. The question now was if Don Arturo really was waiting on the other end.

# ELEVEN

A canopy of trees covered the trail as it inclined in a straight route for more than a quarter of a mile before emerging into the mid-day sun. Monsacro towered over Graham in an aggregate of rocky scarps terraced haphazardly. He could see the slaloming path ahead like a bad stitch being pulled apart by a small gorge. Stray rocks looked like rubble among the scrub brush, a slowly advancing avalanche down the steep slope. Power lines stretched overhead like an abandoned ski lift.

A large, grassy plateau marked the end of the main ascent, offering a panoramic view of the low mountains of Asturias. La Collada was hidden in the trees below, but Graham could clearly see Oviedo. He checked the map on his phone and found he was only seven and a half miles from the cathedral as the bird flies.

He turned back to the field and scanned the area as he crossed it. On the bluff to his right, a small building constructed of stacked stone and a terra cotta roof overlooked the valley. The curved wall of an apsidal chancel broke the rectangular shape, indicating it was the chapel he'd seen on the map—one of two buildings on the mountain. Half a dozen horses milled near a pond in the middle of the expanse, unsaddled and apparently ownerless. A group of hikers were silhouetted on the top of the ridge hedging the area, on their way to the peak.

The second building—his destination—clung to the side of the hill on the far side of the plateau, between the pond and the ridge. The octagonal building used the same light stone and terra cotta roof as its sister. Its apsidal chancel attached to the building at an awkward angle, off-axis from the arched doorway overlooking the expanse of grass. The heavy wooden door was cracked open, and Graham stepped inside.

Plaster walls encompassed a rough stone floor to form a chamber furnished only with a heavy stone altar supporting several statues. Iron bars fenced the apse, making it look like a prison cell. Don Arturo rose from behind the altar, his black clerical clothing contrasted against the light room, giving the impression of a shadow with substance.

"Dr. Eliot. Thank you for meeting this way."

Graham shook hands and scanned the room again. "Where are we, exactly?"

"This is where the Sudarium was hidden during the Muslim conquest. Saint Toribio, the bishop who cared for it, hid it inside the well here." He tapped the surface of the altar.

"Why are you hiding here?"

Don Arturo smiled sadly. "The bishop was not pleased with the plan to photograph the Sudarium. He wants to protect the sanctity of the church from unnecessary distractions. To him, the project appeared too worldly. He does not share my desire to be more active in culture. Especially in the media. He said reacting to cultural whims would send a message that those who want to destroy the church were allowed to decide the church's place in the world. He believes that even if the Sudarium could be conclusively connected to the Shroud, nothing would change. The holy relics would simply be attacked in a different way. He says the project is a response to a question unbelievers will not accept an answer to, and that believers do not have."

Graham sighed. "I'm not surprised, actually. What does surprise me is that the project got this far. I thought as dean of the cathedral it was under your purview."

Don Arturo fished a bottle of water from his backpack and handed it to Graham. "Yes, that is true. But within limits. I acted within my responsibility, but I can be overruled. The funding for this work comes through the diocese. Someone in the bishop's office brought the expense report for your flight and hotel to his attention. He was so displeased with the project that I have been suspended from my duties as dean. Temporarily, Lord willing. I was also told to have no contact with you. That is why we are meeting here."

"You told me it was a secret project, but I didn't think it would be kept from the bishop."

Don Arturo made an empty-handed gesture, an apparent show of innocence. "I assure you it was not my intention to undermine the bishop's authority. But I am afraid his traditionalism, though well-intended, isolates the church from the very people it is trying to reach."

"Careful now," Graham said, raising a warning finger. "You're starting to sound like Martin Luther."

"Better him than Servetus," Don Arturo said.

Graham laughed, instantly recalling the infamous chapter in Reformation history. Michael Servetus was a Spanish scientist, medical doctor, and theologian in the sixteenth century. His theological contributions, however, were not as well-received as his scientific ones. His rejection of the Catholic Church and the doctrine of the Trinity put him at odds with both Rome and the Reformers. Accused of heresy, he fled to Geneva, but found no sanctuary. He was burned at the stake—a sentence falsely attributed to John Calvin by his detractors.

"But all you are trying to do is confirm the claims of the relic that built this church," Graham said. "Authenticating the

Shroud through the Sudarium helps the church, not hurts it. Surely the bishop can understand that."

Don Arturo shrugged. "As I said, the bishop does not disagree with the principle, only the premise. If those who reject the authority of the church can dictate its actions, then what authority does the church really have at all? We both understand the position of the other, but we are at an impasse. I had hoped when the bishop learned about the project, he would see the church acting proactively to engage those outside the church. An intersection of all the interests. And at the very least, I had hoped not to have to explain myself to him until after your work had been done. I apologize for putting you between the sword and the wall."

"And I'm not even sure what to believe about the Sudarium in the first place," Graham said. "Or the Shroud." He finished the rest of the water and set the bottle on the altar covering the well. "So, what will you do now?"

"I have already done it," Don Arturo said. "I sent an email to SIFT—anonymously of course. There is a chapter in Madrid. I informed them you would be at the cathedral this morning to examine the Sudarium. I also told them you would be turned away."

Graham stiffened indignantly. "You tipped them off? Why would you do that?"

"To force the hand of the bishop. SIFT would love to embarrass the church, especially before their publicity campaign. And the church wants to avoid bad publicity."

"As do I," Graham said. "Without my reputation, I can't do my work. Controversy does not instill trust in the people who hold the documents left to digitize."

"And for that, I do apologize," Don Arturo said. "But I sincerely believe if the work is done, you will be vindicated, and therefore become even more trustworthy."

"If the work is done," Graham said pointedly.

"Without contacting SIFT there would be no *if* at all. If—as I think they will—they are able to make something of the footage they shot this morning and post it, it may create an opportunity."

"How so?"

"Hopefully, it will spur the bishop to react and carry out our initial proposal while you are still here. Otherwise, the Sudarium might as well still be hidden in this well."

# TWELVE

From the side of the hill outside the chapel, the small pond at the center of the meadow on the plateau looked like an eye, its dark blue water forming a cornea in a muddy bank sclera. *The sky in the eye*, he thought, laughing to himself. The twist on the title to the Alan Parsons Project song triggered the chorus in his mind.

> *I am the eye in the sky, looking at you.*
> *I can read your mind.*
> *I am the maker of rules, dealing with fools.*
> *I can cheat you blind.*

The events of the day, he realized, were strangely mirrored in the lyrics. He made a note to share the connection with Alexander, anticipating the rejoinder that if the lyrics were applicable, Graham would be the fool.

To the right of the pond on the edge of the meadow, the parallel tracks of a seldom-used utility road cut through the brush, leading to the base of a power line tower. He pivoted, following the road up the hill, behind the chapel and discovered a group of casual hikers who had ascended from the other side of the mountain, dogs in-tow.

He turned back and followed Don Arturo down the slope as he took in the view. A nuclear power plant emitted a vertical cloud, marking the halfway point to Oviedo.

"I suddenly feel like a freed Hebrew slave," Graham said.

Don Arturo stopped and turned to face Graham. "Why is that?"

"The pillar of smoke."

Don Arturo twisted around, following Graham's finger, and laughed. "Let us hope you are misreading the signs. If we followed *that* pillar of smoke, we will never make it to the Sudarium."

"I *did* make it to the Sudarium and there was still nothing to see. Just smoke and mirrors, as your mother's cousin might say."

"The Lord leads us all, Dr. Eliot, whether or not we follow a pillar of smoke or fire. And sometimes, the reason we do not see the pillar is because we choose not to, not because it is invisible."

"I have lived that truth," Graham said on a crooked smile.

"We all have."

As they reached the edge of the plateau, Graham turned around again for a final look at the chapel. The remote location on a mountaintop triggered the memory of the chapel at the peak of the traditional Mount Sinai, as well as the ruins of a chapel on the peak of Cudi Dagh, a mountain in southeast Turkey with an ancient tradition for being the landing place of Noah's Ark. He hadn't envisioned the job of digitizing biblical manuscripts leading to obscure peaks.

"There is a superstition about Monsacro," Don Arturo said, breaking Graham's reverie. "To this day, pilgrims to the Sudarium come here to collect thistles from the mountain. They are said to have miraculous healing powers."

"Like water from Lourdes?" Graham asked.

"Yes, something like that."

"Is that what you believe?"

Don Arturo shrugged. "There are miracles enough in the

Holy Ark holding the Sudarium. I do not need to add miraculous thistles to the treasures it contains. My interest in plants has only to do with the pollen on the Sudarium."

Graham followed the priest onto the switchback trail descending the mountain.

"Why is there pollen on the Sudarium?"

"Because there is pollen on almost everything," Don Arturo said. "And because many plants grow only in certain locations, the pollen found on an object can reveal where it has been."

"Like Sherlock Holmes being able to identify different parts of London by the soil he saw on people's clothes," Graham said.

"An interesting connection to make. The man who discovered the pollen was a forensic scientist from Switzerland. He developed a technique for extracting pollen from the clothes of suspects to learn the locations they had visited. In 1979, this criminologist, Max Frei was his name, took samples from the Sudarium. He identified more than thirty types of pollen."

"And where did he determine it came from?"

Don Arturo swept a hand across the valley. "Some of it came from here, the mountains of Asturias. But he also found pollen that is unique to the regions around Madrid, Cartagena, northeast Africa, and Jerusalem."

Graham mentally plotted the points, forming a route spanning Spain from where he was to its southern port, then across the Mediterranean Sea. "That's quite specific."

"What is more impressive is that it agrees with the history of the Sudarium found in the earliest documents mentioning it."

"How old are the documents?" Graham asked.

"The earliest is from 570. It is a travelogue attributed to Antonius Martyr, although it was most likely written for him by a servant he sent in his place. One of the places this pilgrim visited was the Jordan River, to the spot where Christ was baptized."

"I've been there," Graham said. "Near the monastery of Saint Mark."

"Did you happen to see a cave along the banks?"

"There are caves all over that area. Not too far from the caves where the Dead Sea Scrolls were discovered."

"Yes, this cave was inhabited by seven nuns. The pilgrim states they were the custodians of a chest containing the cloth that had covered the face of Christ on the cross."

"Did the pilgrim see it?"

"Unfortunately, the book does not say. The most important document was written by Bishop Pelayo de Oviedo early in the twelfth century."

"A six-hundred-year gap," Graham noted. "Aren't there any other mentions of it?"

"Yes," Don Arturo said, "but they have been lost to time. Fortunately, like Eusebius before him, Pelayo's history preserves the testimony of those documents. According to Pelayo, the disciples of the apostles constructed the ark to safeguard a number of relics, including the Sudarium. That is apparently what the Antonius Martyr document refers to."

Graham could hear Alexander joking that *The Spelunking Nuns* would make a great band name.

"It was taken to northern Africa—probably Alexandria—in 614, just before the Persians captured Jerusalem. As the Muslim conquest spread to Africa, the ark was placed on a ship to Cartagena. From there, it was transported to Seville in 616. Forty years later, it was moved to Toledo, again because of the Muslim invasion. It was finally hidden here on Monsacro in 711 before King Rodrigo was defeated by the Muslims. After Alfonso, king of Asturias, repelled the Muslims, he established Oviedo as the capital and built the cathedral in the 780s. The ark is still housed in the oldest section of the cathedral, behind what is now the main section of the building. The Cámara Santa, it is called."

The pillar of steam became obscured as they entered the woods.

"That's a fairly impressive historical trail. It would be great if the Shroud of Turin had the same documentary evidence."

Don Arturo looked over his shoulder. "It does have the pollen evidence, but it reveals a different route. The same criminologist, Max Frei, did the work on the Shroud. He collected more than three dozen samples and identified fifty-six plant species. He identified pollen found only in the area of Palestine around Jerusalem. Pollen that is released in spring. In addition, he found pollen from southern Turkey, in the region of Edessa, pollen from Constantinople, France, and northern Italy. Exactly the proposed route suggested by documents if the Image of Edessa is the same as the Shroud of Turin, as I believe it is."

"Remarkable," Graham said. "There is far more evidence than I imagined for both cloths."

Don Arturo glanced over his shoulder again. "Great enough evidence to be seen, and yet little enough to be hidden."

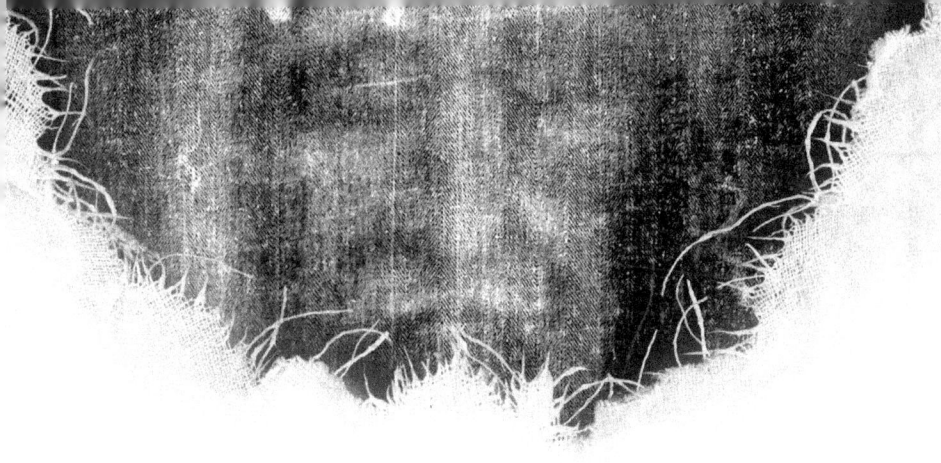

# THIRTEEN

Five minutes after leaving the trailhead, they entered La Collada, a village consisting of several small clusters of buildings connected by streets twining like asphalt tendrils among the foothills. Although there was no central plaza or main hub, the entire community seemed to have gathered outside the parish church next to where Don Arturo had parked. Pallbearers emerged from the open doors, carrying a coffin in short, labored steps to the back of a waiting hearse. Graham and Don Arturo stood respectfully on the fringe of the mourners until they formed a train behind the hearse.

Graham remained silent in the car; his ever-present grief triggered by the unexpected scene. He stared blindly out the side window, oblivious to the serpentine route through the hills.

"Who did you lose?"

The deep compassion in Don Arturo's voice pulled Graham from his reverie as much as the sound itself. He released a heavy sigh, as if expelling the silence.

"How did you know I lost someone?"

"I have not always been an administrator." Don Arturo offered a sad smile on a sidelong glance at Graham. "After seminary, I served for several years as a parish priest at a church much like the one in La Collada. I have seen the look in your eyes many times. Too many."

Graham faced forward before he could say the words, suddenly self-conscious of his countenance. "I lost my family four years ago."

Don Arturo gave a small nod, as if confirming a suspicion. "I am sorry, my friend. What a terrible tragedy."

"It wasn't a tragedy. They were tragedies," Graham said, emphasizing the distinction. "My five-year-old daughter, Alyson, died of cancer after suffering for two years. Six months later, my wife, Olivia, accidentally drowned. She had taken some sedatives for her anxiety and fell asleep in the bath." The words came out dully, grotesquely foreign and familiar. He resented how they had become a script, a mask of words he could recite almost without hearing in order to protect himself emotionally—an act of self-preservation just when he felt he had no self he wanted to preserve.

Don Arturo released his own heavy sigh, a bookend to Graham's. He took a hand from the steering wheel and maneuvered to place it on Graham's shoulder, leaving it there a moment, then squeezing before letting go. "I cannot imagine anything more difficult."

"I'd never struggled with doubt until then," Graham said, surprising himself with his willingness to share with someone he barely knew. "Intellectually, I know all the answers for how a good, all-knowing God is not philosophically incompatible with the existence of evil. But the emotional doubt—it overwhelmed me. I lost my way. I was in a wilderness period for a long time. Half the time I was angry at God, and the rest of the time I tried to deny His existence."

He glanced at Don Arturo, encouraged by an expression that somehow pooled more compassion as Graham spoke. "My favorite verse in the Bible used to be Romans 8:28. 'We know that all things work together for the good of those who love God, who are called according to his purpose.' But I couldn't see any good in the deaths of my daughter and wife. I just went through the motions of living while I waited to join them, I guess."

"How did you find your way out of the wilderness?"

Graham coughed a humorless laugh. "I had to be led out like I had blindfolded myself and walked into a minefield. It's a long story, but it was basically through a treasure hunt. As you know, I inherited the work I do now from Andrew Singer. When he was murdered, I helped investigate why he was killed. And in the process, I almost died. I should have died. When it was over, I could see that my steps had been ordered. It was undeniable. Like providence had left artifacts in its wake. I realized that when I was asking where God was that He was actually with me the entire time. That gave me something to hold onto, a reason to trust Him. I still fall back into that dark place sometimes, but now I know I'm not alone and that it is not without purpose even if I can't see what that purpose is."

Don Arturo allowed a small smile. "Often what we perceive as obstacles, God intends as opportunities. I am not referring to your wife and daughter, or to Dr. Singer, of course, but only to the difficulties you faced in the investigation of Dr. Singer's passing."

Graham nodded. "I see that now. But I have a new favorite verse."

Don Arturo tilted his head expectantly. "And what is that?"

"Mark chapter 9, verse 24. It's the prayer of the father asking Jesus to heal his son. 'I believe; help my unbelief!'"

Don Arturo bobbed his head. "I confess, I have prayed that prayer many times myself."

He stopped the car a block from the plaza, the cathedral tower just visible between buildings.

"It will not be good if we are seen together. Either by the

church or by anyone from SIFT. I trust you can find your way from here. Please do not leave Oviedo just yet. Let us see if SIFT does anything with the video. And if they post it, let us see what impact it has. Wait a day or two before you arrange to return home."

Graham looked away from the plaza where he had been scanning it for the SIFT reporter. "Maybe I should have picked a couple of thistles for luck."

# FOURTEEN

Halfway across the plaza, Graham changed course, deciding to visit the Cámara Santa where the Sudarium was kept, rather than return to the hotel. The plaza was vibrant compared to his arrival at the cathedral that morning. He glanced at the clock on the bell tower and saw it was four p.m. He didn't know if the cathedral closed for siesta, but if so, it should just be opening back up..

He joined the current of pilgrims filtering through the cathedral doors and paid the admission. A self-guided tour was organized into numbered locations that began making a circuit around the interior of the cathedral's sanctuary. Graham skipped through the stops, walking down the right aisle toward the altar.  He turned right, out of the sanctuary and ascended three flights of stairs to a landing with a sign for the Cámara Santa.

A small flight of steps led down to an arched Romanesque doorway at the rear of the Holy Chamber. He stepped into the surprisingly narrow room, a little wider than a single car garage. A high arched ceiling and the lack of furnishings kept the space from becoming claustrophobic. Three pillars supported the side walls, each featuring a pair of Jesus's twelve disciples.

He crossed the floor of the main room to an iron gate

closing off a space with a low arched ceiling. On the other side, each corner of the room contained a tall glass case displaying reliquaries. A fifth glass case occupied the center of the room, enclosing a silver chest large enough to resemble an altar. Graham examined the relief on the silver panel covering the front which showed Jesus surrounded by the disciples, repeating the motif of the main room. A frame rose from behind the chest, exhibiting an exact copy of the Sudarium.

The cloth looked out of place among the bejeweled, polished metal reliquaries. Stains, grime, tears, and deep wrinkles made it look more like a filthy, discarded pillowcase. The incongruity reminded him of *Indiana Jones and the Last Crusade* when Indy selects the most modest, common cup from among dozens of ornate and jeweled pretenders and identified it as the true Holy Grail.

Except the disconnect was even greater. Don Arturo had spoken of it only in the context of the Shroud of Turin and the Resurrection. But taken on its own, Graham forgot about that context and saw only the artifact of a violent, cruel death. It was a rag that had caught blood that had been shed through the torture and execution of an innocent man. From six feet away, the stain's reflected pattern looked like a butterfly, a strange beauty forged from brutal wounds.

As he studied it, the stains began to resemble a faded map. Graham realized that was exactly what it was: a map of his sin, a document of his debt being paid, and the extravagant lengths God went to in His desire to reconcile all who would believe. The thought overwhelmed him, and he folded himself onto one of the two kneelers on either side of the iron gate.

Several tourists entered the room, interrupting his meditation, dissolving the intimacy he'd desired. He rose mechanically, half lost in thought, and saw the back wall for the first time. High above the door, three heads emerged from the wall, as if the figures had been drowning in plaster that had hardened as they took their last breaths. He made his way back through the corridor to the entrance, unaware of the other stops on the tour.

Graham exited the cathedral into the long, dark shadows filling the plaza in the late afternoon. He stopped at the bottom of the steps, fixed on a husband and wife, halfway across the expanse, holding the hands of a small girl walking between them. He was still lost in thought just enough to question if what he saw was real or if the silhouettes were shadows of the past. The buildings catching the sun allowed a wedge of light to slice across the pavement at the spot the family moved into the shade. The father crossed the edge of the darkness first, leaving the mother and daughter momentarily in the light. The moment fixed itself in Graham's memory as if he'd taken a picture.

He had often thought of Olivia and Aly as being in the shadows, while he remained in the light. But the truth was like a negative image, closer to what he was watching. Olivia and Aly were in eternal light. It was Graham still muddling through shadows, through a glass darkly. For the second time that day, his grief came to the surface—or rather, he sank below it. He watched the family leave the square, then drifted back to the hotel, praying to himself.

"I believe; help my unbelief!"

# FIFTEEN

Graham was stirring the next morning—too awake to be restful, too asleep to be alert—when his phone came to life, harshly ending the limbo. He read Alexander's name on the screen as he pulled it from the charger on the nightstand. Alexander started talking before Graham could muster a greeting.

"Dr. E. Are you rocking the province with Spanish Bombs?"

"Not at 5:30 in the morning. Nice deep cut from The Clash, by the way. But you didn't sing it."

"With this cold, I would have sounded like Dylan," Alexander said. "Plus, the words would have come out as 'Spanish Bobs,' which would only be confusing."

"Bob and I both thank you." Graham laughed. "Get your ticket to Nashville?"

"Leaving tomorrow night," Alexander said. "That's why I'm calling. I sent Christopher King an email to let him know to put me on the list. He emailed right back and said he hoped to see me there. He also said he was performing a couple of nights at the magic restaurant."

"Like the Magic Castle?"

"Yeah, except it's called the House of Cards. It's completely unmarked and hidden beneath the Johnny Cash Museum downtown."

"Sounds more like a magic speakeasy than a castle," Graham said.

"Couldn't call it that, though," Alexander said. "Sounds like something Koko the sign-language-speaking gorilla would say. 'Magic. Speak. Easy.'"

Graham laughed thickly, his voice still waking up. "So how are you supposed to find it?"

"I'm really not sure. All I know is I gotta pack a suit. Formal dress is required, like at the Castle. But that's not why I'm calling. King mentioned something in the email you should know about. He said SIFT just dropped a video on their YouTube channel. Some kind of exposé. I clicked the link, and this guy Ben Steele comes on. President of SIFT."

"Ben Steele?" Graham repeated. "That can't be his real name. Wasn't that one of Superman's powers? He could bend steel?"

Alexander chuckled. "Yeah, I guess it comes across differently when you hear it than when you read it. Anyway, the video is kind of like a news report, like he's an anchor, but way more casual."

"Like MTV news."

"I don't even know what that is," Alexander teased. "Way before my time. So, Ben Steele says apparently the Roman Catholic Church brought in someone to examine the alleged cloth that covered the head of Jesus on the cross and was buried with Him."

Graham sat up, rigid with cold needles of anxiety. The abrupt start to the day had begun without the memory of the video reporter outside the cathedral. Now he anticipated Alexander's next words.

"Steele said when the scholar arrived, he was turned away. And then the video cuts to footage of you outside the church.

The reporter started peppering you with questions."

"I got ambushed," Graham said. "I was lost in thought and confused. The last thing I expected was for someone to be waiting outside for me with a camera."

"To be honest, Dr. E., you don't come off so well. Why'd you call it a fake?"

"I don't know what you're talking about," Graham said. "I didn't say it was a fake."

"It sure looks like that on the video. The guy calls out, 'What's your opinion? Is it a fake?' And you just look at the camera with this weird expression and say 'fake.'"

Graham shot out of bed, standing in protest. "That's not what I meant! I was so surprised by the question that I just repeated it back."

"I believe you," Alexander said, "but that's not exactly how it comes across. Check it out. I just sent the link."

"Can't wait," Graham said dully.

"So, what happened? I thought they brought you over there to take pictures of the Sudarium."

"They did. The dean of the cathedral, Don Arturo, did, anyway. But he didn't inform the bishop about the project. The bishop was not on board and was not pleased, so he pulled the plug the night before. I showed up with all my gear. When they told me they had changed their minds, I pushed as hard as I could without burning bridges, but the acting dean was clearly unmovable."

"No way," Alexander groaned. "After you dropped everything to go halfway around the world? So aggravating."

"Thanks for rubbing it in," Graham deadpanned.

"But how did SIFT find out about it?"

"Don Arturo leaked it to them anonymously."

"Really? He was *that* mad?"

"Actually, it's more tactical than spiteful," Graham said. "He thinks if SIFT got wind of what happened and publicized it, then the church would be forced to allow the examination to prove it has nothing to hide. That's why I'm still here. And the fact that the video was posted tells me he might be on to something. Now we'll have to see how the church reacts."

"So, all this was staged?"

"In a way. SIFT is staging one thing and Don Arturo is staging another."

"It certainly paves the way for their announcement of the challenge at the SIFT conference."

"That may just up the ante," Graham said. "Talk about Spanish Bombs. Thanks for the heads-up. I'm going to go watch this video."

# SIXTEEN

Graham opened his laptop and clicked the link in Alexander's text message, opening a browser with SIFT's YouTube channel. Before playing the latest video, Graham scanned the column of thumbnails on the right side of the page noting other topics they addressed. Psychics, paranormal research, homeopathy, chiropractics, Bible errors, evidence-based medicine, and astrology had all been targeted by SIFT, and it was only a partial list, with multiple videos devoted to each one. Ironically, Graham thought, their militant rationalism came across almost as fringe as the ideas they critiqued.

The realization suddenly became a mirror, chastening him with an unexpected empathy. He, too, had fought a certain amount of criticism and misperception after circumstances had compelled him to research things usually associated with pseudo-archaeology. He had followed the treasure map of the Copper Scroll, climbed two different mountains with traditions identifying them as Ararat—each with evidence of Noah's Ark to support them, and investigated ruins in northwest Saudi Arabia that several amateurs had interpreted as artifacts of the Israelites at Mount Sinai. In each case, he was surprised at the evidence, and thankful that his reputation was held in high enough esteem to weather the perception of guilt-by-association.

He pressed Play and an animation of the SIFT logo flew onto the screen, then transitioned to a host. A middle-aged man with a tasteful goatee and hair swept back from his head sat in front of a wall of books. His purple dress shirt was open at the collar and framed by a tailored black suit jacket. A phrenological bust acted as a bookend on one of the shelves, a trophy of an abandoned theory, symbolizing the purpose of the organization.

"Welcome, truth-lovers. I'm Ben Steele from SIFT—the Scientific Inquiry of Free Thinkers. We are doing a special, breaking news edition of the video podcast. I'm sure most of you are familiar with the Shroud of Turin, the cloth that advocates claim is the burial cloth of Jesus Christ, but that experts have conclusively demonstrated is a medieval forgery. But you may not have heard of the Sudarium of Oviedo. Apparently there was more than one cloth buried with Jesus. This one is about the size of a pillow case, and it's called a su-darium, which is a kind of scarf or sweat towel. Believers who visit the cathedral in Oviedo, in northern Spain, claim it was wrapped around the head of Jesus Christ as he died on the cross, and remained on him until he was placed in the tomb. Unlike the Shroud of Turin, there is no image on it. Instead, there are stains they claim are from blood and other bodily fluids. Compared to the Shroud of Turin, there has been little scientific examination of the cloth. But that looked like it was about to change yesterday. Dr. Graham Eliot, a biblical archaeologist who usually focuses on digitizing biblical man-uscripts around the world, arrived at the Oviedo Cathedral yesterday to investigate the alleged relic. We caught wind of it, this is what happened less than an hour after he arrived."

Graham watched himself drag the copy stand case through the cathedral door, frowning in thought, completely unaware of everything around him. He had replayed the scene in his mind so often that seeing his memory from a different angle added a surreal element to it.

"Dr. Eliot, why didn't they let you see the Sudarium?" the accented voice called from offscreen.

He saw his confusion multiply as he looked up and turned toward the camera as the question was repeated.

"Why didn't they let you see the Sudarium?"

The frown contracted into a squint both defensive and confused.

"What is the church trying to hide, Dr. Eliot?"

"I don't know." He remembered intending to say he wasn't sure what was going on, but the stuttered words came across as accepting the premise—that the church was indeed hiding something. He watched himself turn away and start walking, the camera moving with him.

"What is your opinion of the Sudarium? Is it a fake?"

He stopped and looked again at the camera, then repeated the word. He remembered saying the word aloud as if weighing it. Instead, it came across as a statement, an answer. "Fake." The disconnect between his intention and how it appeared shocked and angered him. "Who are you?" he heard himself bark on the video as he studied the screen wondering the same thing about himself.

"I just want the truth. No more hiding. No more lies."

"I'm sorry, I can't help you." Perfect way to put a period on the misconception, Graham thought.

Ben Steele reappeared, a freeze-frame of Graham's scowl over his shoulder like a newscast.

"In case you missed that, here it is again."

The video played a soundbite starting with the question, "Is it a fake?" Again, Graham watched himself say a single word, misinterpreted to say something he didn't mean.

"Fake."

The footage froze again, preserving the dull expression on Graham's face after repeating the word.

"What did Dr. Eliot learn that so quickly convinced him it was a fake?" Steele continued. "And why didn't the church allow him to digitize or even examine the Sudarium? Very strange goings-on, indeed. But no surprise, really. It looks like yet another power-play by the church, which has a history of power-plays. Thankfully, free thinking and critical inquiry have loosened the grip of religious superstition, making the church an increasingly irrelevant leftover of a prescientific mindset.

"Before I go, let me remind you that there is still time to join SIFT for ThinkCon this week in Nashville. Hope to see you there. Now and always, be lovers of truth."

Graham closed his eyes and sighed heavily, as if purging himself of the video in the temporary, blind silence. After a moment of reflection, he copied the link to send it to don Arturo, then remembered he shouldn't make any contact. Given that the video was exactly what don Arturo had hoped for, he was probably monitoring the SIFT site as well as their social media, waiting for something like this to post. Instead, he responded to Alexander's text.

"Just watched it. I don't think Ben Steele's super-power is twisting metal. It's twisting truth."

The retort wasn't the release for his frustration he thought it would be. If anything, his frustration only increased as he stabbed the Send button. Few things angered him more than being misportrayed, and the feeling of impotence over how to combat it amplified his aggravation. SIFT had an outlet and an audience. Graham had academic journals. And if he wrote an article to defend himself, it wouldn't be suitable for that kind of publication. Not only that, it was a story about how there was no story. And what would the church think of the video? Why would they let him view the Sudarium now that he had apparently called it a fake?

The only way to respond in-kind was through social

media—a world he deliberately knew nothing about. Watching his students constantly on their phones and seeing the problems it caused left the impression that social media was nothing more than digital gossip at best. Suddenly he found himself wondering who knew enough about it to help him, and who would have the desire. Alexander would be the obvious go-to, but he was one of the few students he knew who shared his luddite views. He mentally flipped through acquaintances, mumbling social media like a mantra. Suddenly, he knew exactly who to call.

# SEVENTEEN

*"Dígame."*

"Hola?" Graham said, flustered by the clipped greeting he didn't understand, stuttering a rote response. *"Puedo habla con Iris? Es este Iris?"*

"Dr. Eliot?"

The slightly husky voice was more recognizable in English, and Graham inwardly breathed a sigh of relief.

"Yes, thank goodness. Please don't make me inflict any more high school Spanish on you."

"I always imagined the Spanish Inquisition referred to torture inflicted by Spaniards," Iris said, "but you have proven conclusively that the language itself can be tortured."

"No one expects the Spanish Inquisition," Graham exclaimed in a British accent.

Iris laughed. "Monty Python. Very good. You may have just redeemed yourself. What can I do for you?"

"Well, I'm not quite sure how to ask this. I have found my way into some trouble and thought you might be able to help."

"I suppose that depends. What kind of trouble are we talking about?"

"Someone posted a video online making me appear to say something I don't believe. It's really just something embarrassing I need to correct. The matter is a bit urgent, and I think the best way to respond is through social media. But I'm afraid I don't know anything about that stuff. I have a Facebook page I check maybe once a week, but that's it. I don't tweet or anything like that. I had a student call me *Instagrampa*, which probably says it all. I remembered you said you managed social media for the BNE. I don't know anyone else to call about it. Do you think you could help me out?"

"I'll do what I can," Iris said. "What's the link?"

"Just go to YouTube and search for SIFT. Scientific Inquiry of Free Thinkers."

"Sifting facts, I suppose," Iris said over the strokes of a mechanical keyboard clacking in the background. "Very clever."

"It's the latest video," Graham said. "Should be at the top."

"I see it," Iris interrupted. "What cathedral is that?"

"Oviedo," Graham said. "That's where I am. Do you have time to watch it? It's not very long."

"Hitting *play* now," Iris said.

Graham listened to the video and was horrified to discover that without being able to see his expressions, the audio sounded even more damaging.

"So, what do you think?" Graham asked after Ben Steele signed off.

"I had no idea that's why you were in Spain," Iris said.

"No one was supposed to know until after I had digitized the Sudarium."

"Do you know how word got out?"

"The priest who invited me here tipped-off SIFT."

"Really? Why would he do that?"

"His superiors overruled his plan. He hopes SIFT getting the word out will force the church to change its mind."

"Not likely, if the history of the Shroud of Turin is any

indication," Iris said.

"I agree," Graham said. "But I need to do something about the embarrassment this causes me."

"I confess, I am not familiar with this other cloth, the Sudarium. If it's a fake, why is this an issue?"

"That's the thing. I didn't call the Sudarium a fake. It just looks that way on the video. I don't know what to think since I haven't examined it. But you can imagine how interested I was to learn of your research into the Shroud. That's the other thing that made me think of calling you."

"I'm so glad you did," Iris said. "I remember you asked me if I knew about the Sudarium, but it didn't mean anything to me, so I forgot about it. I was entirely unaware of a Shroud connection so close by. I'd be delighted to help you. Did you have anything in particular in mind?"

"All I know is that I look foolish, and I fear it will be exploited. I need a way to protect my reputation. To explain what happened."

"Right. In that case, you should start posting on Facebook, and set up accounts on Twitter, Instagram, and YouTube. That is the best way to respond quickly."

"That's exactly my problem," Graham said. "I know what to do, I just don't know how to do it. Nor do I have the time to learn and respond within a relevant time period. I have to deal with this now. I'm still trying to get in to see the Sudarium."

"After they turned you away?" Iris said skeptically. "You think making a social media post will change their minds?"

"Not by itself, no. I mainly need to do that to set the record straight. But the priest who started all this is still working behind the scenes. I'm waiting in Oviedo for a few days to see if he has any success."

"Good luck with that," Iris said. "Sounds like a regular Martin Luther."

Graham chuckled. "You know, nailing the Ninety-Five Theses to the church door might just be the first social media post."

Iris's throaty laugh was infectious, and he felt the weight of worry lift slightly. "No post in history ever went more viral, that's for certain. Okay, Dr. Eliot, I will set up the accounts for you. In the meantime, think about what you want to say. You have a Mac, right? Use QuickTime to make a video. Keep it short and to the point. Send me a link and we'll talk later today, then I'll post it."

"Iris, I cannot tell you how much I appreciate this. I'll work something up and meet you at the church door, as it were. And please, call me Graham."

# EIGHTEEN

Graham positioned his chair to catch the light from the window, giving him a view of the cathedral tower rising above the rooftops. The screen of his laptop mirrored him, and he pivoted the computer, adjusting the angle of the camera until he was satisfied with the composition. Having a plan to defend himself and a task to perform transformed his anxiety to energy, and he worked with purpose as he thought about what he wanted to say and how to say it. The quicker he could make the video, the sooner Iris could post it, countering the SIFT video before its misperceptions were accepted as truth by default.

He took a sip of water, followed by a deep breath to still himself after the flurry of preparations. He reached toward the keyboard to hit *record*, then froze, suddenly wordless. Everything he planned to say lost its shape, returning to an inarticulate mass of feelings. Extemporaneous speaking had never been a strength. Too many things he wanted to express—details, insights, connections—got accidentally omitted. Others came out in a way he hadn't intended. He developed the discipline of writing down everything he wanted to say. He didn't always refer to what he wrote as he spoke, but it always helped him accurately express himself.

He removed his iPad from his computer bag, deciding to type out his message on a separate device so he could use it as a teleprompter if needed. The words returned as he began typing. After the first pass, he read it aloud, remembering Iris's advice to keep it short. After a few revisions and a rehearsal of the final text, he felt ready enough to record.

"Hello. My name is Graham Eliot. I am a research professor of Ancient Near East Studies at Calbi University in Los Angeles, California. I am speaking to you from Oviedo, Spain. Recently, a video was posted on the internet that showed me exiting the Metropolitan Cathedral Basilica of the Holy Savior where I was approached by a reporter with an organization called the Skeptical Inquiry for Free Thinkers. SIFT for short. The reporter had obviously been waiting in ambush with the intent of trying to embarrass me, as well as the Roman Catholic Church. He was clearly not interested in responsible journalism. The questions shouted at me were framed in ways that either contained a false premise or were exploitative.

"In my confusion at what was happening, I was unprepared to respond articulately. My words have been twisted to ascribe a meaning that I did not intend. I am recording this video to set the record straight. I came to the cathedral at the invitation of the church to examine a relic called the Sudarium of Oviedo, which is purported to be the cloth placed over the head of Jesus as He died on the cross and was buried with Him.

"For reasons I cannot discuss, I was unable to carry out the examination as planned. I had just left the meeting where I learned of the change of plans when I was accosted. My presence of mind was on the unexpected circumstances, and I was preoccupied with how I might be able to salvage my work. In the process of mentally shifting gears, so to speak, I was asked if the Sudarium was a fake. I responded by repeating the key word back. When I said the word fake, I was not making a judgment on the cloth. I was repeating a claim I had not considered.

"Until that moment, I questioned the authenticity of the Sudarium, but not that it was manufactured for deception, which is how I understand the word fake. In other words, I thought the Sudarium might be misidentified as an artifact, but not a forgery. So, I ask the Skeptical Inquiry of Free Thinkers to remove the video and issue a correction or clarification. Thank you very much."

He uploaded the file to Google Drive, then texted the link to Iris. A read receipt appeared, immediately followed by a reply.

"That was fast. Watching now."

Two long minutes later, he answered her call.

*"Dígame."*

Iris chuckled. "Impressive. Fast learner."

"Gracias," Graham said. "So, when can we post this thing?"

"Approximately never."

"What do you mean?" Graham said, realizing she wasn't joking.

"Dr. Eliot—Graham—it's rubbish. You're up against a white wall with bad lighting, and your eyes aren't on the camera half the time. It's like a video of you having your passport photo taken. It's worse than that, actually. It has the aesthetics of a hostage video meant to show proof-of-life."

Graham quickly overcame a defensive impulse and burst into laughter. "Other than that, it's okay, though, right?"

"Since you ask, no," Iris said, apparently encouraged. "Whatever you're reading sounds like you're reciting a memorandum at a technical lecture. It's like you made an exhaustive study of the most interesting presentations ever given, listed their attributes, then avoided all of them."

After another fit of laughter, Graham regained his composure. "I admit it is not the greatest video ever made. But it doesn't really have to be, does it? Everything I said was true.

That's the most important thing. Isn't that enough to justify posting it?"

"Not at all," Iris said. "I may have to take my *fast-learner* comment back."

"But why?"

"Because truth is not enough. Graham, you are not speaking to the academic community now. The way the world is now, the truth will not set you free because everything is about perception. That means you need to be more than true."

"I don't even know what that means," Graham said.

"It means you need to be persuasive. Think about it. Why did you call me? Because of a false perception that will *persuade* people. If you respond with unpersuasive truth, then you'll be right, but no one will care. Posting a video of truth that no one will watch is the proverbial tree falling in the forest with no one to hear the sound you make. You'll just be wasting your time."

"Okay, so what am I supposed to do?"

"I have some holiday time saved up," Iris said. "I can take a few days off from the museum and come to Oviedo to help you. Maybe we can shoot some short videos of you explaining what you do and what the Sudarium is. We can do it with the cathedral in the background or other places slightly more interesting than your dreary hotel wall. I'll take pictures for you to post as well. And in the event you are allowed to examine the Sudarium, perhaps I can document the examination. And as a bonus, I will act as a translator."

"All that sounds amazing, Iris. Let me know your fee and I'll talk to some of my foundation's donors so we can pay for your time."

"That's not really an issue for me, Graham. But thank you. This is a good opportunity for me. Seeing how you work might help me with the project I told you about with the icons. I'll take the train up. I'll be there tonight."

# NINETEEN

It was the laugh. Graham had sensed something vaguely familiar about Iris during their meeting in Madrid, but the connection had escaped him. Her explanation of the iconographic theory had eclipsed everything else trying to claim his attention, so he hadn't thought about it too hard. But the phone isolated her voice, and he realized it was the laugh. He heard Olivia's laugh in Iris.

Maybe it had been Iris's eccentric appearance—so different from Olivia's conventional style—that obscured the resemblance. Graham tried to picture Olivia in the outfit Iris wore at the museum but couldn't imagine Olivia—or anyone else—pulling off the look. Iris had been at once put-together and disheveled, studied and unaffected, stylish, yet without trend. Graham remembered finding her appearance interesting, even as it made him feel self-consciously conventional and strait-laced. Without her visual presence, he felt more at ease—comfortable enough to allow her to help more than he had intended.

Although Iris had laughed, it was Olivia's that lingered, tainting the relief he felt at Iris's willingness to help, making him second-guess reaching out to her. The last thing he wanted to do was send the wrong signals. Since Olivia's death, he had seen only one person—Alexander's aunt, Sarah.

Neither had been looking for a relationship, surprising both of them. Until Sarah, he doubted he had the capacity to love someone the same way he had Olivia. He hadn't even wanted to try. Graham had never believed in the idea of a soul mate, that there was only one perfect person in the world for him, and yet that was exactly how he had lived now that she was gone. Sometimes Olivia seemed more present in her absence than she had been in their time together, but he knew that said more about him than her. Presence had always been something he struggled with.

But that was not the reason he and Sarah hadn't worked out. A bad divorce left her with trust issues she could not overcome. They parted on friendly terms and still ran into each other occasionally through Alexander. In the two years since Sarah, he hadn't seen anyone.

Suddenly, he wondered how Iris interpreted his call. It occurred to him that she had to be at least ten years younger, which only amplified his unease. He wanted to avoid any possible appearance of impropriety, and he worried he had just traded one opportunity for misperception for another. Or worse, added a second. He thought through their conversation and didn't recall saying what hotel he was staying at—something in his favor. He resolved to quickly set boundaries when they talked again.

The notification sound of an arriving email punctuated the end of the reverie, and he woke his laptop to see a message from Father Nikolaos, librarian at Saint Catherine's Monastery. Graham pictured the monastery as he'd seen it from halfway up the traditional Mount Sinai, the view pilgrims to the site had shared since the fortress-like walls were constructed in the sixth century. Scholarly consensus agreed the location was almost certainly not the Sinai of the Bible, and more than two dozen other candidates had been suggested. But the misidentification had not prevented God's providence from using the error for good.

Napoleon Bonaparte had repaired the walls on his visit to the region—a trip that announced the dawn of Egyptology and archaeology. The remote location had protected it from iconoclasts in the eighth and ninth centuries, making it the repository for more icons than anywhere else in the world. The kindness the monks had shown to Muhammad earned its protection as Islam spread, and the compact he'd made with the order—the ashtiname—was still exalted as a model for tolerance between Christians and Muslims.

Its trove of manuscripts was second only to the Vatican archives. In fact, it had been a visit to the monastery that acted as a catalyst for Alexander Pearl to search for the true location of Sinai. And Graham's effort to help him out of the trouble that followed directly led to meeting Sarah.

After Iris had mentioned the monastery's famous Sinai Pantocrator icon, Graham had written to Father Nikolaos, curious to see if the story could be verified. Like all the exchanges he'd had with the monk, the message was brief and austere.

> *Dear Graham, I am happy to help with your*
> *question about the Sinai Pantocrator icon.*
> *Several brothers here know the tradition that*
> *the image was made from the burial Shroud of*
> *Christ, now in Turin. Father Nikolaos.*

The image of the icon Graham had attached for reference looked at him from the bottom of the email window. He double-clicked it to open it at full size, then opened a second window next to it with the face of the Shroud of Turin to compare with. He studied the icon with renewed appreciation for the skill it took to create the image with hot wax. As an image, it carried more immediate impact than the faint discolorations on the Shroud. What had Iris said the Edessenes called it? The *acheiropoietos*—the image not made with hands.

The image made him think of the doctrine of Scripture, that God had revealed Himself clearly and perspicuously. He thought about Natural Theology, how Paul wrote in the first chapter of Romans how God had revealed Himself in what He created. How did the indistinct image of the face on the Shroud fit into God's revelation? Why wasn't it less ambiguous? And yet, Iris had shown how there was a clear connection between the two images if you allowed yourself to be taught how to see.

# TWENTY

Graham walked to the window and stared out at the cathedral tower—near, yet remote—considering what to do with his day. Although it was the focus of his attention, visiting the cathedral would risk encountering someone from the bishop's office. It would also be the most obvious place for a SIFT reporter lying in wait. Leaving the hotel would not only expose him to unwanted contact, it would risk missing another note from Don Arturo. As restless as he was, and as strong as the impulse was to take some kind of action, he needed to stay put.

He decided to redeem the time with research. After Don Arturo had mentioned the most important history of the Sudarium had been written by Bishop Pelayo, Graham had downloaded PDFs of English translations of his works, but he hadn't had time to read the relevant parts.

Pelayo served as the bishop of Oviedo from 1098 to 1130, and again in 1142 to 1143. During that time, he compiled two important collections of documents. One became known as The Book of Testaments. The other, called the Corpus Pelagianum, dealt more specifically with the history of Asturias. Both included histories of the chest of relics, some passages agreeing word-for-word. Yet, each also contained details that supplemented the other. He started with the history in The

Book of Testaments, copied the most relevant passages into a Word doc, then added unique information from the Corpus Pelagianum to create an abridged narrative. After ordering the passages, he reviewed the result.

> *The cathedral of Oviedo is happy with the very numerous garments of the saints. It...has an ark covered with an admirable work of gold in which are contained very valuable aids of the saints, there present for the defense and salvation of the entire peninsula...*

> *When Caesar Phocas obtained the insignia of Roman power, the Persian people, impatient no longer to bear the yoke of the Roman name, waged a most bitter war against that same republic... Heraclius took the scepter of the Empire; in the sixth year of his reign...the Persians took Syria and Egypt from the Romans.*

> *...the ark, which was made in Jerusalem by the disciples of the apostles,...because of the excessive incursions of the pagans and above all because of the fact of the devastation at the hands of Cosroes right there in the temple of the Lord,...was first transferred to Africa by Philip...bishop of Jerusalem, with several citizens of Jerusalem, by way of the Mediterranean...From there, because of an invasion of pagans that occurred in Africa itself, it was transferred to Cartagena in Spain by Fulgentius, bishop of the African Church of Ruspe... After many years it was transferred to Toledo with great veneration of the faithful...until the death*

*of King Rodrigo, at which time it was transferred to Oviedo…They chose this place…because this very region, fenced in by the ruggedness of its mountains, hardly ensured entry to any enemy.*

*Around this time the ark itself remained first in caves and then in tents like the ark of the Lord itself before the construction of the temple…until the reign of Alfonso the Younger. In the third year of his reign, an army of Arabs entered Asturias… After being blocked by the vanguard and defeated by King Alfonso…, seventy-thousand Arabs were killed with iron and mud, and the rest fled…. [He] thought of building a temple where he could rest the ark of holiness… So he had a basilica built in Oviedo…the seat of his kingdom.*

*Anyone God calls to visit such precious and glorious gifts, let them know that by apostolical authority, granted for the purpose by the bishop of this holy church, the third part of the penalty of their merited sins is forgiven, besides which, they obtain one thousand four years and six lents of indulgence.*

Both accounts concluded with an inventory of the chest, which Graham reduced to bullet points.

- Large fragment of the One True Cross
- Eight thorns from the crown of thorns
- Part of "the Shroud of the Lord"

Graham added quotes, unsure what to make of the phrase.

- Part of the reed the Jews used to ridicule Jesus
- Part of Jesus's tunic
- Part of His tomb
- Part of the swaddling clothes that wrapped Him in the manger
- Bread from the Last Supper
- Bread from the feeding of the 5,000
- Manna
- An image of Jesus crucified, one of the three that Nicodemus made of His portrait
- A large piece of the apostle Bartholomew's skin
- A vial of Mary's breastmilk
- Locks of Mary's hair
- Pieces of Mary's robes
- One of the thirty silver coins paid to Judas
- A vial of blood shed from the side of an image of Jesus that had bled
- Dirt from the spot where Jesus ascended
- Part of Lazarus's tomb
- Part of Elijah's mantle
- Part of the forehead and locks of hair from John the Baptist
- A lock of hair Mary Magdalene used to clean the feet of Jesus
- Bones of the babies Herod slaughtered in Bethlehem
- Part of the rock that closed the Holy Sepulchre
- Part of the olive branch Jesus carried in His hand when He entered Jerusalem on Palm Sunday
- A rock from the spot on Mount Sinai where Moses fasted
- Part of Moses's staff
- Roasted fish and honeycomb from the meal Jesus ate with His disciples when He appeared to them after

His Resurrection
- Bones from the hand of Stephen, the first martyr
- Part of Peter's sandal
- Part of a chain that held Peter
- Bones of the twelve apostles
- The pouches of Peter and Andrew
- Water jar from the wedding at Cana

Graham was surprised the Sudarium didn't seem to be the featured object in the chest, but rather a fragment from the alleged One True Cross. Pelayo—or at least his translator—also referred to the face cloth as part of the Shroud. Graham assumed the Sudarium was the only item it could refer to.

His search for the Pelayo source material led to several other sources from the same general time period. *Codex Valenciennes 99* predated Pelayo, proving the bishop had not invented the story. Another history, written around 1075, recorded an attempt was made to open the chest in 1030. However, an intense light burst from inside as the lid was cracked open and it was immediately closed again, but only after permanently blinding some of the people there.

After the successful opening of the chest in 1075, King Alfonso VI commissioned the decorative silver paneling Graham had seen firsthand the day before. A Latin inscription accompanied the reliefs of Christ and the twelve disciples: *Of the Sepulcher of the Lord and of His Sudarium and of His Most Holy Blood.*

He looked over the dubious inventory again—an exhibit that would have made even the shameless P.T. Barnum blush—and felt a mixture of anger and embarrassment welling up. Anger at anonymous hucksters lost to history who profited from the superstitions of the ignorant. Embarrassed that the church had a foot in both camps. Graham felt an impulse to walk away, to just go home. He stared blindly out the window before focusing contemptuously on the cathedral tower. Adding to the assault on his common sense was the incentive to suspend disbelief by the offer of indulgences.

Although he was Presbyterian, Graham had been raised Episcopalian and had frequently attended services of other congregations throughout his spiritual journey, but all the denominations had been Protestant. He had many Catholic friends and colleagues—as well as Eastern Orthodox—but he never understood how Mariology or indulgences could be justified scripturally. He had a higher appreciation for tradition than most Protestants he knew, but he didn't place it on par with Scripture.

As much as he hated how Christians were primarily divided into Roman Catholic, Protestant, and Eastern Orthodox expressions of the faith, these were issues he couldn't see reconciled. He was too committed to the motto of the Reformation—*sola scriptura*, Scripture alone. The relentlessly biblical systematic theology of Calvin made more sense of the whole of Scripture than any other understanding he'd encountered.

The cathedral tower materialized again, piercing his black thoughts. He realized that if he, a Protestant, could see the tower then so could everyone else, including those of other faiths and no faith at all. The tower wasn't merely Roman Catholic, it was *catholic* in the true sense of the word—universal—a symbol of the core doctrines uniting all believers like an architectural Nicene Creed.

Chastened, he decided to try to see the inventory in the most favorable light he could. If the relics could be conclusively proven genuine, what would it mean? Indulgences notwithstanding, the artifacts would be corroboration of biblical and early church history—the work Graham had devoted his life to.

But there were unintended consequences to that kind of proof. Some people would worship the artifacts themselves.

Calvin called the human heart an idol factory. Graham had seen that characterization borne out a number of times, especially at the Holy Sepulchre, where objects and locations—some authentic, others spurious—were literally idolized. One of the principles he taught his students was that—archaeologically speaking—a measure of doubt was a gift from God, divine protection from the human ability to abuse good things.

In their least favorable light, false relics didn't corroborate biblical history, but they did corroborate Christian theology in a backhanded way. They were artifacts of a fallen world, where charlatans preyed on superstitions, where ignorance masqueraded as truth. In the end, dubious relics revealed the need of salvation, and authentic relics corroborated the means of salvation.

Graham studied the inventory again and—aside from the Sudarium—easily categorized the entire list as either patently false or without evidence. The cumulative effect of the absurd claims made him want to avoid guilt by association, and he almost hoped the Sudarium could be easily proved fake to protect his reputation. Yet the cumulative case supporting the Sudarium was stronger than he expected to find. Strong enough not to immediately book a flight home. Strong enough for him to want to contribute to the body of evidence.

Frustratingly, the best-case scenario would please almost no one and leave him open to criticism. Uncritical advocates would not appreciate the concept of benevolent doubt and oversell the evidence. Overcritical skeptics would seize on the lack of certainty as justification to doubt. Graham could be portrayed as a champion by skeptics and a traitor by advocates. To his black-and-white mind, he hated gray area. He realized the view from the window mirrored his thoughts, allegorizing his situation. The cathedral tower sat beneath an overcast sky, a pillar supporting the gray.

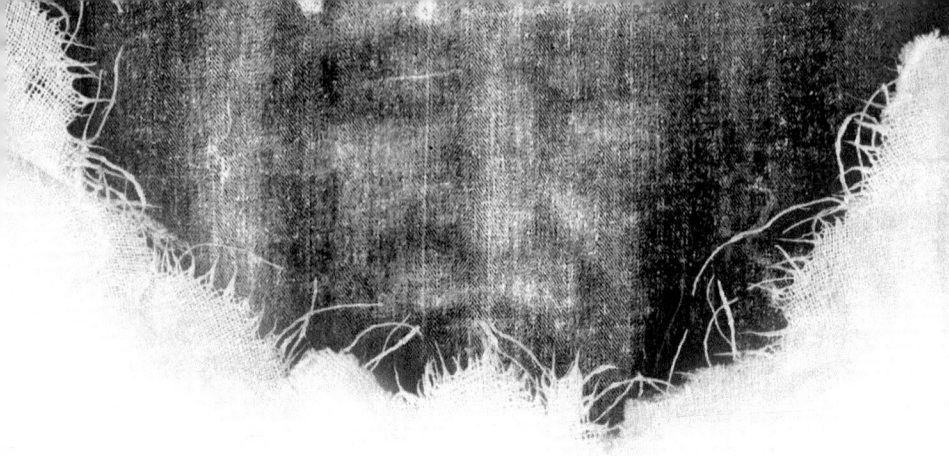

# TWENTY-ONE

Graham returned to the SIFT YouTube channel, hoping to gauge how the video was being received, but the comments section had been turned off. He entered "SIFT Shroud of Turin" into the search bar, curious about the claims of earlier posts. A thumbnail image of Christopher King gesturing to a projection of the Shroud appeared at the top of the column of stacked results, entitled *Shredding the Shroud*. The description listed it as a lecture from five years earlier.

After clicking the link, it was immediately clear the slightly shaky video had been shot by someone in the first few rows. King began with a brief explanation of the Shroud and its known history. Graham was impressed at how the magician conveyed the facts accurately with no editorial or snarky asides. Those were left to the audience members sitting near the camera, mumbling comments to their neighbors, but stopped when King came to his argument.

"The Shroud of Turin is a problem for Christians whether or not it is authentic. In the Gospel of John, chapter twenty, verse twenty-nine, Jesus says to the disciple Thomas, 'Have you believed because you have seen me? Blessed are the people who have not seen and yet have believed.' If people are more blessed because they have not seen Jesus, why would He leave an image of Himself?"

Several chuckles came from the audience as Graham rested his elbows on the table, tenting his arms to support his chin.

"But it gets worse. Exodus chapter twenty, verse four—which is the second commandment—says, 'You shall not make for yourself a carved image or any likeness of anything that is in heaven above or that is on the earth beneath or that is in the water below.' Assume for a moment that the Shroud really is the burial cloth of Jesus. That would mean God violated His own commandment. It would also mean that Peter and John, the men who supposedly discovered the Shroud in the tomb, would have no reason to keep it because they were Jews. How could Jesus fulfill the law and break it at the same time? If anything, Peter and John would have destroyed it to hide Jesus's contradiction.

"But medieval proponents of the Shroud must've understood the problem because they found a loophole in the commandment. They characterized the Shroud as acheiropoieta, not made with hands. If human hands didn't make it, then they could keep it. Now, I am known for sleight of hand, but medieval advocates used no hands at all. That is some serious magic. It transformed a mundane, discarded object into a miraculous creation revered as a relic.

"Even though the Shroud has been scientifically proven to be from the Middle Ages, the legend that inspired its creation goes so far back it can be seen in the gospels themselves. You can actually trace its initial development."

The image on the screen behind King changed to show a passage of Scripture.

"Contrary to the order they are found in most Bibles, the first gospel to be written was probably Mark. According to Mark, chapter fifteen, verse forty-six, 'After Joseph bought a linen cloth and took down the body, he wrapped it in the linen.' Matthew and Luke almost certainly used Mark's gospel as a source for their own gospels. But look what happens."

Two more passages of Scripture faded in, arranged in columns to the right of the quote from Mark.

"Luke's gospel says the same as Mark's—that it was a linen cloth. Matthew, however, adds a detail. He says, 'Joseph took the body, wrapped it in a *clean* linen cloth.' Matthew was allegedly an eyewitness, but Mark was not. So why is Matthew copying Mark's account? Now look at what John says."

A fourth passage filled a column to the right of the other three.

"John wrote his gospel last, probably decades after Luke. He says, 'Then they took Jesus's body and wrapped it, with the aromatic spices, in strips of linen cloth according to Jewish burial customs.' Now the Shroud is accompanied by aromatic spices. What started as a common linen cloth, then became a clean cloth, and then was paired with aromatic spices. You can see the beginnings of a fish story, where repeated tellings add information to make the story better and better.

"Don't believe me? Less than two-hundred years later, church father Origen wrote that the Shroud was cleaner *after* it touched Jesus's body. Not only that, but it cleansed everything it touched—including the tomb itself. Of course, if that's true, then there could be no contamination to skew the radiocarbon test."

This time Graham joined the laughter from the audience despite King overlooking the more commonsense explanation for the differences in the Gospels—that eyewitness accounts rarely share the exact same details. And in the case of the Gospels, the details complimented each other, rather than contradicting themselves. The fish story was Origen's, not the disciples.

"You see the legend even more clearly with the tomb. Mark merely says it was a tomb cut into the rock. Matthew adds the detail that it was a *new* tomb. Luke expands on that and says no one had ever been placed in the tomb. If that sounds strange to you, just know the Jews reused these rock-cut tombs during that period. They would open the tomb after a year and collect the bones in a box for reburial. So then John, decades later, adds another detail—the tomb was in a garden. The stone in front of the tomb even seems to grow. Mark simply calls it a stone, but Matthew calls it 'a great stone.'"

As he spoke, parallel phrases in the passages changed color, highlighting them to make the connections obvious.

"Don't misunderstand me. I do not believe the disciples of Jesus were bad people or con artists. They were uneducated men who were disillusioned and were trying to make sense of how to honor their teacher—a great moral teacher—after his death. I don't believe Peter and John found an empty tomb. And with all the details the gospels provide, you'd think if they really found a miraculous image on the Shroud then it would be mentioned in at least one of the accounts.

"Instead, they talk about the size of the stone, the newness of the tomb, and that it was in a garden. But not that the burial cloth they found had the image of their teacher miraculously imprinted on it. There's no documentary evidence they even kept it.

"I agree with what John Calvin has to say about it, and I don't agree with Calvin about much. He asked how the gospel writers could so carefully relate all the miracles of Christ's death but omit mentioning the image of the Lord on the Shroud. He even goes so far as to admit the image is painted on the linen. He also characterizes the story of King Abgar of Edessa receiving the Shroud as nothing more than a fairy tale. So, in regard to the Shroud, I am a Calvinist." King paused to allow laughter, and again Graham caught himself smiling at the witticism.

"I only wish Calvin had applied his critical thinking skills to the rest of his theology," King continued. "The problem with the church is that it does not have enough Calvins. Or Daniels, for that matter. Daniel is one of the few examples of critical thinking in the Bible—the lions' den notwithstanding. In the book *Bel and the Dragon*—which is really a chapter of Daniel kept out of Protestant Bibles but included in Roman Catholic and Eastern Orthodox Bibles—Cyrus, king of Persia worshipped an idol called Bel.

"Every day the king offered forty sheep, six pitchers of wine, and a ton of flour. He would make the offering in the temple, and the next morning it would be gone. The king said the disappearance was proof Bel existed. But Daniel refused to worship Bel, whom he considered an idol, nothing more than a statue made of clay and brass. Daniel denied it ever ate or drank anything. The king accused Daniel of blasphemy and told him to prove Bel was merely a statue. The king made his offering as usual, then sealed the door with his own signet.

"In the morning, the offering was gone as usual. But Daniel had directed his servants to scatter a layer of ash across the floor. Although the offering was gone, there were footprints in the ash. And they led to a secret door the priests had installed. The priests had been taking the offerings for themselves. It was a magic trick, an illusion. Fast-forward to today and nothing has changed. From the priests of Bel to televangelists to the Shroud of Turin—religion is always about power and control."

Despite some of the loaded phrases, fallacies, and mischaracterizations, Graham found King intelligent and better informed than he expected. More than that, he liked King. The impression proved Iris's point. If Graham's video was proof someone could be right but unpersuasive, King's video proved someone could be wrong and persuasive.

# TWENTY-TWO

Curious what King's background was, Graham opened a new tab on his browser and entered christopherking.com in the address bar. King's face filled the center of the page, surrounded by a halo of five cards, each with a symbol instead of a suit and number. Alexander used cards like that—he called them ESP cards—in a trick Graham had seen him perform several times. Alexander would have two sets of the cards, have a volunteer pick one. Then he'd make a prediction, setting one of the cards facedown, asking the volunteer to place any of their cards facedown.

The sequence was repeated until all five predictions had a pair. When Alexander turned each pair faceup, the symbols matched. The two circles were together, as were the crosses, wavy lines, square, and star.

Graham navigated to the About page to read the biography. The memory of Alexander's trick with the ESP cards reminded him of something Alexander said about the autobiographies of magicians: they often lie. It was part of creating the mystique of the characters they played, a meta-illusion which gave performers a backstory. Sometimes the character created by the magician was their greatest illusion.

He remembered Alexander telling him about Jean Eugéne Robert-Houdin, whom he called the father of modern magic.

After retiring from performing, Robert-Houdin published his memoirs, inspiring thousands of magicians including the son of a rabbi in Appleton, Wisconsin, called Erich Weiss who later renamed himself after the author, adding an i to the name to become *Houdini*.

Robert-Houdin wrote that as an apprentice he was introduced to magic when a shopkeeper mistakenly gave him books on conjuring rather than his craft of clockmaking. Soon after, he fell ill while traveling and lost consciousness on the side of a country road. He awoke in the wagon of a magician named Torrini, who nursed him back to health. Robert-Houdin traveled with Torrini for a time, learning the art and skills of magic.

According to Alexander—Robert-Houdin had invented Torrini and most of his early history. However, even his writing was done with such skill, when the memoir was published, it was admired and reviewed by Charles Dickens, who was also an amateur magician.

Graham wondered how much of King's biography was fictional, then smiled to himself at the irony. King accused the Gospels of being fictional biographies, after all. The difference, of course, was that the Gospels were not intended as entertainments.

King had grown up in Pasadena, the son of a lawyer who was an amateur magician and an original member of the Magic Castle. When the Magic Castle added the Academy of Magical Arts and Science, King was one of the first kids to work through the courses.

On an interesting sidenote that Graham couldn't wait to share with Alexander, when King was in middle school, he could sometimes hear a band practice in the basement of the mansion next door. The neighbor was an eye surgeon, but the son, who was about ten years older than King, sang for a band called Mammoth who played backyard parties almost every weekend around Pasadena.

By the time King was a junior in high school, Mammoth had changed their name to Van Halen. King had once climbed a tree to watch a photoshoot of the band in the backyard. The singer inherited the mansion and still lived in the house.

In his twenties, King met James Randi at the Magic Castle. The Amazing Randi—as he was known on stage—became a mentor not only for his magic, but also heavily influenced his worldview by encouraging King's skepticism. King was inspired to follow Randi into the tradition of magicians who used their knowledge of deceptive practices to expose frauds. Houdini had famously attacked Spiritualism, revealing the methods of mediums, proving they were nothing more than unscrupulous magicians victimizing the distraught and bereaved. Other magicians had similarly exposed those who abused the art and pretended to actually have supernatural abilities.

At the time of their meeting, Randi had just made news with his appearance on The Tonight Show with Johnny Carson. Carson—another amateur magician and member of the Magic Castle—had Randi perform on the show more than two dozen times. But when a self-proclaimed psychic from Israel named Uri Gellar appeared on the show, Randi served as a consultant. Gellar had become well-known for using his mind to bend spoons, make watches stop and start on command, and other minor wonders.

Randi the magician skeptic advised the producers of the Tonight Show, explaining possible methods for performing the trick and how to prepare the props so that Gellar couldn't cheat, but would be able to achieve the result if, in fact, his powers were real.

Graham opened YouTube and found the clip of Gellar's appearance. Gellar failed every demonstration of his abilities and explained he was experiencing a mental block from nerves. Despite the failure, Gellar had maintained a career as a psychic, which Graham thought might be Gellar's greatest trick.

A clip of Randi on *The Tonight Show* was at the top of the column of related videos, captioned "Popoff Exposed!" Graham remembered some scandal involving the televangelist in the 80s but couldn't remember the details. He clicked the link and watched Randi—bald, bearded, and surprisingly small—take the guest chair next to Carson's desk without performing. Randi announced he wanted to show a clip from a Peter Popoff service that had been held and broadcast a few days earlier.

The clip showed Popoff in a packed arena, roaming the area in front of the stage, revving up the congregation, promising the Holy Spirit would heal whatever ailments they suffered from. Popoff halted, strained to listen to the Holy Spirit, then called out a name, pointed into the audience, and walked to the person. Without being told what her affliction was, Popoff asked if she wanted to get rid of the walker next to her. The woman said yes, as he took her hand and declared her street address. Suddenly—violently—he pressed a palm against her forehead and screamed he was burning the arthritis out of her body. He then had the woman take a few steps just to—as he said—"make the Devil mad."

Randi stopped the clip, then explained he wanted to play it again, this time synced to the radio signal he had recorded during the service. As Popoff walked back and forth in front of the stage in the replay, his volume was lowered and a crackle of static sounded, followed by a woman's voice. "Hello, Petey. Can you hear me? If you can't, you're in trouble."

The voice continued, overlapping Popoff's own, prompting every prophetic utterance just before he said it. After the clip was over, Randi explained that Popoff used an earpiece and that his wife was feeding him information gathered from prayer cards filled out by the people as they waited in line to get in.

Graham leaned back in his chair, appreciating the research and work Randi must have done to pull off the exposé of such a despicable charlatan. King attributed the development of his critical thinking skills to Randi's inspiration. But like King's wish for Calvin, Graham wished Randi and King could use their critical thinking to dismantle their own false worldview and the irrational foundations of their own thought.

# TWENTY-THREE

Graham stood, restless with inaction, and decided to visit Camilo de Blas, the gourmet confectionary across from the hotel. A picture of Woody Allen and Scarlet Johansson standing in front of a display case was propped on top the same case in the picture. He hadn't realized some of the movie *Vicki Barcelona* had been filmed in Oviedo. After several failed attempts to communicate with the person behind the counter, he pointed at the the house specialty—a carbayón—and a Coke Zero. Ten minutes later, he opened the door to his room to discover an envelope slipped under the door signed with the letter A. He tore open one end, tilted the note out, and recognized Don Arturo's handwriting.

*Cathedral Cloisters. As soon as you read this.*

He found the map from the cathedral tour and located the cloisters on the other side of the Cámara Santa from the apse. After downing the remainder of the Coke Zero and walked back out the door.

The man in the cathedral ticket book recognized him from earlier and ushered him in with a nod. Graham walked down the right aisle again, but instead of a sharp turn up the stairs, he veered to a side entrance and walked through an open gate. The corridor passed a small gift shop and fed him through another gate, into the cloisters.

A border of gravel surrounded a rectangle of grass with a shrub in each corner of the courtyard. Pointed Romanesque arches fenced the area in, with two stories rising above them. He scanned the colonnades on all sides for Don Arturo, discovered he was alone, and began a slow walk around the perimeter. He'd been in such a rush to reach the museum, it hadn't occurred to him until then that meeting so close to the cathedral office would risk Don Arturo being seen. The priest had gone to great lengths to ensure the secrecy of their last meeting. Did setting a meeting here mean the risk had lessened or that it had increased and left no time for an elaborate plan?

"Excuse me, please."

Graham started as a figure stepped in front of him, exiting a side door in the museum. He angled to move past the man but froze as he sensed something familiar. The hair was different from the last time he'd seen the man—long hair cascading to his shoulders from beneath a beanie—but the goatee and black glasses were the same. It was the SIFT reporter.

"My name is Paco Escarrà." The man nodded once, seemingly confirming Graham's recognition.

"I don't have anything to say to you." He moved to push past the man, hoping Don Arturo did not arrive to see them together.

"Don Arturo sent me."

Graham froze again, then turned back to Paco slowly. "How do I know you're telling the truth? You already twisted my words once."

"I did not do anything wrong," Paco said calmly, shaking his head. "There are no edits on that video. Your words are your own."

"That didn't stop Ben Steele from spinning them against me," Graham said. "They may be my words, but that was not my meaning."

"That is why I am here," Paco said, placatingly. "Don Arturo said you would want to say the truth. He said you would want to tell the people who watched the video. I can help you."

"How can you be working with Don Arturo?" Graham asked, unable to keep a confrontational edge from his voice. "You believe totally different things."

"That is true," Paco said. "I do not believe as he does. But we both want to know the truth about the Sudarium. We do not believe the evidence will say the same thing, but we both want to hear what it says."

"Strange bedfellows," Graham said.

"My English is not so good. I do not understand."

"It means I appreciate the unusual situation," Graham said. "What do you and Don Arturo think we should do?"

"I will make another video. This time I will not surprise you. I will ask what happened, and your opinion about the Sudarium. If you do not like your words, then you can do it again. I promise not to upload anything you do not want me to. Don Arturo is hoping it will change the bishop's mind."

"Yes," Graham nodded. "He told me the same thing."

"It is agreed?" Paco raised his brow expectantly.

Graham closed his eyes, taking a deep breath as he thought it through. "Yes, I agree. But I want your word nothing gets used that I don't approve first."

Paco placed a palm across his heart. "*Tienes mi palabra.* You have my word."

"Okay, so when do you want to do it?" Graham asked.

Paco patted his backpack. "I have my camera. We can do it now. I know the perfect place."

# TWENTY-FOUR

Graham followed Paco to the other side of the cloisters, through a set of iron gates to a triangular gravel yard between the apse and the cloisters. A lone tree sheltered in the far corner, and Paco set his backpack down beneath it. A narrow building with rubble walls looked like it had been spliced into the side of the cloisters, as if parts of it had been trimmed away to make it fit.

"What is this place?" Graham asked, pivoting around.

Paco removed a camera from his bag and pointed at the small structure. "That is the Cámara Santa, where the Sudarium is kept."

Graham studied the building again, trying to orient himself on the internal map he'd build when he visited the inside of the chamber. An incoming text vibrated his phone and he checked the screen to see a message from Iris.

"2 hours out. What hotel are you at?"

Graham responded with the name, deciding against sharing the address, thinking sending the location would also send the wrong impression.

"Gran Hotel? Too posh for my blood," Iris replied. "Just booked a spot off the plaza. Meet for dinner?"

Graham agreed to meet her at a place directly on the plaza at 8:30, then slid the phone into his pocket as Paco finished testing different positions to shoot from.

"Stand by the gate, please, Dr. Eliot." Paco pointed him to a spot, then fine-tuned the angle of Graham's stance and position. After a sound check, Paco nodded at Graham to indicate the camera was recording.

"Please, say your name and where you are."

"I'm Dr. Graham Eliot and I am standing behind the San Salvador Cathedral in Oviedo, Spain."

"Why are you here?" Paco prompted.

"I am an Ancient Near East scholar, a biblical archaeologist. My current focus is digitizing biblical manuscripts in the original language as well as early translations. The work takes me all over the world. I was invited here by the dean of the cathedral to photograph one of the relics in their collection, a cloth called the Sudarium. It is said to be the cloth wrapped around Jesus's head as He died on the cross, which was discarded in the tomb when He was buried."

"Will everyone be able to see the images?"

"There are no images to see. I was not allowed to photograph it."

"Why is that?"

"I'm not sure. When I arrived, I was told the dean who arranged for me to do the work had been replaced the day before, and that the bishop and new dean decided not to go ahead with the project."

"This is the closest you have come?" Paco asked.

"I guess so," Graham said, turning to look up at the cathedral. "It's somewhere in there."

"Is the church hiding something they do not want you to know?"

Graham turned back to Paco, composing his expression to be philosophical, refusing to be provoked. "I am not a conspiracy theorist. It could be a bureaucratic issue. They might be concerned that my lights would damage the cloth or the stains that are on it. It might be that they have someone else to do the work. I wasn't given an explanation, so I am not sure what to believe. But I wouldn't say they are hiding something."

"Do you believe it was the cloth wrapped around the head of Jesus Christ?"

Graham shrugged. "I don't have an opinion yet. I didn't even know it existed until a couple of weeks ago. The documents recording the history are very interesting, though some of the material is almost certainly legendary.

"However, I want to make it very clear that I am not here to determine whether or not the Sudarium is authentic. I was asked to document it with high resolution images using multispectral lights so that it can be studied. Only then can scholars determine the probability of its authenticity. I would hope the church would be interested in having as much information about the Sudarium as possible so that it can be evaluated.

"There really is nothing for the church to fear. If the Sudarium really is the actual cloth that covered the head of Jesus, it is an astonishing archaeological artifact that needs to be studied further. And if it can be shown to be more recent or inauthentic in some other way, I would think it would serve the church well to acknowledge that and stop venerating it. I would think an admission like that would bolster the church's credibility, not do damage to it. Your organization, SIFT, you want the same thing, don't you? You say you are lovers of truth. I am too. That's why I'm here."

Paco smiled broadly, giving him a thumbs-up, and turned off the camera. "*Excelente. Gracias*, Dr. Eliot."

"Thank *you* for giving me the opportunity for both of us to do this right." He offered Paco his hand and shook it holding his eyes. "I'm trusting you."

# TWENTY-FIVE

Hunger—along with a vague, unsettling anticipation—conspired with a lifelong habit of being early to appointments, leaving Graham with a few minutes to spare outside the restaurant in the plaza. Exterior lights illuminated the cathedral, an immovable point against a flow of black and gray clouds. The umbrellas of the open-air seating outside the restaurants lined the perimeter like an encampment. He sauntered away from the cathedral to the fountain in the corner of the plaza.

On the other side of the three-tiered waterfall, he noticed a statue of a woman on the overlook that rose behind the fountain. As he moved around to get a closer look, he realized the bronze figure was larger than life, the top of his head reaching her eyes. The ornately flowered hat, bustled dress hemmed in frills, and ballooned shoulders reminded Graham of a costume from *Hello, Dolly!* A plaque near her feet identified the woman as *La Regenta*.

"Stylish, isn't she?"

Graham turned to find Iris, smiling irreverently. Rays of blonde streaks cascaded from beneath a black velvet floppy beret. A pink sweater covered a tea-length floral dress, complimented with a pair of Doc Martens. She slipped past him before he could reply, walking up to the statue, touching different features of the bronze.

"A hundred years out of fashion, but I could make it work."

Graham laughed. "Any idea who this is?"

"*La Regenta*, of course," Iris said, tapping a toe on the plaque.

"I got that far. Who's that?"

"Seriously?" Iris mocked. "You do know that ancient biblical manuscripts were not the only books ever written, right? Well, one of them was *La Regenta*, by Clarín. Takes place in Oviedo, though it's called something else in the book. This is Ana, the unhappily married wife of the magistrate—the regent. She takes a lover, but a priest—her confessor—falls in love with her as well."

"Which one is she waiting for by the fountain?" Graham asked.

"*La Regenta* waits for no one," Iris said proudly. "Look at her pose. She is caught in mid-turn, and she is positioned at an angle to the church. But is she turning toward it or away from it? Has she just left someone, or is she on her way?"

"She moves in mysterious ways," Graham said.

Iris smiled playfully. "U2. Well done. Unless that was your Bono impression, in which case that was crap."

Graham laughed, then waved a hand, shepherding her toward the restaurant. "Hungry?"

"Positively famished."

Graham was thankful the restaurant was bright and casual, neither a hot spot for nightlife, nor an intimate setting for a date night. Iris slid behind the table, onto a cushioned bench running the length of the wall, while Graham took a chair opposite her.

"Thank you so much for coming," Graham said. "I didn't know who else to call."

"I'm honored," Iris said, bowing her head. "And I'm glad

you did. As I told you at the museum, I'm fascinated by your work. After your lecture, I went to your organization's website to learn more. Even made a donation. Just a widow's mite, but a show of support."

"Very kind," Graham said, echoing her bow. "I appreciate that. Every little bit helps."

"Yes, well, I have to uphold my philanthropic reputation as the Richard Branson of expatriate art historians working as social media coordinators who double as translators."

Graham chuckled. "A heavy crown to wear."

"You have no idea," Iris said with an exaggerated frown. "But it's your reputation I came here to rehabilitate. I have to say I am a bit surprised. Looks like you've started to plot out a social media strategy without me."

"What do you mean?"

"That interview you gave today," Iris said, bending the inflection into a question. "The new SIFT video that posted about an hour ago."

"It posted already?"

Iris cocked her head. "How could you not know?"

"I don't know how long these things take," Graham said. "I got a note from the priest who had approached me origi- nally, Don Arturo. It said to meet at the museum behind the cathedral. I thought I was going to meet him. Instead, it was the guy from SIFT who made the first video.

"When the guy said Don Arturo sent him, I couldn't think of any reason he'd know the priest other than he was telling the truth. And he wasn't aggressive at all. I actually kin- da liked him. He said Don Arturo thought I should be given a chance to explain myself without being ambushed, and he agreed."

"And you trusted him?" Iris asked incredulously.

"Yes," Graham said, "because Don Arturo trusts him. It was an opportunity that just kind of happened."

"Well, let's try to be more cautious in the future, shall we?" Iris scolded mildly. "The good news is that there is no damage done. In fact, you come off quite well. Here."

Iris held her phone in the center of the table, angling it so they could both see it. Ben Steele appeared and announced another breaking news update, then explained SIFT talked with Graham Eliot again about his rejection by the church after arriving to work on the Sudarium of Oviedo. As the video played, it occurred to Graham that Paco hadn't framed the shot to feature the cathedral in the background, but the Cámara Santa.

"Well, he kept his promise," Graham said, sitting back after it was over. "That's exactly what I said. No edits, no ambushes."

Iris raised a finger to make a point. "Most importantly, it was a quick response. Hopefully it'll do some damage control. Now, let's order some food. Then we can talk about next steps."

# TWENTY-SIX

"How was the train?" Graham asked after they had ordered several tapas.

"Brilliant. It gave me time to research the Sudarium." Iris leaned forward, folding her arms on the table. "I've lived in Spain for more than ten years, and I have never heard of it before. Even with all my research into the Shroud. And then when I learned all the ways the Sudarium appears to correspond to the Shroud, I was gobsmacked. Am I right in thinking this is why the dean contacted you? To help develop better evidence that can demonstrate the correspondence?"

"Exactly." Graham nodded. "I hadn't heard of it either until my meeting with Don Arturo. I've been devouring all I can about it, mainly its history. It's really just background information since the scope of my work is to digitize the cloth, not authenticate it. But I am intrigued by it. More than that, actually, which is why I'm still here. So tell me some of the connections you discovered."

"Do you know about the blood type?" Iris asked.

"Don Arturo said they matched."

Iris nodded. "Type AB, in fact, which is not common in Europe, but quite common in the Middle East. Did Don Arturo say anything about testing the DNA?"

"They tried, but he said there was no nuclear DNA to test."

"Unfortunate. Especially since the blood on the Sudarium

and the Shroud are both mixed with pulmonary edema. What are the odds that two relics both contain evidence of asphyxiation? If these are supposed to be forgeries, then the forgers would not only have to understand the physiological process of crucifixion, but also collect the blood of someone from the Middle East who had asphyxiated. Or if they are not forgeries, then we could have the cloths from two different Middle Eastern asphyxiation victims, which seems highly unlikely."

"Agreed," Graham said, not wanting to interrupt. Olivia had been an external processor, and he had developed the instinct of when to affirm and when to contribute.

"Then there's the stains themselves," Iris continued enthusiastically. "The stains on the Sudarium are similar in both shape and size to the Shroud, and they're in the same positions. That makes sense if they're made by the same wound. And yet it's not a perfect match, which makes sense if they were made at different times and the body was moved while the Sudarium was covering the head. Also, the Sudarium has both vital and postmortem blood, but the Shroud only has postmortem. And do you know where the vital blood on the Sudarium is?"

"No, tell me."

"Near the puncture wounds in the cloth where it wrapped around the back of the head. And the holes in the cloth are wider on one side of the fabric, meaning whatever pierced it was conical."

"As in the crown of thorns," Graham finished.

"Some holes were probably made by pins attaching the cloth in the back," Iris said, "but not all of them. So, yes, that would be the implication. Do you recall the researchers I told you about who overlaid the negative image of the face of the Shroud on top of the Christ Pantocrator icon? Well, they overlaid the image of the Sudarium on top of the Shroud and discovered seventy points of congruence on the frontal stains, and fifty points on the rear side."

"Interesting, but remember they are not using photographs of equal resolution or quality, so nothing conclusive can be determined."

"Understood," Iris said, bowing her head in deference. "It would be simply amazing if you had the opportunity to digitize the Shroud as well as the Sudarium."

Graham smiled conspiratorially. "Actually, that's the idea."

"What?" Iris froze in astonishment, her eyes wide as if unhinging to fit the news. "You're serious."

"At least that was the plan," Graham said, bobbing his head slowly. "But not the whole Shroud. Don Arturo's plan was for me to digitize only the area with the head and shoulders. That way there would be photographs made by the same photographer with the same equipment at the same resolution and scale. That would be the closest we'll ever get to having the two cloths in the same location. Actually, it's better since the scans can be overlaid for comparison in ways the cloths themselves cannot."

Iris released a puff of air as if she'd been holding her breath.

"At this point, it doesn't look like I'll see either one of them," Graham continued. "But the project does make sense. It is the best way to discover common elements in the two cloths. Someone needs to do this work even if it's not me."

"I can see why it is so important for you to defend your reputation so quickly," Iris said. "There's never been an opportunity like this before. It's a real cock-up."

Graham gave a crooked smile as he showed his empty palms to the ceiling. "Now you know everything. So, are there any other correspondences you found in your research?"

"Let's see," Iris said on a sigh. "There is evidence on both cloths suggesting the right cheek was swollen. And there is a mark on the right ear of the Shroud that may match a mark on the Sudarium, which would give a reference point for registering overlaid images."

"Excellent," Graham said. "I was hoping there would be something like that."

"There is also a possible scourge wound on the Sudarium that is like the ones all over the Shroud. The barbell shape is the same, and the two balls are the same size and relative distance as on the Shroud."

"Can it be matched to the Shroud for another registration point?"

"No. It's still debated because it's not as defined as the scourge wounds on the Shroud. There are some other less conclusive features that may show correspondence. The nose is about eight centimeters long on the Shroud, which matches the head the Sudarium wrapped. And the point of the nose, the nasal cavities, and the mouth and chin on the Shroud seem to match the Sudarium head as well."

"Fascinating," Graham said, half lost in thought, processing.

"Yeah, but frustrating, too."

"What do you mean?"

"It's evidence, but it's not proof. Even if they allow you to digitize both the Sudarium and the Shroud and prove the two are connected, it adds to the evidence, but without definitive proof of anything except the two are connected."

"I'm not sure what you expected," Graham said. "That's no different than your interest in the iconographic theory."

"Exactly," Iris said. "I confess sometimes it's hard to accept that so much evidence will never bridge the gap to proof. Sometimes it feels like the more I know, the less certain I am. It's like each piece of evidence is a musical note and we're trying to identify the song. The problem is other songs can be made from the same notes. So how can you tell which song we're actually hearing?"

# TWENTY-SEVEN

The conversation paused as a server placed a plate of translucent strips of Iberian ham between them. He returned a moment later with a basket of bread and a plate of cheese on a bed of tomatoes topped with olive oil. He returned again with bowls of rice pudding topped with cinnamon.

Graham bowed his head and offered a silent blessing over his food. He looked up to catch Iris glancing at other tables self-consciously.

"Didn't mean to make you uncomfortable," Graham said with an understanding smile.

"Sorry. It's just not something I'm used to. Is that something you've done since you were a child?"

Graham wobbled his head equivocally as he swallowed a bite. "Yes and no. We always said grace at the dinner table at home, but not when we went out to a restaurant."

"You were raised in a religious home, I take it?"

"We went to church every Sunday, and there was a potluck supper on Wednesday with classes afterward. And I went to youth group every week. But I never really believed any of it. It was just something we did."

"So why do you still do it?" Iris asked.

"When I was a senior in high school I had a kind of Damascus Road experience. You know, like the apostle Paul?"

"Knocked off his horse," Iris said. "A classic scene for painters."

"Right. Except neither of us actually had a horse. But we both had a sudden understanding of the truthfulness of Christianity, of the reality of the risen Christ. And it completely reoriented my life, just as it did Paul's. And with that faith came the habit of prayer."

"And you ended up believing what your parents believed all along," Iris said.

"Not exactly," Graham said. "I am more conservative in my theology than they are. I grew up Episcopalian but started attending a different denomination after becoming a believer. At the time, I couldn't appreciate the liturgy and structure of the service. Now, I've come to appreciate it very much. In fact, the Presbyterian church I belong to now has a high liturgy that is pretty close to what I grew up with. How about you? Grow up in church?"

"It's rather complicated, actually," Iris said. "Technically, my family belongs to the Church of England, but we never attended services except on Christmas and Easter. *Chreasters*, my mother called us. But it never had any meaningful place in our lives. It was just the English thing to do."

"So, what made you believe?" Graham asked.

"I don't." Iris shrugged. "I suppose I am what you might call a theistic agnostic. Or maybe an agnostic theist. I'm not sure. I'm agnostic toward both faith and unbelief."

"I don't understand," Graham said, brow pinched.

"It means I want to believe. I would love to believe in something that could give my life meaning and purpose. But I just don't see much evidence to believe in. Not enough to convince me, anyway. And *yet*," she said, tapping the air between them with a fork loaded with toast and avocado, "I'm still looking."

"Then what makes you so interested in the Shroud of Turin and the iconographic theory?" Graham set his fork down, leaning back to study her. "Did you go to art school because you grew up wanting to be an artist?"

Iris recomposed herself primly. "Actually," she said, affecting a formal tone, "I grew up wanting to be Kate Bush. Only problem was my singing voice is crap, I can't play piano well, couldn't write songs, and couldn't dance."

Graham laughed. "Other than that, how'd it work out?"

"I did have the bangs. Spot on."

"Nice. I used to cut my hair like Sting."

"Do tell," Iris said. "What record?"

"*Zenyatta Mondatta*. I took the album cover in with me and pointed to the pictures of him on the back. But please continue."

"Right. I was in art school when I stumbled across one of Ian Wilson's books on the Shroud in a used bookshop. I was captivated by the image of the face on the cover. Couldn't stop staring at it. Like it was calling to me. I bought the book and got hooked on the topic.

"If there is evidence that could convince me Jesus Christ was truly God incarnate, the Shroud might be it. And given my specialty in art history, the iconographic theory appealed to me on a number of fronts. For me, it's not merely an academic interest. I want it to be authentic. If I had that kind of proof—a kind of ancient photograph of the moment of Resurrection—then I could believe. What was it that convinced you?"

Graham took a moment to collect his thoughts, surprised at the turn the conversation had taken. "The problem with a Damascus Road experience is that it is unique to whoever experiences it. So, my reasons for believing wouldn't be very persuasive to you. Paul tells the story of his conversion three times in the New Testament, but never as evidence for someone else to believe.

"Instead, he gives evidence that can be investigated, or he makes philosophical arguments. He understood that if Christianity is objectively true and God has revealed Himself in Scripture—then what it says about the world we all share is true for everyone whether or not they believe it."

Iris shrugged. "But that is not an argument, just a premise. What would you say to someone like me?"

"First of all, there is no one like you in my experience."

"Thank you very much," Iris said, tilting her head in a curtsey.

"Second of all, the best proof for the existence of God is that without God you can't prove anything at all."

"I don't understand."

Graham nodded, preparing the next link in the logical chain. "If the God of the Bible really does exist, then He didn't merely make all the things that can be known. He is also the source for all the ways by which they can be known. God's existence is the necessary precondition for intelligibility."

Iris squinted in thought. "For example?"

"The laws of logic. There are three of them. The law of identity says that something is itself and not something else. The law of non-contradiction says something can't be true and false in the same way at the same time. And the law of excluded middle says something is either true or false, and that there is no other option.

"Every time we make a statement or articulate a thought, we use all three laws. Otherwise, we don't make any sense. They are unavoidable. Think about it. They can't change or be anything other than what they are. And there could never be a time where they didn't exist. That means they are transcendent, immaterial, eternally existing entities. And because they govern thought, they are personal. Now add that up. A transcendent, personal, eternal, immaterial entity is the classic definition for God."

"Uh huh," Iris mumbled, processing and frowning more deeply.

"The implications are enormous," Graham continued. "It means in order to make a logical argument against God's existence, you can only do it using the intellectual tools that God provides. And that means to argue against God's existence actually proves He exists."

Iris leaned forward, propping her chin on her knitted hands.

"Unbelief is fundamentally irrational," Graham said. "That is the fatal flaw for people like SIFT."

"I'll need some time to think through that," Iris said.

"Yes, but whose tools will you use to do it?" Graham smiled.

Iris chuckled. "I didn't intend to have a conversation about religion over dinner. But if you're willing to work with a filthy heathen, I'd still be happy to help."

"I welcome all the help I can get. If I only worked with people who believed what I did, it would be a very small circle and I would be a much poorer man for it. I appreciate your willingness to help and your expertise."

"Just don't try to force a confession out of me," Iris said, pointing a warning finger. "No Spanish Inquisition."

"No one expects the Spanish Inquisition," Graham shot back with a cartoon British accent.

Iris choked on a bite of food, laughing. "Got me again."

# TWENTY-EIGHT

Gray dawn leaked from behind the closed curtains, framing a void Graham stared into as he lay awake, debating whether to get up. A text alert pinged, and he reached for his phone to see a message from Alexander.

"SIFT just played a video announcing the contest at the conference. They posted it at the same time."

He clicked the link without responding. The SIFT logo animated in, then transitioned to Christopher King standing before a virtual background patterned with the logo.

"I am Christopher King. You may have seen me escape from a straitjacket suspended upside down from a crane, or from handcuffs while submerged in a locked tank of water. I've even been buried alive in a coffin six feet below the ground. But you may not know I'm also a mental escape artist. As a fellow of the Skeptical Inquiry of Free Thinkers—SIFT—I sift fact from fiction, liberating myself and others from lies and legends. And one of the many locks I've picked is religion. To borrow a phrase from the philosopher Santayana, 'Religion is a pack of lies about events that never happened told by people who weren't there.'

"Through critical thinking and a scientific view of the world, religion has been exposed as nothing more than sanctified superstition held over from a prescientific age. And a world without God means religious institutions are nothing more than irrelevant power structures. Their authority is enabled by their ability to manipulate the faithful by preying on ignorance and wish-fulfillment.

"One of the best examples of religious superstition, ignorance, and wish-fulfillment is the Shroud of Turin, the alleged burial cloth of Jesus. Scientific examination has conclusively shown that it is a medieval forgery. And yet superstition blinds many people to the truth, causing them to believe irrational nonsense and embrace it as a genuine historical artifact. They believe there is no earthly way the image on the cloth could have been created by human hands through any artistic or natural methods. Superstition enslaves them.

"So, I am here to announce a contest. This is a call for entries for artists to recreate the image on the Shroud of Turin. The goal is not to prove how the image on the Shroud was actually made. Together we will prove that there are many different ways that the image could have been created. I, myself, produce the image in my stage show. SIFT wants to see how you would do it. Although truth is its own reward, the best image will be awarded a $10,000 prize. And we couldn't think of a more fitting name for the contest than a phrase taken from the Eucharist in the Latin Mass. In the Middle Ages, the Latin form of this is my body was corrupted and became *Hocus Pocus*. Ladies and gentlemen, I give you the *Hocus Pocus Challenge*. Let the contest begin!"

Graham checked the time and subtracted the seven-hour difference. It was 12:30 a.m. in Nashville, and Alexander's body clock was on California time.

Alexander picked up on the second ring and started speaking, skipping the greeting. "You have to hand it to him: *Hocus Pocus* is pretty clever."

"Yeah, but the Gospel has the virtue of truth-in-advertising."

"Hey, I have an idea," Alexander said. "Since King's getting into the religion business, maybe you should get into the magic business. Want me to teach you a couple of tricks?"

"I've already had a career as an escapologist. Without any gimmicks, too. He's never freed himself from beneath the Temple Mount, or from a shaft of ice on the summit of Mount Ararat, or from handcuffs in a Saudi Arabian jail."

"Actually, I freed you from the cuffs in Saudi Arabia. But point taken. So, what do you think of the Hocus Pocus Challenge?"

"I think the waters just got really muddy. There's going to be so much misinformation on the internet about the Shroud that it will be even harder for people to find trustworthy information about it. Of course, that's true of almost anything these days."

"You're right," Alexander said, "unless you're quoting from the internet."

Graham chuckled. "Let's just hope that Don Arturo is right, and the church feels compelled to respond. And quickly."

"Keep me posted. I doubt I'll hear the latest in the honky-tonks here."

"Learned to two-step yet?"

"You know how much I love country music," Alexander said sarcastically. "It's funny—I actually do like the old-school stuff like Hank Williams and Johnny Cash and Waylon Jennings. You can't deny they had an authenticity even though they dressed up in fancy suits with rhinestones. Totally opposite of modern country artists that dress like they're fresh off the farm but sound completely contrived and focus-grouped."

"You have a point," Graham agreed.

"I did have my first star encounter." Alexander paused for effect. "Reba McEntire was on my flight. But Nashville's not at all like I thought it would be. It's got to be the bachelorette party capital of the universe. Really annoying."

Graham laughed. "Have you connected with King yet?"

"Only in passing. I ran into him, but he was surrounded by a bunch of people. He told me to come to the show tonight at the House of Cards and we could hang out there. And he wants to introduce me around to some people at SIFT."

"I forgot about that place. Good luck getting in. Look for the owl and say open sesame with a Tennessee accent."

Graham decided it was too early to text Iris and spent the next hour catching up on emails he had ignored since arriving in Spain. He sent Iris the link to the video at nine a.m. Five minutes later, her name appeared on the phone.

"I wish Peter Gabriel announced my arrival wherever I went," Iris said by way of greeting.

"If he knew I'd reduced his art to a ringtone, I'm sure he'd rethink making any more music," Graham said.

"Your secret's safe with me," Iris laughed. "Apparently, it's time for us to get cracking."

"I was just thinking the same thing."

"See my point, now?" Iris asked. "Christopher King was quite persuasive. Very likable and intelligent."

"And he was completely wrong," Graham added. "Did you hear how many logical fallacies he committed?"

"That is entirely beyond the point. The people he is speaking to don't think like that. He communicated it in the language they understand best, which is perception. They don't care about formal argumentation. He sounded fact-based and had an authoritative air. His demeanor and comportment gave him the kind of credibility they recognize. No one watching cares about whether his syllogism is sound or valid or whatever."

"But I wouldn't know how to respond without making a sound argument," Graham stammered. "Frankly don't even want to try. I feel like Alice falling down the rabbit hole."

"It's not an either-or situation," Iris said. "The point is that the form is as important as the content, and it needs to be delivered in a way that resonates with the people you're trying to reach. I'm sure as a theologian you have some kind of category for that sort of thing. Jesus didn't drop a theology book on a rural, agrarian society, after all. Instead, He told stories, right?"

Graham sighed. "I get the point. What do you propose?"

"Let's meet at the café on the plaza and we can talk about what to do next."

# TWENTY-NINE

Graham opened the door to his room and started at the figure filling the frame. He released a puff of air, laughing at himself as he recognized Don Arturo in full clerical robes.

"Forgive me, Dr. Eliot. I did not intend to surprise you."

"Guess you'll have to hand-deliver the message this time." Graham smiled apologetically.

"Actually, I was coming to see you this time."

"Aren't you afraid to be seen with me?"

"Things have changed," Don Arturo said. "For the better. May I come in?"

Graham stepped back, embarrassed he hadn't asked, and invited him into the room with a sweeping gesture. They seated themselves in the armchairs by the window.

"Your plan appears to be working like you hoped it would," Graham said.

The priest clasped his hands together and bobbed them thankfully. "Yes, there were good signs yesterday after your video was posted. But then the contest was announced, and that made all the difference."

"The Hocus Pocus Challenge," Graham said. "Clever name."

"It profanes the Holy Mass," Don Arturo said seriously. "That is what most upset the bishop. It is one thing to attack the authenticity of a relic. It is quite another to insult the church and the institution established by our Lord.

"So, like Joseph becoming chief advisor to Pharaoh after being sold into slavery by his brothers, what they intend for harm, God will use for good. When the bishop learned you were still in Oviedo and were willing to do the work you came for, they recognized the opportunity to answer SIFT's attack before it could have much impact. But it is better than that, even. If the images show what we believe they will, then we can announce the preliminary results on the very platform they themselves provided for us. We will reach those who need it most—the people who do not believe."

Graham leaned forward as if shortening the distance the news had to travel. "So, you are saying the project is back on? That we can digitize the Sudarium and the Shroud?"

"The Sudarium, yes," Don Arturo said, nodding once. "The Shroud is still being discussed with the dean in Turin. But I have faith that he can be convinced. Especially when he sees your images and understands how allowing the work will be good for Shroud research and the church."

"I confess, Don Arturo, I did not think your plan would work. After reading the history of Shroud research, my perception is that the church moves very slowly in these matters."

"In all matters," Don Arturo said. "Very slow, yes. It is almost unheard of for the church to move this quickly, especially on things having to do with the Shroud. It seems the acting dean, the man you spoke to in the bishop's office, has become sympathetic to our project. He is blessed with the foresight to realize the importance of answering attacks of social media. And he has the ear of the bishop."

"You said *acting dean*. Does that mean you still don't have your position back?"

"For now, I am restored as a co-administrator with Don Gustavo, the priest you met. Together we have agreed on a way to proceed. However, it still must be done without publicity and with as few people knowing about the work as possible. We do not wish to appear to be reacting to the pressure of SIFT."

"It's what I agreed to in the first place," Graham said. "When would you like to begin?"

"During siesta, between 1400 and 1600 hours. Visitors are not allowed in the Cámara Santa during that time. I hope that is time enough to do your work."

"The copy stand can be set up in ten to fifteen minutes. I should be able to photograph both sides easily and pack up in that amount of time."

Don Arturo clasped his hands again. "*Excellente*. Let us meet in the bishop's office at 13:30."

"There's one other thing I need to tell you, Don Arturo. I did not have any confidence that I would be allowed to see the Sudarium. And after the first SIFT video that portrayed me in such a poor light, I reached out to the art historian at the national library. She was my translator for my talk. She has an interest in the Shroud and didn't even know about the Sudarium. She is also in charge of their social media. I asked her to help post material to defend my integrity. I talked to her before you connected me to Paco."

"I understand," Don Arturo said with a benevolent tilt of his head. "She has knowledge of the work?"

"She does. And she arrived last night so that we could create some posts for me to explain more fully why I was here and what I was doing. I would like her to be able to document the work this afternoon."

Don Arturo sighed, staring at the floor, apparently thinking through the implications. "I am afraid that would be very difficult. We do not know anything of her background and if she can be trusted with the information."

"I understand the concern," Graham said, "but that might actually recommend her for the job. Remember that many of the people on the STURP team that examined the Shroud in 1978 were not Christians. Some were Jewish and some were professed atheists. And some of the Christians did not believe the Shroud was authentic. They expected to determine it was a fake.

"If we do this work and publish it without someone observing and documenting the work, then the project will all be for nothing because it will be seen as simply getting the results we desired. There will be questions about methodology, and we could be accused of presenting only the evidence in favor of authenticity while ignoring contraindications—if there are any. She has told me she does not have an opinion on the Sudarium. She only just learned about its existence from me. And she's not convinced about the Shroud, although she is an advocate for it. She's fascinated by the project and wants the chance to help collect evidence."

Don Arturo shook his head regretfully. "There are many reasons it would not be a good idea."

"Think about this," Graham pressed, "there were no women on the STURP team. Another all-male team would give SIFT and other critics another way to dismiss and attack the work. Including her on the team would be a gesture of progress to them, that the church is willing to include women in its work. Plus, she's English, which would make the examination a multinational project."

Don Arturo shrugged, holding it as he spoke. "I can make no promises. I would have to have the approval of the bishop's office. I made a decision once before without consulting him, and it almost cancelled projected. Hopefully, it will be a way of demonstrating that I, too, can learn from past error. But I would need to meet this person first. When can you arrange that?"

"Right now, actually. She's waiting for me at the café on the plaza."

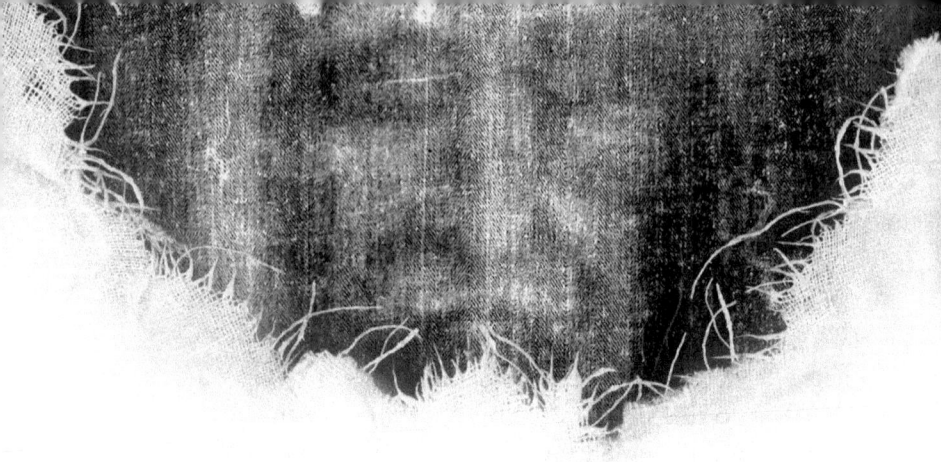

# THIRTY

A text arrived as Graham shut the door to his room, a single question mark sent by Iris.

"Sorry," Graham replied. "On the way. Bringing Don Arturo."

A string of question marks immediately appeared, but he left them unanswered, not wanting to be bad company to Don Arturo as they walked.

The café occupied the corner of the plaza nearest the cathedral entrance, skirted by umbrellas shielding outdoor patrons. Graham spotted Iris beneath a loose red beret draped to one side, complimented by a pink jacket and blue jeans. The colorful ensemble made it unnecessary for her to flag down Graham, but she raised her hand high in a wave as if completely anonymous. She stood in greeting as the men approached and offered a hand as Graham introduced them.

"Don Arturo, this is Iris Elizondo."

Iris released a short blast of rapid Spanish, and Don Arturo responded with a modest smile. "Apologies," she said, noticing Graham's lost expression. "I was just thanking Don Arturo for meeting me under such unusual circumstances."

"If I may, señorita, how does a Spanish girl have an English accent and appearance?"

Iris motioned for them to sit, then held her coffee with

both hands without picking it up. "My father was from Madrid. He met my mother at uni in Cambridge. Her family came from Wales. My grandmother worked in the Hotel Portmeirion, that village where they filmed *The Prisoner*, you know the old spy program?"

"I love that show," Graham said. "XTC shot a couple of music videos there for the *Skylarking* record."

Iris frowned in appreciation. "Peter Gabriel, Kate Bush, XTC, Monty Python, and *The Prisoner?* Dr. Eliot, you're a regular anglophile."

"I come by it naturally. I was named after Graham Greene. My mom had a complete set of his novels."

"Unfortunately, my mother was burdened with a distinctly Welsh maiden name," Iris said. "Cadwallader. It's bad enough on its own. But it makes a ridiculous surname: Elizondo-Cadwallader."

Don Arturo chuckled.

"Apparently, my parents thought the only thing that could make my name more melodious was something old fashioned and dowdy, so I inherited the name of my grandmother. Iris Elizondo-Cadwallader. Sounds like a name made out of spare parts, doesn't it? I grew up in England, but after my father died in a car crash, I moved here. I was a daddy's girl, and he always said my mind was English, but my heart was Spanish. Been here over ten years now, close to twenty, actually."

A waiter served Don Arturo his coffee, and the two bantered briefly. Graham inferred the priest was a familiar face at the café.

"Dr. Eliot tells me you are interested in the Shroud of Turin," Don Arturo said as the server moved to another table.

Iris shook her head, counterintuitively. "I've been fascinated by it for years. I was hoping to contribute to the body of research by possibly photographing medieval and Byzantine paintings that support the iconographic theory. That is why

I am interested in Dr. Eliot's work digitizing biblical manuscripts."

"What is your opinion of the Sudarium?" Don Arturo gestured over his shoulder blindly, toward the cathedral.

"Honestly, I had not even heard of it until Dr. Eliot arrived. I learned about it from the SIFT video. I'm intrigued by it and surprised it's not more well-known. I would love to be a part of any work that would help bring a greater understanding and awareness of it. If it's authentic, the implications are enormous for the dating of the Shroud."

"Indeed, they are." Don Arturo nodded. "May I ask, señorita, what do you believe for religion?"

Graham made a faint nod as Iris glanced at him quickly.

"It's complicated. And please, you may call me Iris."

"Thank you, Iris."

"I'm not quite sure the best way to answer your question." She paused to sigh, looked over Don Arturo's shoulder at the cathedral, then returned her eyes to him. "You know how when you were a child and your parents put you to bed, read a story, tucked you in, then turned off the light and shut the door? Being alone in the dark was scary. It was unnerving. But I could feel the presence of my parents on the other side of the door. I knew they were there.

"In a way, my religious beliefs are like that, except no one read a story and tucked me in, but I am alone in the dark. And yet, I feel the presence of someone caring for me, keeping me safe. I want to meet this person so badly, but I don't know how to do it. I can't find the door in the dark. I'm terrified what will happen if I *do* meet this person watching over me, but don't recognize them." She punctuated the explanation with a shrug.

"That is a wonderful description," Don Arturo said, smiling compassionately. "However, you are mistaken about one thing, señorita—Iris. You *have* been told a story. It is the word of God. *That* is the light in the dark that will show you the door."

"I wish I could believe that," Iris said.

"Saint Augustine would say your thinking is backward," Don Arturo said. "*Credo ut intelligam*. I believe in order that I may understand."

"But I need evidence, a map to the door. I don't want to believe it just because my grandmother did or because it makes me feel good. I'm not looking for a benevolent lie."

"I appreciate that. I would, however, ask you to think about what you accept as evidence. It is all around you. What you lack is the seeing of it."

"The Shroud and the Sudarium are not things to base your faith on, ultimately," Graham said. "They could both be forgeries or frauds, and it wouldn't say anything about the truthfulness of Jesus's Resurrection."

Iris nodded. "I understand that. I really do. But if they are authentic, then the Shroud is quite possibly an image—a kind of proto-photograph—of Jesus Christ at the moment of His Resurrection. That is what draws me to it. And that is why I am interested in helping Graham to collect evidence that may corroborate it. As an art historian, I am incredibly visual. The face on that Shroud just might belong to the presence I feel on the other side of the dark."

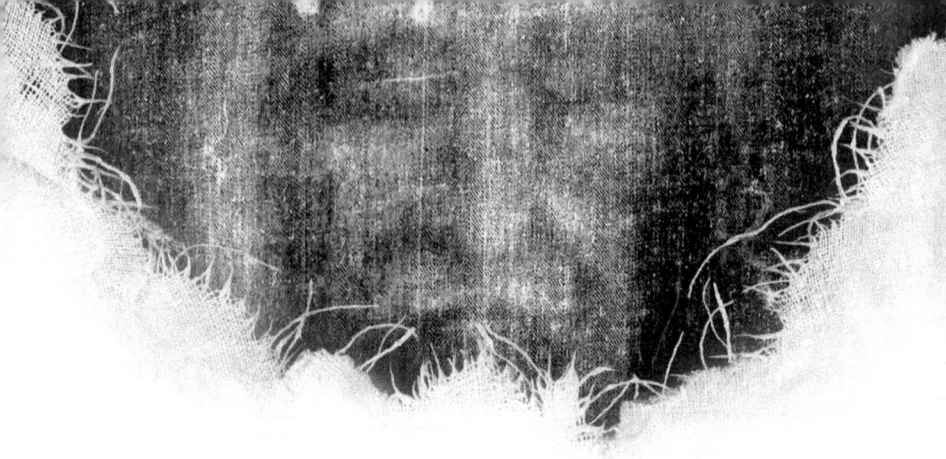

# THIRTY-ONE

The architectural patchwork of additions to the cathedral complex formed an irregular box canyon of shadows along the south side of the church. Iron bars spanned an awkward niche below a second, smaller bell tower.

"It's like an empty zoo exhibit," Graham said, looking into the space.

"I feel more like a mouse in a laboratory maze," Iris said, scanning the alley.

After receiving permission to accompany Graham, Iris had changed into a conservative, all-black outfit with a long skirt, collarless jacket with flared sleeves, and a scarf tied around her neck. Her hair had been tamed into a bun, like a knot tying off her eccentricities. An expensive digital camera hung from her neck in place of any accessory, and she had already taken several photos of Graham with his gear.

"I hope the unannounced closing of the cathedral for siesta doesn't look too suspicious," Graham said, checking his watch again and glancing at the door.

"They're only five minutes past when they said to meet here," Iris said. "They're probably still ushering visitors out."

"I'm still surprised we're getting to do this at all. And I'm especially surprised you won over Don Arturo."

Iris curtsied. "Thank you for the vote of confidence. Good thing I'm charming."

The side entrance—a single black metal door engraved with biblical scenes—opened to reveal Don Arturo. He emerged with a set of keys in his hand and briskly moved to unlock the gate. *"Excellente.* Very nice to see you again, señorita. Hurry please. We must be quick."

They followed the black robe into a hallway joining the cathedral to adjacent buildings. After passing a small gift shop, they entered the cathedral on the right side of the altar. They turned left and Graham recognized the stairs that led to the Cámara Santa. Although he had been there two days earlier, the air felt like a different place as they ascended. The gate dividing the chamber of relics stood open, like a window admitting action and purpose into the room. The priest who had denied Graham access to the Sudarium stood in front of the silver chest, reaching across it to remove the facsimile that hid the reliquary. Don Arturo helped him extract the case containing the Sudarium and place it reverently on the glass top. The second priest turned and smiled modestly with a nod.

"Dr. Eliot, you have met Don Gustavo."

"Your help is appreciated." Don Gustavo offered his hand, then enclosed Graham's hand with his left in a two-handed greeting. "Especially after our first meeting. Thank you."

"Thank *you* for reconsidering your position," Graham said. "It is a privilege and an honor to help the church."

"And this is Iris Elizondo. She is who will be photographing the examination."

Don Gustavo repeated his double-handed shake. "The photographer of the photographer. Welcome. You understand you may not publish the images without the permission of the church, yes?"

"You have my word," Iris said, nodding once earnestly.

Graham half expected an irreverent rejoinder and was relieved by her understated demeanor. His eye caught the frame over Don Gustavo's shoulder, and he realized it contained a duplicate Sudarium.

"The one that is displayed is a replica," Don Gustavo said. "The actual Sudarium is removed only three times a year to be used in benedictions on certain holy days."

"We have a table for your equipment, Dr. Eliot," Don Arturo said, gesturing to the room. "Where would you like me to set it up?"

"In front of the chest is fine."

Graham opened his case and assembled the equipment to the intermittent, soft clicks of Iris's camera. He concentrated on his task, ignoring her as she changed positions, orbiting him like a satellite.

She paused and looked at Don Gustavo. "I may ask, why is the chest so large for such a small cloth?"

Graham glanced at the priests, wondering how they would characterize the contents.

"The Sudarium was not the only precious relic that came to Oviedo in the chest," Don Arturo said.

"I was reading Pelayo's history and was impressed by the inventory he listed," Graham said. "A water jug from Cana; part of the crown of thorns; part of Moses's staff. Quite an amazing collection." He could sense Iris's gaze bouncing from his face to Don Arturo's. "Is this the same ark that transported them from Jerusalem?"

"That is what we believe," Don Gustavo said. "Although it was not ornamented in such a way."

Graham looked to his left, directly at the central image of the silver relief on the front of the chest—Christ enthroned, surrounded by the twelve disciples. "The chest itself is probably quite valuable for historical reasons."

"Without question," Don Arturo said. "But it is also important because it provides protection."

Graham assumed this was an allusion to superstitious powers ascribed to the chest. "Are you talking about how the

Muslims were unable to take Asturias?"

"That is one of many examples. The chest was built by the disciples of the apostles. It is not ordinary."

Don Gustavo paused from his work freeing the Sudarium from its frame. "That tradition was put to the test in 1934. Miners protesting against the government set off a bomb in the crypt of Saint Leocadia, just below us."

"Saint Leocadia?" Iris asked.

"A martyr from the time of the persecution of Diocletian," Don Arturo said.

Don Gustavo returned his attention to the cloth as he explained.

"She was symbolically martyred again with dynamite set off by the explosion. It did great damage to the chamber. The cover of the ark was blown off. Relics were scattered throughout the debris. General Franco himself had the Cámara Santa and the crypt restored."

"How much damage was done to the Sudarium?" Graham asked.

Don Gustavo looked up. "None. There was no harm done to the Sudarium. It was a miracle."

"Looks like it protected all these relics," Astrid said.

"No, the relics you see did not come from the ark," Don Gustavo said, looking around the room. "They were acquired later. Two pieces of the True Cross, thorns from the Lord's crown, one of St. Peter's sandals, a fragment of St. John the Baptist's skull, dirt from the house of the Virgin Mary, and a fragment of of the Lord's burial shroud."

At the mention of the shroud, Graham looked at Don Arturo who shook his head. "The material is not the same as the Shroud of Turin."

As he tested the connection to his laptop, controlling the lights and camera, Graham wondered if the heat and chemicals from the explosion could cause a chemical reaction on the material that would alter the results of a radiocarbon test on the linen.

By the time he finished preparing the stand, Don Gustavo had slipped on cotton gloves and opened the reliquary case.

"I'm ready to begin."

Don Gustavo pinched two corners of the Sudarium, lifted it, and draped it onto a pane of glass laying across the cradle of the stand. Because the copy stand had been designed to protect the spines of fragile books, the cradle where the books were placed could open only to 105 degrees—the angle Graham currently had it set to. As they slid the glass into place, a look of concern clouded Don Gustavo's face as he realized the Sudarium was almost twice as large as the stand was designed for.

"Will you be able to adjust the stand to fit the cloth?"

Graham fine-tuned the position as he looked at the laptop screen. "Not with this lens. I'll have to use a wide-angle lens and extend the camera mount all the way back. Every once in a while, I have to use it to digitize oversized manuscripts."

"Will the wide angle distort the image?" Iris asked.

"The software corrects the distortion for whatever lens is used." Graham swapped lenses as he explained. "This stand has a laser that ensures the focal point will give us the sharpest images possible. That's one of the most important parts of this project. It will ensure these images are being captured with the same precision as what we will hopefully take on the Shroud. Distance, focus, scale—this takes all the guesswork out of the process. It's one of the tools the STURP team did not have in 1978."

"*Excellente,*" Don Arturo said as Don Gustavo made an impressed frown.

Graham placed a color bar and a ruler next to the side of the Sudarium, then made a final adjustment on the laptop.

"Here we go."

The shutter noise of Iris's camera created an arhythmic

counterpoint between the slow clicks made by the camera on the copy stand. Between each shot, Graham adjusted the lights, capturing the cloth in different frequencies.

"What will the different kinds of light show?" Don Gustavo asked.

"I'm not sure." Graham studied the screen, working as he responded. "We won't know what we have until they are processed. Then we can manipulate the images in a variety of ways and see if anything is revealed we couldn't see otherwise. Will one of you turn the cloth over, please?"

Don Gustavo delicately flipped the Sudarium and repositioned it.

"This side is dirtier," Graham said.

"It is the side of the cloth that was actually touching the face of Christ," Don Arturo said, then pointed to an area to the left side of the cloth, near the asymmetrical stains. "See the holes? They were probably made by thin, sharp bones used to pin the cloth to His hair."

Iris came closer and leaned over Graham's shoulder, documenting as well as looking herself. "What about holes from the crown of thorns?"

Don Arturo shifted his finger. "This pattern of holes is almost identical to a pattern of wounds on the back of the head of the image on the Shroud." He indicated another place. "And here is where the cloth was folded back on itself because Christ's head was resting on His right shoulder. Instead of moving His head, they just folded the cloth back."

"I wondered why the stain had a mirrored look," Iris said.

"Where are the finger marks?" Graham asked.

Don Arturo repositioned himself behind the cradle and reached over from behind, making a pinching gesture. "Someone held the cloth to Christ's face like this, probably as He was taken down from the cross or as He was moved to the tomb. Here is the thumb, and this one is the finger," he said, pointing to the faint smudges.

Graham digitized the reverse side with each of the same light settings, stepped away from the laptop, and stared directly at the cloth. "As interesting as this is, these stains and smears—most of them seem too vague to be matched to the Shroud with precision."

"That is one of the reasons the work you are doing is important," Don Arturo said. "The images may uncover a connection with the Shroud that had not been seen before."

"And if the images don't?" Graham asked.

Don Arturo pointed to a small, butterfly-shaped stain near the bottom left corner of the cloth. "Then we will use this stain to register it to the Shroud. A similar shape is found on the back of the head."

"*If* we get permission," Graham said, emphasizing the problem. "It may take a miracle to photograph another miracle."

Don Gustavo lifted the cloth and returned it to its original position, then removed the glass from the cradle. Don Arturo helped him reinstall the relic in its frame under the watch of Iris's camera eye.

"Dr. Eliot, what is the next step?" Don Arturo asked.

"The downside of having to use the wide-angle lens is that it captures so much." Graham collapsed the copy stand, talking as he worked. "I'll have to crop each image and make sure I do it so all the images from each side align correctly. Once that's done, we can do some manipulation to emphasize certain features. Blood, for example. And I'll back up the images so you can access them as well."

Don Arturo glanced up from his work. "I look forward to learning what the camera sees that my own eyes cannot."

"It'll be like Christmas morning," Iris said, lowering her camera.

"Like Easter, you mean," Graham said, on a crooked smile.

Don Gustavo replaced the frame in the chest. "Miss Elizondo, please include your photographs from this afternoon so that we may also have a record of those."

"Of course. Thank you for allowing me to be included this afternoon."

"What is your opinion of the Sudarium now that you have seen it, señorita?" Don Arturo asked.

"I confess I'm a bit conflicted. Part of me sees it as an unremarkable dirty rag. But another part of me feels a kind of—I don't know—a spiritual thickness surrounds it. Reverence, I suppose. But I suspect it's just some superstitious desire in myself, a will to believe rather than something I'm recognizing in the cloth. Do you have any doubts at all?"

Don Arturo offered his compassionate smile. "I have the same confession. I understand your feelings. On some days, at least. I do not believe all the things said about the relics here. And yet, I also do not reject them all. I do believe the biblical account of what happened to Christ is historically true. I do believe the Shroud and face cloth were found in the empty tomb. But sometimes I do find myself re-examining my reasons for believing in their authenticity."

Graham noticed Don Gustavo raise his brows, then saw Iris had done the same.

"Are you saying you have doubts?" Iris asked.

"The Bible uses several words that are translated as *doubt*. One of them means to reason or think through different viewpoints. It is a dialogue inside yourself. We all do such things naturally when we examine our beliefs. It is one way we test what is true, and that is how our trust becomes stronger. That is what I mean about not believing these things simply because of the claims of tradition. It is because of that kind of doubt that I am happy to be the dean and the custodian of the Sudarium. I believe because I question. The mistake is to question without leaving room for the answer."

# THIRTY-TWO

The silence of empty churches held a holy ambience different from what Graham felt in a worship service. Without a congregation, it was as if God's presence was his alone to experience, like Moses encountering the burning bush. It always called to mind the Hebrew word *kavod*. Most of the time the word was translated *glory*, but it also meant *weight*. And when he found himself alone in a church, he felt both—the weight of glory.

He felt it now in the deserted halls of the cathedral, *kavod* manifesting in the weight of the copy stand case, and in his thoughts about the cloth that he was becoming more convinced could be authentic. The image of Don Gustavo staying behind to lock the gate added a sense of drifting away, as if he'd shifted across some unseen fulcrum.

Ahead, Don Arturo's black robe billowed as he shepherded them down the stairs and out the side door of the cathedral. They emerged from the alley into the plaza and turned into the office of the dioceses where he guided them into a conference room.

"I cannot stay. I have much to do after being gone."

"You won't be missing anything exciting," Graham said. "It'll take me a couple of hours to crop the images and do some initial processing."

As Don Arturo excused himself, Graham opened the laptop, then cropped the first image and saved it, recording the actions. He used the actions to set up an automated process that he applied to the entire folder of images. As he monitored the progress—each file taking a while to process because of its large size—he chatted with Iris.

"I didn't want to say anything in the Cámara Santa," Iris said, just above a whisper, "but when I did my research into the Sudarium, I came across Pelayo's inventory."

"You have an excellent poker face," Graham said.

"Almost bit clear through my tongue. Mary's breastmilk?" Iris raised her brow skeptically. "Do you know how bad it must smell?"

Graham laughed silently. "Funny you should say that. I thought the same thing about the manna from the desert. If I remember my Exodus correctly, it started stinking the day after it was collected. And it got worms."

Iris exaggerated a sincere face. "That almost makes the fish and honeycomb Jesus fed the apostles look fresh. But I guess when You're the Creator of the universe, it follows that You're also the ultimate preservative."

"Ever been to the Topkapi Museum in Istanbul?" Graham asked, keeping one eye on the screen. "They have some alleged biblical relics there, too. Including Moses's staff. It'd be interesting to see if the wood is the same kind and age as the fragment they have here."

"Please tell me you don't actually believe this inventory," Iris said, suddenly serious. "I mean, a water jug from the wedding at Cana? A vial of Christ's blood? Bread from the Last Supper?"

Graham raised his hands, shielding himself from the accusation. "I have never been impressed by relics."

"That's an interesting confession coming from an archaeologist."

"It's not the same thing as a relic hunter," Graham said. "No one ever fell down and worshipped any of the artifacts I've recovered. And even though I reject almost all relics, I have to admit that some of them could possibly be authentic. There's just no way to authenticate most of them. Even if the wood from the staff of Moses in the Topkapi Museum was 3,500 years old and the same kind of wood as the one in the Cámara Santa, there would be no way to know if it was actually Moses's or not."

"Yes," Iris said, touching his shoulder as if illustrating the connection. "My thoughts exactly."

"Which is actually a good thing," Graham said, a crooked smile creasing his face as confusion clouded Iris's.

"Why do you say that?"

"Because the only thing more dangerous than a fake relic is an authentic one."

"You've completely lost me," Iris said. "Why would the real thing be worse than the fake."

"Because some people would worship them. They'd make idols of them. Instead of the Creator they would worship the creation. They would use a good thing in a bad way."

"I get that," Iris said. "And yet, you're here."

Graham sighed, collecting his thoughts. "This is a unique situation. I came as a skeptic. I doubted the authenticity of both the Shroud and the Sudarium. But the more I've learned about them, the more plausible they seem. The evidence for each is far more impressive than I imagined, especially the Shroud, which I'd completely written off. The fact that both these artifacts can be examined scientifically takes it out of the realm of wishful thinking or superstition."

"You mean it's not a question of faith?"

"I mean that the scientific results do not rely on the personal faith of the scientist. If the tests are properly conducted, the same results should be obtained by a Christian or atheist or Jew or whatever. And that is what makes me interested in this project. It's an opportunity to test the historicity of an object that possibly corroborates the Gospel accounts of Jesus's death. I'm looking for truth, not for a reason to believe the relics, and not for reasons to support my faith."

Iris cocked her head, looking askance. "But you're starting from faith. I'm trying to be neutral."

"Neutrality is an illusion. Remember the reason I gave you to believe? All the intellectual tools we are using to evaluate the evidence—like the induction necessary for scientific inquiry—must come from somewhere."

"But you just said the test results don't rely on the faith of the scientist."

"They don't," Graham said. "Everyone uses the same tools. And people who are not Christians have unquestionably discovered great truth about the world. Truth is true wherever it's found, regardless of who finds it. The question is if your worldview makes sense of the tools. What makes truth true?"

Iris raised her hands in surrender. "This is getting too deep for me."

Graham tipped his head, relenting. "Just be doubtful like Don Arturo is doubtful. Examine how it is you can examine anything at all."

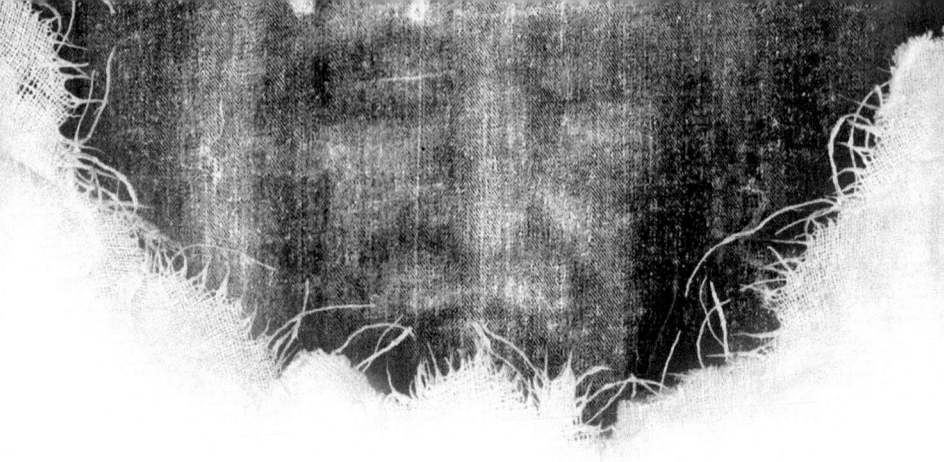

# THIRTY-THREE

Inky blackness hovered over the plaza, a blanket of clouds blotting out stars. Café umbrellas that had provided shade by day now created pools of light. The languid siesta of the afternoon had transformed into a center of activity.

Graham stepped through the cathedral door and stopped, taken by surprise, his head still full of his work, thinking for a moment it was a photographic negative of the world they left.

It hadn't been until Don Arturo had asked how much longer they planned to be that Graham realized it was 9:30 p.m. After processing the images, he began studying the results and had lost track of time. He experimented with different filters as he overlaid the new Sudarium images onto the 1978 Shroud photograph, using the small butterfly shape as the registration point. The correspondence was compelling—Iris had gasped looking over his shoulder—but would be even stronger if they were able to get permission to digitize the Shroud.

As he turned to Iris to say good night, the sound of his name spun him back toward the café where they had met that morning. He found Paco motioning an invitation to join him at a table.

"Who's your friend?" Iris asked, following Graham to the café.

"My favorite SIFT reporter. The guy who made the videos you saw."

Paco stood and offered Graham his hand. "Dr. Eliot, happy to see you."

"You as well, Paco. This is my friend, Iris Elizondo."

"Sit, please, sit, sit," Paco said, shaking Iris's hand warmly, then gesturing to the empty chairs. "You have equipment. Does this mean the church changed their minds?"

As soon as Graham spotted Paco, he began deliberating how forthcoming to be. Given that Paco's help with the second video had been pivotal for gaining permission, and that Paco knew that was its goal, he chose to speak candidly.

"Between the video you shot and the SIFT announcement of the Hocus Pocus Challenge, they decided the best course of action would be to go ahead with the digitization while I was still here."

"Beautiful!" Paco beamed, turning the smile to Iris. "Good news, yes?"

"Absolutely." Iris smiled back.

"And the work was good? No trouble?"

"Everything went according to plan," Graham said. "We made almost fifty images. More visual data than has ever been captured on the Sudarium. I hope the evidence they collected will provide some new insights."

Paco tilted his head to look over his glasses. "Is it real?"

Graham made a crooked smile. "If you are asking if it is authentic or not, I don't know. That is for others to determine."

"What is your opinion?"

"I'm still processing everything. It's compelling, but I haven't been convinced one way or the other."

Paco squinted, apparently parsing the words, searching for something unsaid. He broke off and turned to Iris. "And what did you do?"

"I'm the documentary photographer."

"I see. The proof of the proof." Paco chuckled. "And you

are part of the church?"

"Actually, I do not believe."

Paco blinked theatrically. "A photographer who does not believe the Sudarium?"

"Or anything else," Iris said. "I don't work for the church. And I'm what you might call a reluctant agnostic."

Paco nodded from one face to another, looking impressed. "Bible scholar and free thinker. It is an unusual team."

Graham wondered if Paco was trying out an angle on a new story and decided to change the subject. "Do you usually come to this café?"

"No, no. I hoped to see you here."

"Really? You sat here hoping I would walk by this café?"

Paco lifted his hands in a guilty shrug. "Truly, this afternoon, after siesta, I waited in the line of tourists to enter the Cámara Santa. I wanted to shoot some video and take some pictures. I tried to do it yesterday, but too many people. Photography is not allowed, so I must be very, very discreet." He smiled conspiratorially. "This afternoon I saw you with your equipment, coming from the cathedral to the offices. I assumed you photographed the cloth. But Don Arturo was there, and I did not want to make a bad situation. I have waited in the plaza for you to come out."

"I don't know whether to feel flattered or stalked," Graham said. "Is SIFT paying you to stake me out now?"

"SIFT does not pay me at all. I do their work because I believe in skeptical inquiry."

"And what is it you do for a living," Iris asked, "that gives you the ability to donate your time to them?"

"I edit video for the news at the local television station," Paco said. "Many, many years I have done this."

"Is that where you learned your style of reporting?" Graham asked.

Paco chuckled. "If you had not acted like a sheep, maybe I

would not have looked like a wolf."

"Fair enough." Graham laughed. "So, you spend your spare time pretty much doing the same thing you do for a living, just for someone else."

"Yes, yes. That and painting."

"You're a painter?" Iris asked. "What do you paint?"

"It is very, very abstract," Paco said, earnestly. "Do you study art?"

"As a matter of fact, I took my degree in art history," Iris said, looking pleased to be able to share the personal detail.

"And do you study a certain period?"

"Byzantine iconography," Iris said, studying his response.

Paco leaned forward, folding his arms on the table. "Very, very interesting. It is—how you say—both representational and abstract."

"Yes," Iris said. "I suppose it is."

Graham sensed a connection between the two, as well as a slight pang of jealousy—an emotional reaction he knew was irrational. Again, he changed the subject.

"Paco, are you going to submit an image to the Hocus Pocus Challenge?"

"Yes, yes," he said, enthusiastically embracing the new topic. "I have been deciding how to do it."

"What techniques do you know that could recreate the image?" Iris asked.

"That is what I have been thinking of. First, I decide to make paint as in the thirteenth century. Mix iron oxide and vermilion to make red ocher. But also, I am thinking brushing powder onto cloth that is wet. Also maybe acid to stain the cloth. Or maybe also creating a bas relief, heating it, and burning the cloth."

"Those methods have already been tried," Iris said. "What would you do different, Paco?"

"I am thinking if I can make them better. The problem

to solve for me is to make the image on the cloth a negative. Why would an artist do that? Very, very strange. Then I say to myself it looks like a cloth that sits in the window of a shop and fades. That is what makes the shape of a man. I have an idea to paint the man on glass and shine light through it onto the cloth."

"That's quite clever of you," Iris said. "I'll be interested to see the results."

Paco smiled apologetically. "You will be home in the U.K. before I have it to show."

Iris smiled. "Actually, I live in Madrid."

Graham inserted himself, noting the spark of interest in Paco's eyes. "Here's another feature of the Shroud you'll have to consider in your recreation. You mentioned the image on the cloth is a negative image. What color hair would the man have to have to look like this?" He displayed a close-up of the face of the image on his phone.

Paco frowned as he realized the implications. "His hair is dark."

"Not if this is a negative image. It's dark on the Shroud, which means the hair must be…"

"White," Paco finished, still working through an observation he seemed surprised not to have made before.

"The hair on his head was white," Graham said. "Like white wool, like snow. That's the description of the risen Jesus in Revelation 1:14. It's one more thing that makes forgery hard to explain."

"I have never noticed that," Paco said.

"Well, I'll leave you to mull it over. I'm exhausted. I am going to head back to the hotel."

"Thank you for the update, Dr. Eliot. I hope we see each other again."

"I'm going to stay a bit longer," Iris said. "Feeling a little peckish. I'll call you in the morning."

# THIRTY-FOUR

A faint cloud of jealousy followed Graham from the café to the hotel, fogging his thoughts like an internal shadow. He had worked to keep the connection he felt with Iris at bay. Even if he planned to stay in Spain longer than a few days, he knew it was unwise to encourage a relationship with someone who didn't share his faith. The difference in worldviews would ultimately cause too much conflict. And yet, when he saw the instant chemistry between Iris and Paco, he felt a sense of loss. He was self-aware enough to recognize the irrationality of his reaction, but too emotionally vulnerable to be armored against it. He craved for a connection like he'd had with Olivia and had to be vigilant not to project his need on a substitute.

He climbed into bed and pulled the sheet over his head, as if hiding from his own distractions. Lying on his back, he realized he was in the same position as the man in the Shroud. The pose reminded him of Paco's list of artistic techniques for recreating the image, and he started working his way through them, analyzing each one.

The sensation of the cloth on his face and chest made him think of Paco's idea to lay the linen sheet across a heated bas relief. The contact would scorch the material, imprinting an image. Graham felt the cloth on the sides of his head and arms, conforming to his body, and knew the technique would fail. Even if an image was left behind, it would become distorted when the sheet was laid flat. Any method that used contact to create the image—such as paint or dye on the body—would fail for the same reason. The blood and dirt would be transferred by contact, of course, but not the image.

Paco had said he was thinking about making his own red ocher paint in the same way as it had been made in thirteenth century Europe—vermilion and iron oxide. He made a mental note to see if the STURP findings mentioned iron oxide on the cloth. In his work with manuscripts, Graham grew to appreciate how strokes used in writing showed directionality and a subtle variance in the way pressure was applied at different points on the line. Again, those would be characteristics STURP might have detected if the image had been created with a brush.

Powder applied with a dry brush—another method suggested by Paco—would also leave traces of directionality and variant density. But it would also leave grains of powder caught in the weave. Yet another feature STURP may have detected or tested for.

The technique suggested by Paco that made the most sense to Graham is how light could be projected through a glass painting to discolor the cloth. It was clearly within the reach of the imagination of a thirteenth-century forger, but it had a number of practical problems. The amount of sunlight needed to create the discoloration would require multiple exposures for long periods of time. Given the changing angle of light from a moving sun, the image would be blurred. Either that or the glass would have to move with great precision and be mounted in such a way as to change the angle as well.

Graham doubted a medieval forger would have that kind of knowledge, let alone go to such trouble. What would be the upside to the effort? And even if he correctly made the calculations and the apparatus, how would the forger know to collect and apply pollen from the regions where the Shroud had apparently been kept prior to its appearance in Europe? Paco's favored method dropped from ingenious to wildly improbable.

Haunting all the methods was the question Paco himself asked: Why would an artist make a negative image if the idea was to convince people the image of Jesus had been imprinted on the cloth? It's a strange choice for someone pulling a con. Especially for one that did not bring the con man fame or fortune.

As Graham reflected on the implausibility of the methods, he became more aware of the weight of the sheet pressing against him. The perspective from beneath the linen gave him a new insight, a truth he accidentally stumbled upon. He had always thought of the Shroud as covering Jesus, when the truth was that people were the ones enShrouded. They wore the veil of sin, of unbelief, of self-deceit. They were cloaked in mortality and finitude. The Shroud didn't trap darkness, it enveloped light—Jesus.

Moses had veiled his face after beholding God's glory because the light from His countenance shone so brightly. The light was where shadow should have been. The Holy of Holies—the location of God's immediate presence on Earth—was obscured by a curtain, ultimate reality condescending to be with His people. It was this same curtain-veil-Shroud the writer of Hebrews referenced when he wrote, "We have this hope as an anchor for the soul, sure and steadfast, which reaches inside behind the curtain."

From beneath his bedsheet, behind closed eyes, Graham imagined himself bathed in light, and fell asleep.

# THIRTY-FIVE

*Graaahammm.*

*He opened his eyes, vaguely aware of the sound of his name. The sheet still covered his face, but now weighed so heavily on him that he felt restrained. His eyes shifted from side to side, alarmingly disconnected from his body, which refused to move.*

*Graaahammm.*

*His name, unmistakable, slipped quietly—directionless—into the lightless void. He continued to struggle against the invisible bonds without success.*

*Graaahammm.*

*"Hello?" His voice sounded too loud, as if the darkness refused to admit it. "Hello." The cloth across his face moved, or rather his head moved slightly. Immobility fell away in chunks like melting ice, freeing him incrementally.*

*Relief flooded him as he pulled the sheet away, revealing more nothingness. Except for the sheet in his hand, which seemed to be illuminating itself. He held it out in front of him, shaking out the wrinkles to discover the imprint of his wife, Olivia, in repose.*

*His eyes slammed shut, shielding himself from the stabbing vision of a truth he still wrestled with.*

*"Olivia." His whisper had the force of a shout, but with none of the volume.*

He suddenly awoke again, this time fully from sleep. After

Aly's death, he began suffering from nightmares that grew worse following the loss of Olivia. Not just nightmares, but false awakenings. A dream within a dream. The experience gave a new perspective on a poem he had loved by Edgar Allan Poe. The verse almost became a kind of scripture, a black psalm recited as he questioned his faith during the darkest time in his life. Waking from one always recalled its words.

> *I stand amid the roar*
> *Of a surf-tormented shore,*
> *And I hold within my hand*
> *Grains of the golden sand—*
> *How few! yet how they creep*
> *Through my fingers to the deep,*
> *While I weep—while I weep!*
> *O God! can I not grasp*
> *Them with a tighter clasp?*
> *O God! can I not save*
> *One from the pitiless wave?*
> *Is all that we see or seem*
> *But a dream within a dream?*

Graham glanced at the clock: seven a.m. He never slept this late.

He reached for his laptop on the bedside table and opened a browser to the news. The headline screamed across the width of the page, making him wonder if he was still within a dream within a dream.

Magician King Dead.

# THIRTY-SIX

*Magician Christopher King was found dead this evening inside the House of Cards, a magic-themed restaurant in Nashville where he was appearing this week. He was 61.*

*His body was discovered backstage between shows at the time his next performance was to begin. The cause of death was not released, but sources say it did not appear to be natural. Police are seeking a person of interest seen talking with King shortly before his death.*

*King, an award-winning illusionist and close-up magician, was well-known for using his knowledge of deception to expose faith healers, psychics, superstitions, and urban legends as frauds. His investigative work ranged from UFOs, ghosts, and sponta- neous human combustion to religious miracles.*

*His death comes the day after he revealed his latest project, the Hocus Pocus Challenge. The contest is a critical investigation into methods used to create the Shroud of Turin. He made the announcement at ThinkCon, the annual meeting of the Skeptical Inquiry of Free Thinkers (also known as SIFT), for which he was a Fellow.*

A series of real-time updates from the reporter's social me- dia accounts followed the article. The first showed an ambu- lance amid police cars outside the Johnny Cash Museum with the caption, "Emergency personnel arrived at the House of

Cards at 9:32 p.m., responding to Christopher King's death."

The second update came at 10:45 p.m. Jostled footage apparently shot with a cell phone showed the police parting a crowd of revelers in cowboy hats and bachelorette tiaras taking pictures and videos as the body was removed to the ambulance. Several live bands could be heard in the background, creating a cacophony of country music, oblivious to the scene outside the honky-tonks.

The caption read, "Christopher King removed from scene as police continue their investigation. Anyone who dined at the House of Cards last night is encouraged to contact police."

Graham frowned, wondering if King's death was suspicious in some way. He hit Alexander's number on his phone but was sent immediately to voicemail and settled for a text.

"Just saw the news about King. What's happening?"

He scrolled to the final update, a video posted at 11:15 p.m. The ambulance was gone, but police cars still sat outside the museum, red and blue lights adding a disco element to the redneck soundtrack. A man in a tailored suit, made unsteady by the buffeting crowd, answered questions, raising his voice to be heard by the reporter offscreen.

"You were at the House of Cards tonight when Christopher King's body was discovered. Can you tell us what's going on inside the restaurant?"

"Yeah, so, the police are talking to everyone who was there at the time." He glanced behind him, annoyed by a shove. "They wanted to know if we saw anything unusual or out of place. People acting strange. That sort of thing."

"Did you share any information they seemed to think was useful."

"I really don't know. Probably not. They asked if we'd taken any pictures, but they don't allow photography in the House of Cards, so we didn't have any. And reception is bad down there, so you can't even get texts or anything. We're here for an anniversary dinner. We did see Christopher King do the show right before they, you know, found him. He seemed fine to us."

"We've heard the police are wanting to speak to someone in particular. Did they ask you about that?"

"Right, yeah, they did. I think we saw the guy they were talking about. Young guy, kinda tall, really skinny, long hair in a ponytail, and a kind of hip beard. Dressed in all black. He was at the same show we saw. He hung out with King at the bar, but we really didn't pay attention. I didn't think anything of it."

"Did they seem like they were arguing, or that the guy was upset?"

"No, not at all. I mean, like I said, I didn't pay much attention. But they looked like friends. So, you know— It's just kinda freaking us out to think that we saw the last show."

"Was there anything unusual about his performance?"

"I don't know. I'd never seen him in person. He joked a bit with us. He pulled my wife up as a volunteer and read her mind. That's a trick I've never been able to do." The man chuckled guiltily. "And the last trick he did was he made the image of Jesus's face appear on a blank cloth. Just like the Shroud of Turin, you know, in Italy. All he did was speak and told it to appear, and it just kind of spread like a stain across the cloth. I can't believe we're some of the last people to see him alive."

Graham refreshed the page to see if any more updates had been posted and found none. Alarm sang through his thoughts, almost physically vibrating him. Why were the police interested in Alexander? And why couldn't they find him?

# THIRTY-SEVEN

Being so far from Nashville, unable to help, left Graham rattled in a worried, impotent restlessness. He was, by nature, a fixer, calmed by having a task that helped solve a problem. But there was nothing to do. The only person who might know more about what was going on was Sarah. That's who Alexander would reach out to first, since she'd been his legal guardian, raising him through his adolescence after his mom died. Graham sent a text, not wanting to tie up her phone.

"Sarah, it's Graham. I just saw the news. Any word from Alexander? Please let me know if there is anything I can do to help. Very worried."

He busied himself with a shower, rushing through it as if late for an appointment, not wanting to miss a call. As he dried off, he checked his phone to discover it was still set to Do Not Disturb from the night before, and that Sarah had left a voice message. He tapped the call-back button, and she answered on the first ring.

"Graham, I'm so glad you called. I just got off the phone with Zander. He said you were somewhere in Spain."

"I am. But where is he? I tried to call him."

"He's at the police station."

Graham heard the studied calm of Sarah's voice and remembered the look of anxiety in her eyes that accompanied it. The expression had become familiar when they had illegally entered Saudi Arabia to track Alexander to the possible site of the biblical Mount Sinai.

"He's at the police station," she continued. "Apparently, he was the last person to see Christopher King alive. He stayed in the theater to chat with King after the last show."

"They don't think he had anything to do with it, do they? Have they arrested him?"

"No, they're just questioning him. Right now he's not under arrest, but he's worried they might. He said he was cooperating and trying to help any way he can. But it doesn't look good. He said he's starting to see how everything he tells them could get twisted against him."

"What did he say happened?"

Sarah released a rush of air, as if she'd been holding her breath. "He told me so much so fast. He didn't have a lot of time to talk. But he said King had invited him to Nashville to the SIFT convention. ThinkCon, or something like that. He said they'd met at the Magic Castle a week or so ago and hit it off. They talked magic, but also philosophy and religion, and that's how he got invited. He said he went because you'd sent him, and for some reason that's why you were in Spain?"

"I'll explain later," Graham said. "But I did pay for the tickets and hotel for him so he could take King up on the offer to get to the convention."

"Okay, so, King told him he was doing a couple of nights at the House of Cards while the convention was going on, and Zander went to see him. The theater there is small, and there is really no backstage area. Just enough room to store some props offstage, but no major illusions or anything. Zander said he did a stripped-down show. Mostly mentalism. And the gear he did use packed flat, which is how magicians say it's easy to carry. One of the tricks was with a blank canvas in a frame, and when he says the magic word or whatever, the image of the face of Jesus from the Shroud of Turin appears."

"I saw him do that at the Magic Castle a couple of weeks ago myself," Graham said. "That's really why he went to the Magic Castle. And partly why I'm here."

"Hmm," Sarah noised, noncommittal. "King showed Zander how it was done. It's a chemical thing. One kind of chemical—I think he said it was bismuth nitrate—gets painted onto the material. When it dries, it's invisible. Then there is another chemical that is used as a reagent. Apparently, he had a remote-control atomizer that shoots a mist onto the back of the cloth. That's what makes the invisible image appear in light brownish yellow."

"Clever," Graham said. "What was the chemical for the reagent?"

"King wouldn't tell him. He only said he had to mix it with water before each performance and put it in the atomizer. King claimed it was dangerous if used incorrectly and he didn't want to let the secret get out. While he was explaining all this, someone from the restaurant came in and said there were some customers who wanted to get a picture with King. He left the theater for a minute or two, and Zander looked in King's equipment bag. He pulled out the two bottles from a little side pouch. One was liquid and had a commercial label that said it was bismuth nitrate. The other was a powder. The label was a sticker with handwriting that said it was powdered sugar."

"Powdered sugar was the reagent?"

"Zander wondered the same thing. So he opened it. He said it did look a lot like powdered sugar, but something about it was different. He said it smelled more like almonds than sugar. He was about to touch it when he heard King's voice getting closer to the door, so he quickly put the lid back on.

"He had just returned the bottles when King came back

in. Zander said the police asked him if he was certain he had put the lid back tightly. Zander said he did because King had told him it was dangerous. At first, when he saw the powdered sugar label, he thought King might have been putting him on, like he had some private joke with himself, you know, another layer of misdirection. It wasn't until he had opened it that he thought King might mislabel the bottle to protect it. But like I said, he swears he put the lid back on tight."

"I see why he's worried," Graham said. "So, what was in the bottle? Did they tell him?"

Sarah hesitated, as if avoiding the answer. "Cyanide."

"What?" Graham exclaimed.

"The police could tell King had been poisoned. That's why they knew the death wasn't natural. I looked it up. Cyanide poisoning happens very quickly. Doesn't take hardly anything for a fatal dose, even if it just gets on your skin. If Zander had touched it, he might have been the one who died. And guess what cyanide smells like? Almonds."

"I can't believe King was carrying around cyanide for a magic trick," Graham said, suddenly alarmed he'd been in the same room, sitting so close to it.

"At first, the police didn't know it was part of a trick. They didn't know why he had cyanide in the first place, or why it was mislabeled. When Zander told them the story, he said they hadn't announced anything about poisoning or cyanide to the press, so it filled in some blanks. And they found Zander's fingerprints on the cyanide bottle. Now he's second-guessing himself about putting the lid back on correctly. He thinks it might be his fault, that he accidentally killed someone. He's completely destroyed."

Graham groaned empathetically. "I feel so helpless being this far away."

"I get it. I'd be on a plane right now, but I need to stay available to arrange a lawyer and anything else he needs immediately," Sarah said.

"I can see how it might look like he was negligent and caused King's death, like manslaughter. And that it could even be seen as homicide."

"He sees that, too," Sarah said. "And to make him look even guiltier, Zander left and went back to the hotel before the body was discovered. I've never heard him so scared."

"King could have been the one who mishandled it," Graham said. "If it's such dangerous stuff, it could've been an accident that would've happened without Alexander there at all. It's possible it could even be suicide."

"Zander thinks that's what the police were trying to figure out. But when he told them about handling the bottle without permission, it gave them a whole new avenue to investigate. Oh, hey, the lawyer I contacted is calling me back. Gotta go. I'll let you know if anything else happens."

# THIRTY-EIGHT

The phone felt heavy in Graham's hand as he waited for Don Arturo to answer, the time between rings feeling unusually long. He hung up as voicemail kicked in, opting to send a text instead.

"Call me. We need to talk."

His hand fell to the bed, weighed down by the phone, and he sat paralyzed with his eyes closed. The depression that had swallowed him after Olivia and Aly died spread into his thoughts, toxic vines raising themselves up by pulling him down.

*Had I not come to Spain, Alexander would not have met King, and King might still be alive. And Alexander's life might not be ruined.*

Graham shook his head, casting out the incriminating voice. He needed action, something to occupy his mind, to keep him from indulging his worst instincts. He grabbed a coat and left the hotel, thankful for the cold, overcast morning that slapped his face as he crossed the street.

The alley leading to the archaeological museum was thankfully empty, the only sound made by his slow footfalls. He reached the small plaza where Paco had shot the second video, and stopped at the gate, staring at the Cámara Santa. An image of the Sudarium filled his mind. Had he come halfway around the world to photograph the ancient bloody cloth only to get blood on his own hands?

He expelled the thought, violently exhaling his breath, blowing it away. An afterimage of Christopher King's face remained, a stain of grief for the man tinted with an ironic gratitude for the unintentional gift he gave. Without King, Graham would never have had the privilege of photographing the Sudarium and Shroud. He found himself actually thankful for the Hocus Pocus Challenge.

Hocus Pocus. *This is my body.*

It suddenly occurred to Graham that King had missed the point. Of everything. Proving the image of the Shroud could be replicated wouldn't change anything about the reality of the Resurrection. It was a straw man. Or, given that the Shroud was made of linen, a flax man. Not only that, but King was attacking only half of the holy sacrament of communion.

After offering His body, signified by the breaking of bread at the Last Supper, Jesus took a cup of wine and said, "Drink from it, all of you, for this is my blood, the blood of the covenant, that is poured out for many for the forgiveness of sins." The Sudarium contained lifeblood, blood actively being shed by whoever was wrapped in the cloth—possibly Jesus. Graham had been so focused on capturing the image of the Sudarium and approaching it as a scientific examination that he hadn't fully considered the theological implications of what he was looking at. He firmly believed that Jesus had shed His blood for the forgiveness of sins, but there had also been an abstract quality to the idea. If the Sudarium was authentic, then those stains—that lifeblood—was the actual blood that bought his forgiveness. The Sudarium was a fragmented, earthly receipt for the divine transaction that accomplished salvation.

That thought carried Graham around the corner of the

cathedral complex, past the door beneath the tower they had entered the day before. He crossed the empty plaza and sat on the edge of the fountain, staring at the facade of the church.

Worry for Alexander, sorrow for King, and a confused malaise mingled in a haze he knew accumulated near the edge of depression. In the past three years he'd come to recognize this place and had worked to develop strategies to cope with it. It was a spiritual exercise developed by nineteenth-century Scottish pastor Robert Murray M'Cheyne that had helped him most. M'Cheyne taught that for every look at yourself, take ten looks at Christ. It was a kind of cognitive behavioral therapy that had come to his rescue many times.

Graham studied the cathedral as he enumerated ten things he knew about Christ. The list changed depending on the situation and his emotional state, but regardless of the circumstance, the first thing he listed every time was the most important to him. Without it, the other nine didn't matter. Christ was sovereign over all things. There was no darkness that could not be overcome by His light. After reminding himself of that, other attributes fell into place. Gracious. Merciful. Forgiving. Patient. Omniscient. Good. Knowable. Faithful provider. Extravagantly loving. He let his mind linger on each one, meditating on it.

When he reached the tenth, he thought again about all that had happened and no longer felt vulnerable to depression. He didn't feel good about the situation, but he didn't feel hopeless. Iris had described feeling God just outside the door of the dark room. Graham knew that as much as he appreciated the description, God wasn't outside the room. He was in it. God was in the darkness, present but working in a way not always obvious from Graham's earthly point of view.

As if in answer, the vibration of the phone in his pocket jolted him from his musings. He saw it was Alexander and stabbed the *answer* button.

"Alexander, I'm so glad you called. What is happening? How are you holding up?"

"Good to hear your voice, Dr. E." Alexander's voice sounded hoarse and weak. "Aunt Sarah said you guys talked."

"She told me as much as she could. Are you still at the police station?"

"No, thank God. I'm not under arrest or anything. Not yet, anyway. They let me go back to the hotel, but I need to stay in Nashville for now."

"Stay as long as you need," Graham said. "I'll cover it. Sounds like you could use some rest."

"I'm too exhausted for sleep. I just keep replaying what happened over and over. I feel so guilty about what happened."

"Alexander, you didn't do anything wrong." Graham heard himself emulate Don Arturo's pastoral voice.

"I should've never snooped in his bag. It's not like I was going to steal the trick or anything. I was just curious."

"I'm sure the police understand that."

"Not sure that matters. I was handling the thing that killed him minutes before he died."

"If they thought you were trying to kill him, they wouldn't have let you walk out of there. Plus, you had no reason to commit murder. It's absurd."

"I don't know," Alexander said. "The more I explained, the more I felt guilty. But I swear I put that lid on tight. And I had no idea it was cyanide. I don't know anything about that stuff. I was about to touch it when I heard him coming and put it back. I actually had my index finger extended. I mean, I could've died just from that. I had no idea until they told me. If I'd have known what it was, I wouldn't have gone near that bag."

Graham puffed incredulously. "I can't believe he put his audience at that kind of risk at all. I was only a couple rows away when I saw it."

"I know, right?" Alexander said. "But if they somehow determine the lid was loose when he took it out of the bag, I don't know what I'll do. I don't know if I can live with that."

"I'm not sure how they could detect something like that," Graham said, trying to be encouraging.

"Sorry, man, I have to go," Alexander said. "Connecting with the lawyer Aunt Sarah got me."

"Let me know if there's anything I can do," Graham said. "And call with an update when you can."

He stared at the phone, his mind still focused on the image conjured by the timbre and tone of Alexander's voice—haggard and drawn, sunken and distorted by stress and depression. He looked up, wanting to unsee the imagined portrait, and fixed on a couple making their way across the plaza toward the café near the cathedral entrance. He recognized Iris's bright red beret, then realized the other person was Paco. He stood to catch up to them, but immediately froze again as their angle changed, revealing the space between them. The two were holding hands.

# THIRTY-NINE

Graham changed course, crossing the back of the plaza into a side street to avoid being seen by Iris and Paco. Halfway back to the hotel, a text arrived from Iris saying she was at the café.

He stopped on the sidewalk, thinking through how he'd respond if he hadn't seen what he just saw.

"On the way."

As he turned into the lane leading from the hotel to the café, he prepared himself to look pleasantly surprised at Paco's presence, rehearsing a line to mask his conflicting emotions. He spotted them under an umbrella, and Iris waved him over.

"Look who I found lurking around here again," Iris said, after greeting him with a traditional Spanish perfunctory kiss on each cheek.

Graham hoped his expression didn't betray the effort of ignoring her deception as he shook Paco's hand and took a seat.

"You know, Paco, according to Ian Fleming, once is happenstance, twice is coincidence, the third time it's enemy action."

Paco made a failed attempt at a smile that didn't reach his smoldering eyes. "You have heard the news?"

"About Christopher King?" Graham asked, suddenly chastened by his miscalculation. In his desire to act surprised at seeing them together, he'd forgotten for a moment the bigger picture. "I have. I am still in shock. Have they said how he died?"

Paco glared pointedly. "You should be telling us."

Iris put a hand on Paco's, apparently attempting to attenuate the sharp tone. She glanced at Graham and withdrew her hand self-consciously.

Graham turned back to Paco. "I'm not sure what you mean."

"You are professor at Calbi University, yes?" Paco said, his frown deepening. "Professor of Ancient Near East Studies?"

"Yes," Graham said, wondering where this was going.

"The police have been questioning a student from Calbi University," Paco said, pointing a finger, tapping the air for emphasis. "A student in Ancient Near East Studies who just happened to be in Nashville at the conference held by SIFT. The very people you say you are trying to speak to. What would Ian Fleming say about that?"

Graham stammered, feeling foolish for being unprepared. This time it was Iris who returned a disappointed, accusatory look when their eyes met.

"I know how it must look," he said, lifting his hands in defense, "but I promise you, no one did anything wrong."

Paco spit air out of his mouth. "Except send a spy to the conference."

"No one sent Alexander, and he wasn't spying. He was personally invited by King. They were new friends. And it was an opportunity to hear firsthand what objections would need to be answered. It was a way to go to the source."

Paco pointed his finger again. "It was not honest of him not to say."

"Say what? He was never asked. And why would it have changed anything? What kind of society of free thinkers wouldn't welcome people who disagreed with them? Isn't the whole idea of SIFT to disabuse people of their misconceptions? Isn't that the goal of all people who seek the truth? Look at Iris. Even the church allowed her to accompany me to photograph the Sudarium, and she is a skeptic herself. I would expect the same from SIFT."

"That is my point exactly," Paco said, opening his arms as if illustrating the widening gap between them. "You know she is a skeptic because *she told you*."

"Yes, but ultimately her belief was irrelevant because we were seeking the truth. Both of us were. The church, too, for that matter. That should be the only criteria."

"Is that an excuse for murder?"

"Come on, Paco, that is absurd."

"It is? A man publicly challenging the church and skeptical of its claims is dead just a day after a major announcement. Convenient, yes? And he was killed by a kind of divinity student. Very, very convenient." Paco folded his arms, as if making his own challenge.

"First, I repeat, there was *no murder*." Graham left a beat of silence to emphasize the point. "Second, murder by a divinity student seems ironic, I agree. Although, Moses and David were both—"

"That is not what I am talking about," Paco interrupted. "Houdini was killed by a divinity student from McGill University. He accepted Houdini's challenge to punch him in the stomach as hard as he could. But before Houdini could tighten his abdominal muscles, the student hit him hard several times. Houdini's appendix ruptured, and two weeks later he died of peritonitis. Poisoned."

Graham chuckled incredulously. "Are you seriously suggesting that I sent a graduate student to not only murder Christopher King, but to do it in a way that alluded to how Houdini died?"

"It is suspicious," Paco said, backing down a notch. "Suspicious of the whole thing. I feel you were not true with me. You tricked me and used me."

Graham turned to Iris. "Do you feel that way too?"

Conflict warred in her eyes, part embarrassed, part agreeing.

"I am sorry you feel that way," Graham said. "There was no deception on my part. Regardless of how it may appear to you. What was not shared was not mine to share. Surely you can understand that. I am genuinely thankful to you both for your help, and it was my desire that it would benefit us all to work together. That way each side—skeptics and believers—would stop demonizing the other."

Paco made a dismissive gesture and looked away.

"Paco, I did not tell you about my student there because there was nothing to tell. He was simply providing feedback and was a barometer for the mood of the conference so we would know how to best reach people. It really is as simple as that. I know it might be hard for you to believe, but when I spoke to Alexander just a little while ago, he was absolutely devastated. The thought of being part of anybody's death, let alone someone who he admired—and he did admire King—has completely broken him.

"Please withhold judgment until all the facts come out. At least do that based on the trust that we had developed ourselves. I'm sorry our collaboration has to end this way, and that we couldn't keep working together. I wish you both the best."

Iris reached for his hand as he stood.

"Graham. I—" She left the sentence unfinished and looked down.

He turned and walked into the cathedral, the one place he was certain they wouldn't follow.

# FORTY

"Ah, Dr. Eliot, I am glad you are here." Don Arturo broke away from Don Gustavo as Graham entered the office. "I assume you have heard the news."

"Unfortunately. It still doesn't seem real to me. I spoke with Alexander, my graduate student, not long ago. He spent several hours being interviewed by the police. Evidently, he was the last person to see King alive. He was in the theater between shows just before whatever happened."

"Very tragic," Don Gustavo said through a frown. "Do they believe he has done something wrong?"

"He's not sure. He's afraid it might appear that he had."

"Does your student, Alexander, know how King died?" Don Arturo asked.

"Cyanide poisoning."

Don Gustavo raised a hand to his mouth and collapsed heavily into his chair.

"That is terrible," Don Arturo said. "You do not think the police believe your student poisoned King, surely?"

"Not intentionally," Graham said. "Maybe not at all. Alexander said King told him how he performed the trick where the face of the Shroud appears on the blank cloth. Two chemicals need to be combined. One is used to paint the image but is invisible when it dries. The other is the reagent that makes it appear. He told him the name of one of the chemicals, but not the other. Alexander was left alone in the theater for a few minutes and looked in King's bag. The cyanide was in a jar labeled 'powdered sugar.' He opened it to see if that was really what it was but heard King coming. He had just put the lid on when King came back in the theater. Alexander went to his hotel, and in that time is when King was discovered dead."

"It was an accident, possibly?" Don Gustavo asked.

"As far as I know, there was no indication King committed suicide," Graham said. "And Alexander swears the lid was on tight when he returned it. But as you can imagine, he is wracked with guilt at the possibility he may have made a mistake."

"We shall pray for him," Don Arturo said. "And for Christopher King and his family."

"But I am afraid we have a more immediate problem of our own," Graham said.

Don Gustavo arched his brow. "And what is that?"

"I just saw Paco, the reporter from SIFT, outside. He's the one who posted the videos of me on their site."

"Did you speak with him?" Don Arturo asked. "Did he ask you about King?"

"I did speak with him, yes. And of course, it was all about King. He is seeing all the evidence in a very poor light. He hinted that King may have been murdered in retaliation for the Hocus Pocus Challenge. That the church might be involved in—"

"Outrageous!" Don Gustavo erupted, leaping to his feet. "We cannot let such things be said."

"I agree," Graham said. "Especially because I fear he may publish his view and pour fuel on this rumor about murder. He even framed it as some kind of conspiracy of poetic justice paralleling Houdini's death."

Don Gustavo glanced at Don Arturo. "I do not understand."

"It's not important," Graham said. "I think the worst

thing we can do to combat them is to sit back and wait for the facts to take care of themselves. We cannot trust SIFT to interpret them correctly."

"What do you suggest?" Don Arturo asked.

"I think the best distraction from that news would be bigger news," Graham said.

"Do you have something in mind?" Don Gustavo asked.

"We need to go to Turin." Graham let a beat of silence punctuate the idea. "We need to complete this project. If the two burial cloths can be shown to correspond, then that conclusively shows there is a problem with the carbon dating. And the carbon dating of the Shroud of Turin being proven to be inaccurate is huge news. Way bigger than King's death."

Don Gustavo shook his head. "That is not possible. Things do not move so quickly in the church."

Don Arturo shrugged reluctantly in agreement. "The archbishop there would take too much convincing even without the urgent timeline."

"But I thought that's why I came here in the first place," Graham said.

Don Arturo repeated the shrug. "He had agreed, yes, but only after much persuasion. This new controversy will only give him more reason to leave the Shroud unexamined."

"Wouldn't it be worth at least trying to explain to him what I just told you. Surely he can see how important it is to act quickly. As you said when you approached me, the church is not obliged to release the results if they are not in your favor. And if we do it without announcing it, then there would be no one to reveal to the public that it was being examined again."

Don Arturo looked at Don Gustavo, each apparently searching the other for a response.

Don Gustavo broke the connection to turn to Graham. "Dr. Eliot, I would like to have a word in private with Don Arturo. Would you please be so gracious as to excuse us."

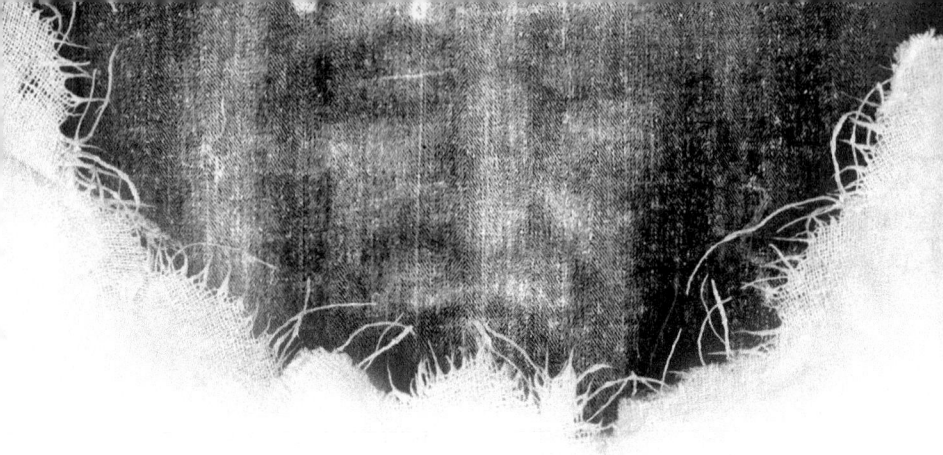

# FORTY-ONE

Fog crawled through the foothills like wayward clouds, separated from the gray billows impaled by the mountain peaks. The mixture of stone and mist reminded Graham seeing is not believing. Vapor obscured the range in places, but the mountains were always there, reliable, substantive, even where they were hidden. And the clouds obscuring the mountains could not provide a foundation, appearing substantive only from a distance.

The first verse of Joni Mitchell's "Both Sides Now," the one about clouds, began to play in his head. He remembered Iris mocking the song when they first met. Now she was one of the clouds he'd seen from both sides. Not for the first time, he noticed his knee bouncing with nervous energy and self-consciously calmed himself as he studied the changing perspective slipping past him from the passenger seat of a small SUV.

"I promise, this is better than flying to Turin," Don Arturo said, glancing at him from behind the wheel.

Graham kept his eyes fixed on the landscape. "I just want to get this done as quickly as possible before something else can go wrong."

"This way it is safer," Don Arturo said. "A few hours longer, maybe. Even if there was a direct flight from Oviedo to Turin, we would not be able to see the Shroud until the cathedral was empty. If we drive, we arrive after midnight. No one to see us go in or out."

"That's if we are allowed in at all," Graham said.

"Don Gustavo is a good friend of the archbishop of Turin. As well, we are friendly. He is the Papal Guardian of the Shroud, and he is quite protective of it. But he did agree to my proposal the first time. With Don Gustavo now seeing you work, we are hopeful he will permit us again. It will also I think be much harder for him to reject us if he learns we are on the way."

"I hope you're right," Graham said, sounding unconvinced. "Please forgive me for saying so, but it seems like the archbishop of Turin has a great deal of power over the Shroud. Almost dictatorial."

Don Arturo bobbed his head in agreement. "Yes, he is more controlling than I am with the Sudarium. But I understand. We both are trying to protect treasures of the church."

"It's amazing that the 1978 STURP investigation ever happened at all," Graham said. "More than two dozen American scientists and all of that equipment?"

"Ah, but you must remember that at the time the Shroud of our Lord was not the property of the church. Not officially."

Graham looked at Don Arturo. "Wait. Really? I thought it's been in the church for five hundred years."

"The cathedral was only its keeper, not its owner. At that time the Shroud belonged to the king of Savoy. The king took possession of it in the sixteenth century. When he moved the capital of Savoy from Chambéry to Turin, the Shroud went with it. But the kingdom of Savoy was annexed by France in the nineteenth century, and the province including Turin became part of Italy. The final king, Umberto II, was deposed after World War II. At his death in 1984, the Shroud was given to the Roman Catholic Church."

"So, it was the king of Savoy who gave permission for the 1978 scientific examination?" Graham asked.

"Yes, that is true. And when the STURP team proposed another round of tests to take place in 1988, the Shroud was owned by the church and in the care of the archbishop." Don Arturo gestured as he spoke, navigating the winding highway one-handed, adding to Graham's anxiety. "The archbishop agreed to STURP's proposal of a new series of tests. One of them was radiocarbon dating. He asked the scientists to create a plan with a representative of the Vatican, and then gave them permission."

"What were the other tests they did?" Graham kept his eyes fixed on the road, hoping Don Arturo would not gesture if no one was looking.

"I do not remember what was suggested, but I do know they were never done. For reasons I do not know, the radio-carbon testing was separated from the other tests and treated on its own. The plan was for seven different laboratories to test samples taken from at least three different locations on the Shroud. At that time, there were two methods available to perform the test. Some labs used one method, the rest used the other. I do not understand why, but shortly before the samples were taken, the archbishop changed the plan without explanation. He allowed only three labs to do the work, and one single sample was taken that was divided between them. Not only that, but all of the labs used the same method, which was the older technique."

"The archbishop just suddenly changed the rules of the agreement?"

"Unfortunately," Don Arturo said, stealing a glance at Graham.

"Without any explanation whatsoever? Not even to the scientists?"

"It was a very strange decision. After the controversy that

came next, it would have been better not to have allowed the testing." Don Arturo looked fully at Graham. "I mean that from an earthly mindset, you understand."

Graham shook his head uncomprehendingly. "For someone predisposed to scientific inquiry, that seems about as unscientific as it can get."

"But he did more than that," Don Arturo said. "He ignored the places the scientists wanted to take the samples from and chose his own spot. And the spot he picked was the one area the scientists said should not be used in the test. They said it had the most contamination and results from a test there would not be reliable."

"It almost sounds like he was trying to undermine the test," Graham said. "Do you think the archbishop thought that if the most contaminated spot on the cloth was dated to the first century it would somehow make the results more believable. You know, like the saying that a chain is only as strong as the weakest link? If the most questionable part of the Shroud was dated to the first century, then surely the rest would be as well. That sort of thing."

Don Arturo shrugged, keeping his hands on the wheel. "I do not know what he was thinking, my friend. I have never doubted the work of the scientists who dated the material. It is not reasonable to believe the labs all conspired to change their findings or misrepresent them. Their professional reputations were at stake, and I do not believe they would allow their religious beliefs—or lack of them—to influence the results. I have always believed keeping to the original plan would not have resulted in the medieval dating. That result comes from the most contaminated part of the Shroud. I understand that the fires it survived may have possibly changed the chemical composition of the material. But by sampling the one spot the scientists all agreed should not be used for the test is hard for me to understand."

Graham threw up his hands and let them drop into his lap. "Unfortunately, that test gave skeptics like SIFT some real ammunition against the church. The way the church treats the Shroud makes it look like they are anti-scientific, promoting a lie for the sake of tourist money."

"Graham, you and I both know that skeptics would have still rejected the Shroud as the authentic burial cloth of Jesus even if the radiocarbon dating indicated it was from the first century. The recent chemical analysis on the sample used in the carbon dating proved that."

"I don't know what you're talking about," Graham said.

"A chemist from Los Alamos who was a part of the STURP investigation did an analysis on the sample and compared it to a known fiber from another part of the Shroud. The sample proved to be from an entirely different cloth."

"How is that even possible?"

"The Shroud has a backing cloth on it. And the Shroud has been repaired in several places. The sample was taken from material added during the Middle Ages."

Graham rocked his head back in thought. "I haven't heard of any of this before."

"Which proves my point," Don Arturo said. "It was published in an academic journal for professional chemists, not television shows concerned with ratings or conspiracy websites. That information is ignored by skeptics because the radiocarbon test is better for business. It became a popular controversial narrative in the media. But there is some good in this, as there always is in God's providence."

"What's that?" Graham asked.

"It gives us—you and me—the opportunity to personally encounter what may be the very cloths our Lord was buried in. Few people have ever had such a privilege."

"Just like Peter and John," Graham said. "Except in an SUV, driving as fast as we can instead of running."

# FORTY-TWO

A lull in conversation left Graham to his thoughts, their speed making the car feel sluggish. He considered asking Don Arturo if he knew of M'Cheyne's exercise for spiritual discipline and keeping emotions in check, but decided against it, appreciating the comfortable silence they shared. Instead, he opened his phone and navigated to SIFT's site, hoping to survey the comments on the videos. As the page loaded, he saw a new video had been published.

"Looks like SIFT just posted an update."

"Please turn the volume loud," Don Arturo said, "so I may listen as well."

Graham steadied the phone on the console between the seats and pressed play. The SIFT logo animation transitioned to a bleary, exhausted looking Ben Steele standing in front of the Johnny Cash Museum. Night still enabled the riot of lights to color the scene, but the cacophony from the honkytonks had died down significantly.

"Hey, guys, Ben Steele back with some breaking news. I'm in Nashville, Tennessee, for ThinkCon. By now I'm sure you've heard about Christopher King. He was found dead in the theater of the House of Cards, a magic restaurant in the basement of the building behind me. So far, the only thing the police have said about the death was that it did not appear to be natural. But SIFT has learned that Christopher King died of cyanide poisoning."

Graham started to wonder how Steele knew about the cyanide, then answered himself in an epiphany that burst in a gasp. The information came from him. He told Paco, and Paco must have passed it on. The guilt hit him in a wave of nausea as Steele continued.

"We've also learned police have been interviewing a person of interest. For legal reasons, we won't release the person's name, but I can tell you that this person is a graduate student at Calbi University, a private Christian school in Los Angeles. It turns out, he was in Nashville to attend the SIFT conference, which immediately raises a red flag. Why would a young Christian scholar fly across the country to be part of a conference of skeptics? According to the people I've talked to, he didn't seem to be proselytizing or trying to convert anyone or anything like that. In fact, no one we've spoken to even knew he was a Christian or what school he went to."

Don Arturo glanced away from the road long enough to tap pause. "You are certain your student would not be influenced by arguments against the existence of God and against Christianity?"

Graham choked on a laugh. "It's way more likely he'd persuade them than the other way around. He's an excellent debater, quick on his feet, and totally unflappable. And he's an iconoclast in many ways, so he's hard to peg down. Not at all like the conformist, unimaginative, mindless believer that skeptics like SIFT like to picture. Way too smart and too informed to fall for the new-atheist arguments."

"Is it possible he lost his faith or his temper?" Don Arturo asked.

The quick denial Graham wanted to give caught in his throat as he remembered how his own faith seemed suddenly dead to him—an unimaginable state before it happened.

He covered the unexpected emotional land mine with a fake cough, then found the words again.[j3]

"Not Alexander," he said, then unpaused the video.

"Witnesses at the restaurant said this man and King appeared to be on friendly terms, even sharing a meal at the bar together before the first show of the night. The student was also visiting with King in the theater between shows, just before King's body was discovered. By that time the student had left the restaurant to return to his hotel. As I said, so far he appears to be a person of interest and has not been arrested or named as a suspect."

Don Arturo shook his head. "I am happy to hear that last part."

"Very," Graham said. "Hope the mob hears that caveat before they storm the hotel."

"But there is another twist to the story," Steele continued. "Calbi University is also the school where Graham Eliot is a research professor. Dr. Eliot is the scholar who is in Spain right now to photograph the Sudarium of Oviedo, the cloth alleged to have been placed on the head of Jesus Christ while He died on the cross and was then buried with Him. It turns out that this person of interest is actually his graduate assistant. Coincidence, or is something more sinister going on? It appears that Dr. Eliot may have sent his student to spy on SIFT after he heard about the Hocus Pocus Challenge. It looks like a coordinated effort."

Graham looked up, exasperated. "Is everything a conspiracy to these people? Aren't they the ones who ambushed me outside the cathedral?"

Don Arturo smiled ironically. "Be careful who you curse. Without them, you would not have photographed the Sudarium. Right now, you would be in America, not on the way to view the Shroud of Turin in private."

"You do know how to put the shine on the apple," Graham said.

Don Arturo raised a brow knowingly, then transformed it to a frown as the video played on.

"It makes you wonder just what the church is afraid of. What are they trying to hide? It doesn't exactly seem like the behavior of saints, does it? If Jesus really is the light of the world, it seems to me He needs to start shining in the church first. He needs to expose these deceptions. The church needs to be candid and transparent—two things that are not its strong suit, historically." Ben Steele paused, seeming to gather himself for what he had to say next.

"Christopher King was a friend and was a source of great encouragement to me over the years. But more than anything, he was a brilliant critical thinker, and a passionate lover of truth. Let's honor him by finding the truth about what happened. This is why now, more than ever, we need things like the Hocus Pocus Challenge. Friends, now and always, be lovers of truth."

Graham copied the link and texted it to Alexander and Sarah along with the caption, "Seen this? We need to get the police to clear this up ASAP."

Don Arturo's silence had the fragrance of safety, patiently waiting to be filled. Graham massaged his forehead, then spoke without looking up.

"I feel so helpless. I can't believe people can twist the truth so irresponsibly. It's like untrue truth. Like they hollowed it out and filled it with something rotten."

The SUV wove slightly and corrected as Don Arturo stole a glance across the car. "It is a dangerous time for truth, my friend. To you and me, truth is a rock, a foundation. To people like that, the rock is—at most—raw material to be shaped and sculpted, unwanted parts chipped away. And if the result is still missing something, they manufacture it, trying to make it match the look of the rock."

"The problem," Graham said, "is that I supplied the rock."

"But we always supply the rock, my friend, just by speaking truth."

"You don't understand." Graham fixed his eyes on the road before them, as if in a mobile confessional without a screen. "The only way SIFT could know about the cyanide is because I told Paco about it. I only shared that information to regain his trust. And now it's being used to make Alexander look guilty. They complain about the church not being transparent and forthcoming but look what they do with the information when they get what they want. This is my fault. I was a fool to ever trust him. If anyone's the spy it's Paco, not Alexander."

Don Arturo's countenance filled with compassion. "Graham, my friend, this is not your fault. You did not share the information recklessly. As you said, it was an act of good faith, done to repair harm. What they do with that knowledge cannot be held against you. All good things can be abused and made to be bad. Truth is never an error."

The vibration of the road gave a physical sensation to the static in Graham's thoughts. "Thank you. I know you're right. It would be exhausting to see everything as some grand conspiracy like they do. As if every group they disagree with is part of some secret society."

"I agree," Don Arturo said. "Unfortunately, there is already too much of such things in the history of the Shroud."

"What do you mean?"

Don Arturo looked askance at Graham. "Have you not heard of the Shroud's connection to the Knights Templar?"

# FORTY-THREE

"The Knights Templar." Graham repeated the name flatly, as if parroting a fib back to a child.

"You have studied them?" Don Arturo asked in a knowing lilt that hinted the claim could withstand scrutiny.

"I was very interested in them for a time. Definitely mysterious and fascinating. Not sure what happened, but somehow they started to get blamed for everything. They became the root of every conspiracy and secret society. And their spiritual descendants, like the Masons, supposedly control the world today. Crazy stuff. They got credited with so much it's hard to credit them with anything anymore."

"I understand what you say," Don Arturo said, then raised a finger in exception. "But remember what it was about them that made you interested in the first place. Before the legends started, they were truly a secret society. That gave them much power at first, and later became a weakness."

"Okay," Graham said, shrugging with his hands. "So how are they related to the Shroud of Turin?"

"Do you remember anything about the Templar's rites of initiation, or what they used in worship?"

"As a secret society we don't know a lot about such things."

"But we do know some. When the Templars were declared enemies of the church, some details of their rituals were revealed."

"Exacted by torture," Graham objected.

Don Arturo nodded reluctantly. "Yes, but that does not mean what they confessed was false. One of the revelations was that they worshipped an image of a bearded head. They would touch the face with the ropes they used as belts to receive a blessing."

"Interesting." Graham frowned thoughtfully. "I hadn't read that. And you think it was the Shroud?"

"Is there another face it could be?" Don Arturo looked sidelong across the SUV. "What if it had been folded to show the face, just as the Image of Edessa."

"I suppose that's possible," Graham said, "but it's not particularly compelling."

"What other portraits were believed to be true images of Jesus Christ? The Image of Edessa—the Mandylion—is the most logical, if not the only option. Remember that the image disappeared from Constantinople in 1204 during the Fourth Crusade. That was the time when the Knights Templar were at their most powerful."

"You're still a long way from convincing proof," Graham said. "It's not even great evidence. Interesting, but completely circumstantial."

Don Arturo's eyes brimmed with more information. "How do you explain the Templecombe discovery?"

"I can't say I've heard of it."

"There were descriptions of the bearded head given during the confessions, but they did not say where the images were. But in 1951 a storm with strong winds shook the plaster from the ceiling of a medieval structure in Templecombe, England. The building had been used by the Templars as a preceptory, but by this time it was being used as the outhouse for the cottage. Behind the plaster, there was a painting on the inner side of the roof. It was of a face that looks very much like the

Shroud of Turin."

Graham took out his phone, did a search for the image, then studied the face. "It does look remarkably like paintings of the Mandylion that Iris showed me. Given the iconographic theory of the resemblance of the Shroud to so many Byzantine icons after discovery of the Image of Edessa, I have to say it makes a lot of sense. But it's still not a direct connection. Even if they were aware of the Shroud, it doesn't mean they possessed it."

"Do you remember the leader of the Knights Templar?" Don Arturo asked.

"Jacques de Molay."

"And do you remember the name of the officer of the Templars who was executed alongside de Molay in 1314?"

Graham chuckled. "I have no idea."

"A man named Geoffrey de Charnay." Don Arturo paused, waiting for Graham to recognize the name.

"And who was he?"

"And what was the name of the man who first displayed the Shroud in Europe in 1355?"

"I remember that it appeared in Europe at that time," Graham said, "but I don't remember the knight who displayed it."

Don Arturo's eyes brimmed again. "A man named Geoffrey de Charny."

"I don't understand. If de Charnay died in 1314, how could he have displayed the Shroud forty years later?"

"Obviously, he could not," Don Arturo said. "But one of his descendants could. The names are not spelled exactly the same—the younger de Charny uses only one a—but spelling rules at that time were not as they are now. The name of the Templar knight is the same as the Crusader knight who showed the Shroud in 1355. The time that had passed between the two men might mean the Crusader could be the nephew or some other relative of the Templar.

"After the Fourth Crusade, the church had to give permission for someone to display relics. That is probably why the Shroud was kept hidden for 150 years. The name de Charnay is a connection to the most obvious group to have had possession after the fall of Constantinople. It bridges a gap in the historical record."

Graham acquiesced, turning his palms up. "It is a far more persuasive case than I thought it was going to be."

"There is another possible connection," Don Arturo said, "maybe even more strong. The younger de Charny's wife was the great-great-granddaughter of a knight in the Fourth Crusade who was at the fall of Constantinople. Afterwards, he became the duke of Athens. If you are skeptical of bringing Templars into the history, this man is another candidate for ownership. The chest that was said to contain the Shroud is still on display at a castle in Besacon, France owned by the de la Roche family. The Shroud then passed down through her family to Geoffrey de Charny through marriage. This gives de Charny a way to receive the Shroud even if he was not a descendant of the Templar. However, by the mid-fifteenth century, the finances of de Charny descendants were not in a healthy state, and they sold the Shroud to the king of Savoy to raise funds."

"Honestly, both seem plausible to me," Graham said. "But what most impresses me about the Shroud is that for something I never considered to have much evidence, I am completely overwhelmed by all the information surrounding it. And I keep learning more. Scientific results, historical documents, icon correspondence—if it's a fake, it's got to be the most successful fraud in history. And yet, if it's real, there is still room for doubt."

"I know exactly what you mean," Don Arturo said on a sigh. "It is often called the most studied object in history for good reasons. There does not seem to be a lack of desire to study it. Only a lack of desire to follow where the evidence leads."

# FORTY-FOUR

The car decelerated as sleep drained away from Graham, his awakening mind vaguely linking the simultaneous events. Fatigue had claimed him unexpectedly, and he awoke to the lane subdividing into a fan of checkpoints.

"My apologies," Don Arturo said, as if he'd had an option. "This is the border with France."

The priest displayed a mastery of French as he and the guard exchanged a volley of words beyond Graham's ability to follow. The guard glanced across the car at Graham as Don Arturo explained their business accompanied with a flurry of gestures.

The guard responded by asking Graham for his passport, then studied the document as he asked Graham's business.

"Tourist," Graham said, deciding to use as few words as possible to keep his tortured French to a minimum for both their sakes. "Going to Italy."

By the time he'd finished, the guard had handed the passport back and waved them through as he focused attention on the next car.

"What did you tell him?" Graham asked. "I said four words to him, and he was bored before I finished."

Don Arturo glanced at him with a mischievous spark in his eyes. "I told him the truth. That you are a university professor who photographs old Bibles."

"You made it sound so glamorous," Graham said. "And what did he say to that?"

"He asked why anyone would do such a thing. I told him the Bible was a mirror that shows us how we appear spiritually. By taking pictures of Bibles, you were helping to make its reflection more precise. Fortunately, he did not seem interested in a theological discussion."

Graham laughed. "Know your audience, then do the opposite. Brilliant! You probably just made some watchlist. Or maybe an ignore list of known bores. Even better."

"To tell the truth," Don Arturo said, "as a young parish priest I became very familiar with that look of boredom. It is good to know I still have the gift."

A lapse into silence allowed Graham to refresh the SIFT site on his phone. Two breaking news updates had been added. The first was a repost of an image from social media showing several police cars and a crime scene unit van outside the hotel where Alexander was staying. The caption burst off the screen like a shockwave without an explosion.

BREAKING! POLICE RAID ROOM OF
PERSON OF INTEREST IN KING DEATH!

The second update was another photo from outside the hotel, zoomed in on police officers passing through the lobby. Again, the headline forced him back into his seat.

ANONYMOUS SOURCE: LOOKING FOR CYANIDE!

Graham sucked in a breath as if he'd been submerged. "What is it?" Don Arturo asked.

"Alexander," Graham rasped as he started to compose a text, then abandoned it and called, putting it on speakerphone.

Three rings drilled holes into the silence, filling it with anxiety.

"Everything's okay," Alexander answered in singsong calm. "No one's hurt. I'm fine."

"Tell me what's happening." Graham's intensity sounded incongruous next to Alexander's tone. "The SIFT site says they're looking for cyanide in your room. They're basically implying that the police are looking for a murder weapon."

"Another win for critical thinking. That's your problem right there: the SIFT site. Actually, it's my problem."

"What do you mean?" Graham anchored his gaze on the phone, reining in his panic. "Start from the beginning."

"You know how you said SIFT has a gift for stating the truth in a way that misleads people to a lie? They're doing it again. Within an hour after they posted that new video you sent, someone had slipped an envelope under my door." Alexander's facade cracked, sending a slight quaver into his voice. "I opened it up and it contained white powder. I completely freaked and called the police."

"Someone tried to poison you?" The guilt Graham felt over putting Alexander into this circumstance ballooned.

"That's the thing. The cops told me not to touch it and to stay away from it. They showed up with a special team with hazmat suits. But pretty quick, they figured out it was powdered sugar. I was never in any actual danger. Someone just wanted to scare the crap out of me. And it worked."

Graham traded glances with Don Arturo. "I'm so glad it was just a threat and not the real thing."

"You and me both," Alexander said. "Not sure I'll ever be able to eat beignets again."

Graham laughed in relief. "And don't order any French toast from room service."

"Aunt Sarah has a friend who's a professor at Vanderbilt. She gave him a call, and it turns out he and his wife have a guesthouse behind their pool. His wife is some bigwig in the healthcare industry, so this little guesthouse is nicer and bigger than anywhere I've ever lived. That's where I'm at now."

"Ah, the old Martin Luther ploy," Graham said. "Good thinking. But instead of hiding in Wartburg Castle to escape a death sentence at the Diet of Worms, you're in some swank guesthouse in Tennessee."

"Here I sit, I can do no other," Alexander proclaimed, twisting Luther's famous defense.

"Careful with your Luther quotes," Graham warned with a crooked smile. "I'm sitting next to a Catholic priest."

"To ignore the conscience is neither right nor smart," Don Arturo said, with a slight nod of bravado.

"You can quote Luther?" Graham looked at Don Arturo, impressed. "No wonder you got in trouble."

Don Arturo made a noncommittal shrug.

"Seriously, Alexander," Graham said, "I hope no one saw you leave. They're clearly watching you."

"One of the good things about Nashville is that they're used to accommodating celebrities when they want to go unnoticed. The police helped me get out some back way and get me over here. But they still don't want me to leave town. Speaking of: where are you? Sounds like you're driving."

"On the way to Turin with Don Arturo."

"You got permission to shoot the Shroud?"

"Working on it." Graham glanced at Don Arturo hopefully. "Better to ask forgiveness than permission."

"If it's forgiveness you need, you're going to the right place," Alexander said. "It is Jesus, after all."

Graham chuckled, the stress of anxiety draining from him. "Stay safe and do what the police tell you for now. And whatever your lawyer says. It may have only been powdered sugar, but it was still a threat meant to intimidate you."

"Roger that," Alexander responded without levity. "And

Dr. E.?" He paused, prompting Graham to answer.

"Yes?"

Alexander allowed another loaded silence to pass.

"Thanks."

"Thanks for what?"

"Thanks for believing in me."

"Of course. You're Alexander the Great."

"Right now I don't feel so great. Besides, remember what happened to the other Alexander the Great? He was assassinated by being poisoned."

Don Arturo wheezed a suppressed laugh.

"First of all," Graham said, "it's a compliment to be assassinated. It means you carry enough influence that someone wants to stop you."

"Um hm," Alexander hummed, unconvinced. "With powdered sugar. Doesn't make me sound very tough, does it. It's not exactly kryptonite."

"Second of all," Graham continued, ignoring the comment, "Alexander the Great was in his thirties, so you probably got another ten years before someone takes a real shot at you."

"Maybe I'm an overachiever," Alexander said.

"That really is a trait you share with the other Alexander. At least you're in good company. I took a personality test once. The university made each department do it. When I got the results, it included biblical figures who shared those personality traits. I got John the Baptizer and the apostle Paul."

"Pretty good company to keep, Dr. E."

"I thought so, too, at first. Then I realized both of them made people so angry that they were beheaded. So I got that going for me."

He studied the sound of Alexander's laugh after ending the call, turning it over in his mind. Was it genuine or was it a mask contrived to pacify Graham's culpability?

# FORTY-FIVE

"I hope he will be safe there." Don Arturo's words sounded like a prayer as they broke the silence. "But I would be surprised if SIFT did not have someone at the hotel watching for him."

"I was just thinking the same thing. I keep checking for an update that exposes him." Graham dropped his phone in his lap and held his hands away, theatrically restraining himself. "But I assume anyone with a guesthouse like that probably also has a security system. Even if someone spotted him leaving and was able to follow, they wouldn't be able to get to him without being seen. And maybe the police have someone watching the house. That'd make sense given that he was just threatened."

Don Arturo huffed, shaking his head in disappointment. "What most disturbs me is Paco. To me he has been thoughtful, and a seeker of truth. Did he tell you how we met?"

"It never came up," Graham said, making an effort to listen, worry over Alexander dividing his attention.

"We sat next to each other at The Secular Humanist Forum."

Graham looked to see if Don Arturo was joking. "You went to a conference on secular humanism?"

"It is the truth, I did." Don Arturo smiled slyly at the

confession. "Without my clerical collar, of course. I was not trying to be provocative. During one of the breaks, we talked about whether ethics requires religious belief. That was the theme of the conference. He was obviously intelligent and had clearly studied Camus, Wittgenstein, Voltaire—philosophers who argued it does not."

"Wait a second. You did the same thing Alexander did? You went undercover to a conference of skeptics and atheists?"

"There was no deception." Don Arturo pinched his face reproachfully. "As Christians we invite those who do not believe to hear truth, yes? And if what we believe as Christians is true, then it can be examined and survive attacks. By attending the conference, I was allowing my faith to be tested by the most intellectually sophisticated atheists in Spain. Philosophy is, after all, literally the love of wisdom."

"And did you tell this to Paco?"

"I did. I was very open with him. I told him I agreed that ethics does not require religion."

"You did?" Graham asked, looking again at Don Arturo.

"I told him ethics requires God. That is quite a different thing."

Graham laughed. "I love that. Very clever. What did he say to that?"

"It became a conversation that required a meal at a café after the forum ended. And it has continued since then. Every few months, he challenges me with some new argument, and we debate it. Sometimes we will meet at a café. There have been times when I think I see his heart softening. That is what makes his actions now so difficult for me to believe."

"Is he who warned you about the Hocus Pocus Challenge?" Graham asked.

Don Arturo nodded several times. "Yes."

"I had the same impression of him you did," Graham said. "When we made the second video—the one where I explained myself—I really got to like him. And I could see that he was intelligent and appeared to be asking the right questions. I think he's just angry at me and confused by the whole situation. Hopefully, when he calms down he'll see I wasn't being deceptive. Maybe he'll even see it's not so different from how you two met."

"I pray you are right," Don Arturo said.

"Did you know he's an artist?" Graham asked. "He said he's even thinking about submitting something to the Hocus Pocus Challenge."

"Did he say how he was going to do it?"

"One idea was to use paint formulated the same way as it was in the thirteenth century. Something like iron oxide mixed with vermilion and maybe something else; I forget. He said it was found on the Shroud. I didn't know paint had been detected on the Shroud. I didn't know what to make of it, especially since you said the image wasn't made by paint."

"It was not," Don Arturo said, then raised a finger. "But he is correct. Paint was found on the Shroud. What he did not tell you is that the paint was discovered on areas without the image as well as with the image."

"I don't understand."

"When the Shroud became known in Europe, copies were made of it to be displayed elsewhere. Like museum replicas. When a copy was completed, it was laid across the Shroud to compare them, and to sanctify them. Flecks of paint from the copy probably came off on the Shroud."

"Makes sense."

"Iron oxide was found all across the Shroud, not just on the area with the image. Although it is an ingredient of the paint of that time, it is also a possible by-product of how flax is made into linen."

"Sounds like paint might be able to recreate the image without replicating the way it was made," Graham said.

Don Arturo raised his finger again, as if to poke another hole in the hypothesis. "The image on the Shroud has no directionality. No brushstrokes. The pressure of a brush at the beginning of a stroke is different from at the end. And the amount of paint left behind changes as well. The differences reveal the direction of a stroke. The image on the Shroud has no such evidence of that."

Graham rubbed his chin thoughtfully. "I'd never considered any of that. How about powdered pigment? Has any of that been found on the Shroud? That was Paco's next idea—that the image could be made by brushing dry powder onto wet cloth."

"That technique would leave particles of pigment within the weave of the material. The image is only on the outside part of the threads, not on the interior parts of the fabric, which is what would hold the powder. And brushing dry powder onto wet material would show directionality." Don Arturo raised his brow, looking sidelong at Graham. "Did all of Paco's ideas have brushing?"

"Actually, no, but he did have one more. And in this variation, the brushing is indirect. Sounded pretty clever to me. And it was the one he sounded most hopeful about. Instead of painting the image directly on the cloth, he wanted to paint the image on a pane of glass, then let the sun shine through the glass and onto the linen sheet. He thought if he left it long enough, it would fade the cloth where the light came through the strongest."

Don Arturo pursed his lips and nodded. "Yes, very clever. But there are still features in the image that could not be recreated using this method."

"For example?" Graham prompted.

"The image is not on the outer side of the section of the cloth that was beneath him. Only on the inner side. But it is on both sides of the section of cloth covering his front."

"Huh," Graham noised. "That is strange. But a skeptic might explain that as being an oversight by the forger. Or maybe a flaw in the execution."

"When every other detail was so well thought-out?" Don Arturo said incredulously. "Now I am the skeptic. But there is another feature difficult to explain. The image on the Shroud has a three-dimensional quality. The different densities in the image indicate the distance between the cloth and the body below it. For example, if the cloth was laying across the nose, the chemical change making the image would be more dense than the area showing the side of the face or leg or another place not touching the cloth. The image shows there was space between the body that is pictured and the cloth itself."

"Do you mean like a photograph?" Graham asked.

"Exactly. In fact, one of the STURP team members used an image analyzer that was very sophisticated for its time. It interpreted the different densities in the image and created a three-dimensional image."

Graham pictured a digitally sculpted face rendered in shades of green on a black background. "I think I've seen that image."

"It is very well-known," Don Arturo said. "A powerful image, even after all these years."

A Google image search created a mosaic on Graham's phone, each tile showing the face created from the Shroud of Turin in digital green relief.

"You're right, that's amazing technology for 1978."

"The STURP team used the best equipment available at the time," Don Arturo said. "And they were highly qualified experts in their fields. Another reason why the carbon-14 test alone should not outweigh the results of the evidence collected from the other tests."

"Speaking of three dimensions," Graham said, "Paco said he thought the image might be created by heating a metal statue, like bronze, and then laying the cloth on it. He thought that might scorch the image onto the material."

Don Arturo glanced across the car. "You see the problem with this, yes?"

"I told him even if the heat did transfer the image to the cloth, it would only look correct when the cloth was contoured around the shape of a body. But the image would become distorted when it was laid flat."

"Exactly so." Don Arturo bobbed his head once on each word.

"The only question Paco didn't have an answer for was why a forger would create a negative image. What would be the point? I don't know if the medieval mind could even comprehend exactly what a negative image was."

"That is a difficult problem for any explanation. But there is an even more difficult problem."

"What's that?" Graham asked.

"The STURP team found the image is made of a change in the chemical composition of only the outside parts of the threads, the ones on the very surface, not by any medium used by artists. No one at that time had a way of thinking of such a thing, and certainly no way to create it. Especially since the only explanation that can explain all the features of the image is difficult for even the scientists on the STURP team to accept. Some of them still do not."

Graham cocked his head. "Why not?"

"Because it is not possible. As I said, the image on the surface parts of the linen has different densities."

"Which is how that three-dimensional image was made that you just talked about." Graham held up his phone with the image still displayed.

"According to the physicist who led the STURP team, to create an image with like that requires a corpse to become volumetrically radiant in the vacuum ultraviolet range while simultaneously becoming mechanically transparent."

"I have no idea what that means," Graham said.

"Basically, it means that the body emitted a burst of radiation as it dematerialized, which enabled the top half of the cloth to fall through the body as it disappeared."

"Sounds a little science fiction-y to me."

"Science, yes. Fiction, no. It has been modeled using a computer. And now, a physicist from Harvard has a variation on the hypothesis. He suggested something called neutron flux phenomenon could be another factor. Neutron flux phenomenon effects the ratio of carbon-14 to carbon-12, and therefore would skew any radiocarbon dating results. It would also leave rare radioactive isotopes of chlorine and calcium that could still be detected if the proper tests were done. I do not fully understand these things, but I memorize what they say. If these tests confirm their presence, then it would help explain the 1988 dating results."

"In other words," Graham said, "the Shroud very well could be a picture of the moment of the Resurrection."

"Not precisely," Don Arturo said, spearing Graham's words with his finger. "That explanation makes sense of the evidence, but goes beyond it, out of what science can show."

"But it's what you believe, right? It's a miracle?" Graham asked, confused.

"Absolutely. But science is observation and description of natural phenomenon. A miracle is not something to be replicated and tested. Science is limited in how much it can explain miraculous events. It can give context for a miracle. But the real explanation is in what it cannot see. The fall-through radiation hypothesis is an explanation of the evidence for an event that does not occur naturally and has never been observed. That is the most you can say, scientifically speaking. The rest is interpretation."

"Understood," Graham admitted, "but there's a very powerful implication in the data."

"I agree, absolutely. And yet, as I said, even some members of the STURP team do not accept the explanation."

"I think I see your point." Graham folded his arms and processed the information. "Regardless, I think the Hocus Pocus Challenge might actually help vindicate the Shroud by failing to account for all of its features."

"I wish that were true. But some people—including a scientist who was part of the STURP team—have misrepresented the results of the tests."

Graham huffed incredulously. "You're kidding."

Don Arturo shrugged an apology. "This scientist, a microscopist, claimed to have found evidence of paint on the cloth, but no evidence of blood."

"You lost me." Graham frowned across the car. "That is the opposite of what you said earlier."

"Exactly my point," Don Arturo said. "And the SIFT members—such as Paco—always use that particular scientist's findings. He was an expert in his field, but his claim is confusing, especially within the STURP team itself since it contradicts the findings of other tests. And blood experts have contradicted his conclusions."

"I guess the Hocus Pocus Challenge requires what all magic relies on," Graham said. "Misdirection."

# FORTY-SIX

Night had fallen as worry gnawed at Graham, as if dimming the day. He watched the light dissipate from a shell of detachment, not registering it until Don Arturo broke the monotonous thrum of the highway, slowing to take an exit. Graham glanced at the clock, for a moment not processing the pattern of ones and zeroes as eleven o'clock exactly.

"Sorry. Zoned out there for a bit. How far are we from Turin?"

"We have still two hours and a half to drive," Don Arturo said. "But first we need gasoline."

"I could use a little fuel myself," Graham said.

"Yes, me too. This should answer our prayers."

Don Arturo pulled into a twenty-four-hour market and guided the SUV to a pump. Graham unfolded himself as the tank filled, stretching his legs as well as working out kinks from stress.

After reseating the nozzle, the priest started toward the market entrance with Graham at his side.

"Chambéry is near to here," Don Arturo said, pointing vaguely to their left. "That is where the Shroud was before moving to Turin."

"That's where the knight, de Charny, lived?"

"No, no, no." Don Arturo shook his head as he held the

door open, ushering Graham inside the store. "When the king of Savoy bought the Shroud from the de Charny family, his capital was still at Chambéry. It is the location mentioned by Calvin as the home of the Shroud in his treatise on relics."

"First you quote Luther, and now you cite Calvin?" Graham said in mock confusion. "Are you sure you're showing up to the right church on Sundays?"

Don Arturo chuckled. "No need for whatever the Protestant equivalent of the inquisition is. Calvin's treatise on relics is all I have read of him. I discovered it through a reference in a footnote and went to the source. His criticism of relics in general is actually close to mine. But I do not agree with his explanation of the Shroud. Calvin believed the image was painted on the cloth."

"Maybe he was actually talking about one of the copies of the Shroud you mentioned."

"Interesting you should say that," Don Arturo said. "Calvin mentions that there are six copies of the Shroud that he knows of. But the text reads as if his criticism is of the original. Except for one thing. When he describes the Shroud, he says the image of the body is wrapped in a loin cloth."

"Like a modesty covering?" Graham asked.

"That is what it sounds like. But that is a feature that is obviously not on the Shroud we are studying. Maybe it was yet another painting. Maybe he never saw the Shroud himself and is repeating a misconception. There is no way to be certain. He did record a variation of how the Shroud came to be in France, but he presents it as a legend more than history."

Graham selected a protein bar to go with his Diet Coke, while Don Arturo poured a cup of espresso topped with layers of honey, steamed milk, and cinnamon.

"The story told by Calvin is that the Shroud was moved from Jerusalem to protect it from Titus before he sacked the city in AD 70. But he says it was returned in 640. That would fit with the recovery of the Image of Edessa. However, he said it was Jerusalem where the Crusaders discovered it and took it to Europe where it eventually came into the possession of de Charny."

"For something he doesn't believe in, he seems to know an awful lot about it," Graham said.

"That is not so different from today is it?" Don Arturo asked. "The SIFT challenge is proof of that."

"That is true," Graham said. "What do you think of his version of events?"

Don Arturo waited to answer until they had paid out and began moving back to the car.

"I do not see how Calvin's story makes sense of the other historical evidence we have. Either he is mistaken, or he did not have access to the sources we do. Such as Robert de Clari's writings."

"Maybe Calvin was filling in a hole in the timeline. The Crusaders could have taken the Shroud to Jerusalem after the sacking of Constantinople."

Don Arturo nodded, mulling over the suggestion. "Yes, I suppose that could be true. But if that happened, I think there would be some historical record of it. And none of the story would explain the loin cloth."

"That is a problem, I agree," Graham admitted. "Any idea what Calvin's sources were?"

"Unfortunately—"

Don Arturo abandoned the sentence as Graham opened the car door and froze, the air suddenly brittle. Graham spun around, frantically scanning the parking lot before focusing again on the passenger seat.

He reached for the object that had been left while they were inside and held it up to show Don Arturo. Iris's red beret.

# FORTY-SEVEN

"I don't see her anywhere." Graham pivoted around once more, stopping to face Don Arturo. "She must be here somewhere."

"Maybe. We do not know who put the hat there." Don Arturo raised his brow to offer the suggestion.

"What do you mean?" Graham asked.

"You say you saw her with Paco this morning, yes? At the café. And when you left, they were together."

"But that doesn't—" Graham began but was silenced by Don Arturo's raised finger.

"We know they both are interested in the Shroud. And they know you are to photograph the Shroud, so they know where we are going. And we know that Paco has stalked before you to get video of you."

"That's true," Graham said. "But why would Paco leave the hat? It makes more sense that Iris is signaling us that we're being followed. She seemed conflicted at the café. Maybe she's had a change of heart and sees my side now."

"Ah, but see how quickly you look for a way to trust her?" Don Arturo asked. "Maybe that is what Paco is wanting you to think. Maybe the hat is misdirection. A signal he hopes for you to misunderstand."

"For what reason?"

"When you left the café, they lost their connections. Iris lost a chance to see the Shroud, and Paco lost his source of inside information. They need a way back into our project. If you believe Iris has repented by leaving the hat to warn us that we are being followed, then you will have a reason to trust her again. That may be what they are counting on. Because if Iris has not repented, if she still is bitter and suspicious of you, then her sign of good faith makes her a wolf in sheep's clothing."

Graham ran a hand through his hair, releasing a heavy breath. "Hadn't considered that. You know, you have a pretty devious mind for a priest."

Don Arturo curled his mouth in a cynical smile. "I wish I could blame it on all the confessions I have heard. But the truth is I have never heard a confession worse than the sins I commit in my own heart."

"I know how you feel," Graham said.

They settled themselves in the car. Graham studied Iris's round hat on his lap as if it were the dot detached from the tail of a question mark.

Don Arturo sat for a moment without starting the car and studied the map on his phone. "You know, I think it might be time for some misdirection of our own."

"What do you have in mind?"

"We are near Chambéry. Less than fifteen kilometers or so."

"The place where the Shroud was kept before it was moved to Turin?"

"Yes. Sainte-Chapelle."

"Is it on the way to Turin?"

"No. But that is the plan. There is another highway that connects to this one very close. They will not expect us to turn north onto the highway. If they follow us, maybe we will see them and maybe even confront them."

"But we haven't noticed anyone following us so far," Graham said.

"We have not been watching for anyone to follow us. And if they do not follow, we know they will be in Turin waiting for us. Then we can plan to enter the cathedral through a side door as we did for the Sudarium."

"So, what exactly do we do when we get to Chambéry?" Graham asked. "It's almost midnight. It's not like we can tour the church."

"The plan is to force them to reveal themselves, if we can," Don Arturo said. "Once we leave the highway, we will be on a main road through the city. It would be harder to follow us without being seen at this time of night. But whether they follow or not, I have something I want to show you."

# FORTY-EIGHT

"I still can't tell if anyone's following us," Graham said. "Nothing suspicious, anyway."

He'd kept his eyes glued to the sideview mirror for the duration of the trip to Chambéry, the fifteen minutes feeling more like an hour as he scrutinized the headlights in their wake. None followed them through the avenue into the heart of the city.

"Nothing," Graham reported. "Unless they're driving without their lights on."

"It is better this way," Don Arturo said. "If they went to Turin, then we have a better chance of avoiding them."

Graham turned away from the mirror to focus his words on Don Arturo. "Unless Paco has SIFT contacts in Turin who will help him be on the lookout."

"I had not thought of that. But I know an entrance that will be safe, I think. Even if we were seen, they could take pictures only from a distance."

Don Arturo parked on a side street near the start of a narrow cobblestone lane closed to cars. They walked into the canyon of shadows cast by shops with several floors of apartments above them. As they followed the jagged path, the priest picked up the thread of conversation left at the gas station.

"Earlier, you asked me what Calvin's sources were for

his criticism of the Shroud. I think one of them must be the letters to Pope Clement VII from Bishop d'Arcis."

"I'm not familiar with that," Graham said.

"It is a controversial part of the Shroud story. People who are for it and who are against it both use it as evidence."

"Assuming Calvin cared what Pope Clement VII thought," Graham teased, half-joking.

"Heresy does have a way of corrupting the mind," Don Arturo retorted with his own half-smile. "The letters began with Bishop d'Arcis asking the Pope to not allow the Shroud to be exhibited at Lirey. This was in 1389, thirty years after the first public display of the Shroud in Europe."

"Why would the bishop not want the Shroud to be displayed? It seems to me that it would be an excellent source of revenue for the church at the very least. Especially given the interest in relics at the time."

"That is true, but the bishop claimed that the Shroud was not a true relic. He said that the image had been painted. Not only that, but the bishop of Lirey himself was also suspicious of it."

"And this was 1389," Graham said. "Just after the time range indicated by the radiocarbon test."

"Some skeptics today say the letter is evidence that supports that result."

"What was the pope's reaction? He didn't agree, did he?"

"It is more complicated than that. We now know that bishop d'Arcis composed two drafts of the memo. And there is no evidence the final draft was ever sent. Nothing like it has been found in the Vatican archives. The first version contains the more damning claims. It is the one that says the bishop of Lirey was skeptical of the Shroud. That is nothing more than hearsay. There is no other record supporting that claim."

"How do you keep all this stuff straight?" Graham asked. "There are so many rabbit holes to go down."

Don Arturo chortled. "I have spent years in those rabbit holes. It just gets curiouser."

"Nice," Graham said. *"Alice in Wonderland* quote this time. So, if there are two drafts of the memo and the early one has the more spurious accusations, what is the issue?"

"The problem is that skeptics of the Shroud quote the two drafts as if they were one. And they assume a final version was sent, which—as I said—has no evidence in the archives. Skeptics use the drafts as proof the Shroud was known to be a medieval fraud. Some even claim the artist was known, although no one is named in the letter."

"They're misrepresenting a draft that was itself a misrepresentation? Strange. But I suppose there is still some historical value in the Shroud being documented at that time. Enemy attestation, as it were."

They emerged from the lane and stepped into a small plaza. To their right, a tower rose against the night sky, and Graham could just make it out as the apse of a church on a bluff above them, its walls extending down to the plaza. Don Arturo stopped on the other side of the plaza at the foot of a flight of stone steps.

"This is Sainte-Chapelle, where the Shroud was kept for a hundred years beginning in the mid-fifteenth century." He gestured to the archway in the wall on the landing at the top of the stairs. "Unfortunately, we cannot go see the church at this time of day."

"Doesn't sound like there's anything to see," Graham said.

"No, but it is still important. While the Shroud was here, the church caught fire. This was 1532. Do you recall the pattern of triangular holes?"

Graham nodded. "You told me that was damage done by a fire."

"The Shroud had been folded and placed in a metal box. The fire was so hot that one of the corners began to melt and

225

dripped onto the cloth, burning all the way through. The patches you see in the pictures were added by the nuns here. They also added the backing cloth."

Graham stared up at the church. "It's really pretty amazing the cloth has survived all this time."

"I have thought the same things many times," Don Arturo said. "But it is time we left to see it for ourselves."

Halfway back down the lane, angry shouts reverberated off the stone and plaster. A man's voice erupted in a furious torrent of Spanish but was cut off by a woman's voice issuing an even more intense blast of words. The two voices twined, opposing forces refusing to surrender, each unable to vanquish the other. The exchange abruptly ended, punctuated by a slamming car door and the blast of a horn as the car sped away.

Graham and Don Arturo traded glad-that-wasn't-me looks and moved forward again from where they had stopped to listen. The street where they parked came into view from around a bend in the alley, and they saw a figure sitting on the curb, hunched over, sobbing into her hands. They stepped out of the lane and approached the woman, instinctively wanting to offer help. When she looked up, Graham broke into a run for the last few steps. But somehow, he knew who it would be before Iris revealed her face.

# FORTY-NINE

Graham fell to his knees and put a hand on her shoulder. "Iris, are you hurt?"

Iris buried her head in her hands, shaking it, releasing more sobs.

Graham glanced at Don Arturo, remembering the theory that the hat was a ploy to regain access to the Shroud, but the priest's face was a mask of compassion.

"I am so, so sorry." Iris's muffled voice was strained through her hands. "Please forgive me, Graham. I never meant for this to happen." She risked a look, meeting Graham's eyes, triggering a spring of tears as she shivered.

"Did Paco hurt you?"

She closed her eyes and shook her head. "No. Thank God." She stole a glimpse of Don Arturo, apparently checking his reaction.

Graham repositioned himself next to her and put an arm around her shoulders as the priest crouched in front of her.

"Señorita Elizondo—Iris, how can we help you?"

Once again, Graham was moved by the tender manner of Don Arturo, noting the calming effect it had on Iris. Graham knew he was a fixer, a problem solver, and he remembered how Olivia told him that sometimes she didn't want to be solved, just heard. But for all of Don Arturo's talent at engineering schemes, he was foremost an empath.

"It's okay." Graham realized he was imitating Don Arturo's voice. "You can trust us."

Iris looked up again, gaining control of herself. "I know I can trust you. But you can't trust me." She peered into each of their faces, her eyes unfiltered and confessional.

Don Arturo formed a melancholy smile. "Iris, please tell us what has happened."

She held his eyes a moment, released a heavy sigh, and turned to Graham. "He used me. Paco did. He pretended to be interested in me to get more information about you."

"It didn't look that way to me." Graham hoped he didn't come across as a jealous rival. "What makes you think that?"

"Paco was watching the area around the cathedral the whole time. The night I arrived in Oviedo, he saw us meet for dinner. And the next day he waited for us to enter the church. He watched us meet at the café, and he also saw us go into the gate by the tower to photograph the Sudarium."

Graham searched his memory for Paco hiding in the background. "I never saw him. I had no idea."

"He was there," Iris continued. "And that night, when we came out of the cathedral after processing the photos and sat down at the café with him, he was waiting."

"Yes, but he told us that," Graham said. "And you two seemed to hit it off."

"Seemed that way, yes. After you left, we talked forever."

"What did you talk about?"

"About lots of things," Iris said. "A lot about you, actually. And the Shroud. But he asked a lot about me." Her face grew dark again. "I feel so stupid. I thought he was interested in me. I don't have much experience, romantically speaking. I was so flattered, I found myself saying things I didn't necessarily believe just to agree with him, to increase our connection. Or what I thought was a connection. Imbecile."

"That does not make you an imbecile, Iris," Don Arturo said. "It makes you human."

"Maybe, in some way, you saw your father in him." Graham searched her eyes for the words to take hold. "Like you were living out a variation of the story of how your parents met. Regardless, you are not an imbecile. If anyone is, it's Paco for not seeing how special you are."

"Thank you for saying so." Iris sniffled. "Even if it's not true."

"I wouldn't say it if it wasn't true." Graham's eyes finally caught hers, underscoring his sincerity.

"Iris, please help us understand what is happening," Don Arturo said. "Exactly why would he want to follow us to Turin? He cannot join us inside. What does he want to happen?"

"Revenge. He's blinded by it."

"Revenge for what?" Graham asked. "We didn't do anything to harm him. In fact, we helped each other."

"Revenge for the death of Christopher King," Iris said. "It has become like a crusade for him."

"He's the one who told SIFT about the cyanide, wasn't he?"

Iris nodded. "I told him not to. I said the information wasn't his to share or theirs to publish. It's a police matter. But he wouldn't listen."

Don Arturo shifted his crouch to kneel. "Why did King's death mean so much to him that he felt he had to take revenge somehow?"

"There's no evidence he was even murdered," Graham added.

"It's what King stood for—free inquiry, critical thinking, science-based fact. All that lot. He was a hero to Paco, like he was to many others. And now it's like he's a martyr." She met Don Arturo's eyes, seemingly apologizing as she continued. "And he has a suspicion of the church that is almost irrational."

"I found the same in our conversations," Don Arturo said without offense. "He is very intelligent, and I have enjoyed our talks. But I feel he is not truly interested in answers. For him, an open mind is the greatest virtue. Becoming convicted of a position is almost a heresy for his skepticism."

"He didn't come across that way to me when we met to make the second video," Graham said. "He seemed happy to help."

"Because you had something he wanted," Iris said. "Information about the Sudarium that could be twisted into whatever he wanted it to say like a wax nose. You also did not blindly accept what the church was telling you. You were a Christian who was secure enough in his faith to ask questions. That's what he kept asking me about at the café after you left. What you truly believed, and if you could be trusted."

"He certainly didn't give me the benefit of the doubt this morning," Graham retorted, cocking his head.

"King's death has really shaken him. You are collateral damage. But last night, when he told me what he believed and how he questioned everything, it sounded so intelligent and rational. It made me question myself. I told him what I believed, that it wasn't the same as you. He said that intuition I have about sensing God's presence is just a natural desire not to be alone in the dark, and that people invent God to give that darkness meaning."

"People aren't afraid of being alone in the dark," Graham said, unable to resist fixer-mode. "They are afraid of not being alone. That's what terrifies Paco. It would be better to pretend God exists when He doesn't than pretend He doesn't exist when He does."

"Pascal's wager," Don Arturo said. "Now you are quoting Catholics."

A trace of a confused smile bent Iris's lips, apparently

appreciating the attempt to lighten the mood even with an inside joke she wasn't privy to.

"He had me second-guessing myself so much that I wondered if I'd been wasting my life on the iconographic theory. He said the images were pictures of a collective imagination. Christian herd mentality. He said they shared the same features because Christians were too lazy to use their imaginations, just like they didn't use whatever intelligence they had to think critically."

Graham restrained the impulse to explain how the argument was philosophically bankrupt.

"His words—it was like he claimed to see clearly, but all he did was create fog. And I got lost in it. All it took was a bit of flattery and attention. It's so obvious now. That's where I was this morning when we found out the person the police were talking to was your student. And that made me second-guess you. After you were so kind. Both of you."

"Iris, you are too hard on yourself," Don Arturo said. "You are with friends here. You are safe."

"Thank you, Father," Iris said. "But I am not sure how safe you are. Paco wants to embarrass the church any way he can. Instead of watching the cathedral for your next move, he watched the hotel."

"How would watching my hotel help him embarrass the church?" Graham squinted.

"He thought you would leave soon for the airport. If you flew to America, it was because you were going to help your student, which would make you an accomplice in his eyes. And if you flew to Turin, then he could follow and expose the plan like he did when you first arrived at Oviedo. But when you didn't go to the airport, he just kept following you. And it became obvious rather quickly that you were going to Turin."

"And you agreed to go with him." Don Arturo's voice was not angry or accusatory but filled in the blanks to keep Iris from saying the words.

"And you were behind us the whole time?" Graham asked.

"Paco tried to follow as best he could, but he drives a Renault Zoe—fully electric—and it was almost out of charge when we left, so we lost an hour plugging in. We didn't think we'd find you until Turin. Paco said it would be hard to park near the cathedral without being seen, but he still went as fast as he could trying to catch up to you. It was a bit of a death-ride, to tell the truth. We only stopped twice, and that was to use the loo and get something to eat. The second time, when we pulled into a petrol station, we saw your car already there. It was like a miracle."

"Skeptics don't believe in miracles," Graham said.

Iris ignored the joke. "He stopped behind a lorry in the car park so we couldn't be seen, and then he reached beneath his seat and pulled out an envelope that he said contained powdered sugar. I think he had planned to slip it under your hotel door to frighten you."

Graham and Don Arturo traded looks.

"What?" Iris asked. "What did I miss?"

"The same thing happened to Alexander. A harmless threat. He's okay. Go on."

"I told him I didn't think that was funny at all. He said he wasn't trying to be funny. And then he told me to get out and put it under your windscreen wiper. When I refused, he became quite upset. I thought he might become violent. I didn't know what to do. Given his reaction, I didn't feel I had a choice.

"I went to the car, praying you wouldn't see me. I tried the door, and it was unlocked. I wanted so bad to just get in, but I didn't think you'd want me. I left my hat to let you know you were being followed, but without the threat of the powdered sugar. I threw the envelope in the bin on the way back to his car. He started screaming at me to go back and put it right, but just then you walked out of the shop."

"I knew it was yours, of course," Graham said, "but I never saw you."

"We watched you look. But you didn't know what kind of car Paco drove, and like I said, we were mostly hidden from view. But when you left, we did follow you. We couldn't figure out why you turned to Chambéry, but we knew we hadn't lost you. Whatever the reason was, he blamed me for it because of the hat. Once he found your car, I was supposed to put another envelope of powdered sugar under the wiper."

"How many envelopes did he have?" Graham asked.

"Just the one at the petrol station, actually. He had the bag of sugar in the car still, but he had to improvise a packet from some notebook paper. Again, I refused to do it and he completely lost the plot. Started screaming. I truly thought he might hurt me, so I decided to leg it. I thought it would calm him down. But he drove off. Just left me." Iris wiped fresh tears away with the heels of her palms.

"Iris, you are safe with us," Don Arturo repeated.

Iris locked eyes with him. "But you're not safe with me."

"Nonsense. What you did was admirable. You chose not to do what you knew was wrong although it put you at risk. For that we thank you."

An expression of disbelieving thankfulness washed over her face as she turned to each of them.

"You'll have to come with us if you want your hat back," Graham said. "Besides, I have a weakness for powdered sugar."

# FIFTY

The vibration of the phone yanked Graham back from the brink of sleep. Alexander's name appeared on the screen. He showed the call to Don Arturo, then glanced into the back seat to see if Iris was still asleep before answering sotto voce.

"Hey, you okay?"

"Dr. E., I'm fantastic. At least as good as I could be under the circumstances. Police just called and said they've cleared me. They're about to have a press conference that will announce King's death was accidental and that I had nothing to do with it."

"That's great news," Graham rasped, quietly enthusiastic. "What happened? Did they tell you?"

"Yeah, it's kind of crazy. So, you know how the cyanide was the reagent that made the image appear?"

"Uh huh," Graham noised. "Sarah told me. But I don't know how it worked exactly."

Don Arturo caught Graham's attention with a look asking what was going on. Graham replied with a thumbs-up, refocusing on Alexander.

"King dissolved the cyanide in water, and then put it in an atomizer that would mist the back of the cloth. He had some kind of remote control to trigger it. Pretty clever set up. And no one would ever guess it was done that way. The funny thing is that King told me the trick dates back over a hundred years. He just updated it with an electric atomizer instead of relying on a stooge backstage to do it manually."

"Makes sense," Graham said. "Did he accidentally spill it when he was trying to load it or pour it out or whatever?"

"Close. This was a new trick in King's act. He'd only been doing it a few months, so the atomizer was still new to him. He got it just for this trick. According to what the police could figure out, while he was setting up for the next show, he saw that the nozzle was clogged or about to be. They think he pulled the nozzle out to clean it before he remembered to put on gloves."

"And it had cyanide on it," Graham finished.

"That's what they think," Alexander said. "I didn't see it, but maybe it looked like that crusty stuff left from minerals in hard water. Or maybe it really was hard water minerals but had cyanide residue on it. Maybe he just tried to wipe it with his fingers before remembering what it was. Or if he tapped it to knock out the clog, he may have touched that."

Graham nodded reassuringly for Don Arturo's benefit. "Why did it take this long to figure all that out?"

"Because the nozzle was screwed halfway back into place. He got it on far enough not to look out of place unless you knew what it was supposed to look like. But even half-on, it was enough time for the cyanide to take effect."

"At least they figured it out," Graham said. "Better late than never."

"For what it's worth, I think the detectives wanted to believe me. It just took them a while to find a way to check out my story. Without that, they really only had my word that King told me he used the cyanide for the trick. I guess I could see how they thought I might have planted the bottle of cyanide there."

"But they had no reason why you'd want to do that."

"That's what the detective said who just called. How'd he put it? How plus why equals who. He said they had no why. Anyway, they tried to replicate the trick to see how much cyanide it took to make the image. They figured if they compared that to how much was missing from the bottle and how much of the cyanide water was missing from the atomizer reservoir, then they could determine if it was enough to kill. But the atomizer didn't work. It was clogged. So, they took it apart, and that's when they noticed the nozzle wasn't on all the way. And that's how they found the deposits around the nozzle, and that it had been partially wiped down."

Graham made a sigh of relief into the phone. "Thank God for the police. I mean, I know their interest in you didn't make your life very pleasant for a while, but without them, your conscience might have never been totally at ease. You may have always wondered if you really did put the lid back on correctly."

"I thought the exact same thing," Alexander said. "It's like a massive weight has been lifted off me. The weird thing is that it's kind of like what happened to Chung Ling Soo."

"Who?"

"Chung Ling Soo. His posters are all around the foyer outside the Palace of Mystery at the Magic Castle."

"That was a lifetime ago," Graham said. "I don't remember. And I didn't know who most of those people in the posters were, anyway."

"Chung Ling Soo was famous for doing a trick called the bullet catch, which is exactly what it sounds like. He wasn't the only one who performed it, but not many magicians worked it into their acts.

"He would have an audience member mark a bullet somehow—scratch their initials into it or something—then load it into a rifle. He'd walk to the other side of the stage and hold a plate up in front of his chest like a target. He let the volun-

236

teer from the audience fire the gun to make it look as fair as possible. And when the shot was fired, he caught the marked bullet on the plate."

"That's insane," Graham exclaimed. "Must've been a fool-proof method to trust the gun with an audience member. How'd he do it?"

"The way Chung Ling Soo did it was to switch out the bullet when it was loaded. And when the substitute bullet was loaded, it dropped into a hidden chamber in the gun. This was long enough ago that he used an old rifle that you poured powder in and then packed wadding into the barrel. When the gun was fired, the powder ignited and made the flash and smoke and sound, but the bullet wasn't in the actual chamber, so nothing was actually shot out of the gun. Essentially, it fired a blank.

"But one night in London—it was like 1918 or some-thing—somehow the bullet actually fired, and Chung Ling Soo was shot and killed. Afterward, they figured out that the metal shim that divided the blank from the hidden chamber had worn away and that powder had gotten in the chamber with the bullet. And that night, when the powder ignited, it fired the bullet in the secret compartment."

"Crazy story," Graham mused. "And a way stronger coin-cidence than the Houdini retribution theory."

"The what?"

"Some bizarre theory one of the SIFT guys came up with. Not important."

"The story isn't over," Alexander said. "And it gets crazier. Chung Ling Soo turned out to be an American named Wil-liam Robinson. He wasn't Asian at all. He just made himself look Asian. He shaved his head, dressed in robes, and never spoke English in public. His whole, entire life was an elabo-rate act. Can you imagine someone trying that now? They'd totally be canceled."

"Well, he was killed," Graham said. "Doesn't get much more cancelled than that. But I think for your next trick you need to disappear and get home as quickly as possible."

"Already working on it." Alexander's tone closed the subject. "What's up with you? How far are you from Turin?"

"We've still got about an hour. They have decided to let us see it, but it has to be tonight. They don't want word getting out like what happened with the Sudarium. We've got to be done by dawn and it's already one a.m."

"Amazing that it's happening so fast," Alexander said.

"It's amazing that it's happening at all."

"You must've made a good impression on the church for them to trust you so much."

"What do you mean?"

"You're not Roman Catholic, and you're not a Shroud advocate. And yet you've been pulled out of the audience to take the shot."

Graham chuckled. "And this time there's no switching the bullet."

# FIFTY-ONE

According to the map on Graham's phone, the exit off the highway would deposit them on a direct route that passed within a block of the Cathedral of Saint John the Baptist, home of the Shroud. Instead, Don Arturo turned into the first side street he came to and dialed Monsignor Roberto, Keeper of the Shroud. After explaining the need for extra secrecy and giving their location, Don Arturo navigated the side streets of the city, following Monsignor Roberto's turn-by-turn directions to a back entrance.

Graham kept an eye on the sideview mirror, once again looking for Paco, just in case he had been waiting near the exit. The fatigue that mired him since talking with Alexander quickly thawed when the lights of Turin came into view, and he was now fully awake.

Iris woke as the SUV serpentined through the city, remaining silent as Don Arturo received guidance. Graham saw her open her phone's map app and study their course, watching for any sign of sharing their location with Paco. To his relief, she looked out the window, comparing their surroundings with their progress on the screen, but never texted or made a call.

They left the backstreets for a major road directly in front of the Royal Palace. Almost immediately, they slipped through a vaulted, quadruple underpass that cut through the ground floor of a wide, shallow building. The passage deposited them in a park.

"We are here," Don Arturo said, slowing. "The Royal Gardens."

He brought the car to a full stop opposite an ornate, wrought-iron gate.

"No one's there," Iris said.

Don Arturo held up a finger. "Monsignor Roberto is speaking with security. This is the entrance to where the archbishop and his staff park. It is private. Very secure. No one can follow us or photograph us here."

"C'mon, c'mon, c'mon," Graham chanted under his breath, feeling increasingly vulnerable without a sense of motion.

As if in response, the gate began to retract to one side. Don Arturo inched the SUV forward in anticipation, then shot through the opening and descended the ramp to the underground parking structure. He maneuvered through the concrete maze and into a space reserved for the archbishop's office.

"Enormous car park for cathedral employees," Iris said, scanning the cavern.

"It is not all for the cathedral," Don Arturo said. "The Royal Palace uses it, too. It is an art museum now. Ah, there is Monsignor Roberto. Please wait while I speak to him."

A stocky man in a black clerical suit with a silver cross hanging from his neck waited just outside the nondescript door he'd slipped through. His receding white hair formed a natural tonsure, like quotation marks pinching his face into a pensive squint. He smiled modestly as he gave Don Arturo a two-handed shake. The two priests spent several moments speaking, frequently glancing and gesturing toward the SUV.

"Graham, this is a terrible mistake," Iris said. "I should

not be here. I've spoiled everything."

"Why would you say that?" Graham turned to see her shrink into the back seat. "There's no—"

Iris cut him off with a sharp nod. "He's coming back."

Don Arturo opened the driver's door and leaned in. "It is all arranged. They are ready for us. Please, come."

He pressed the button to open the hatch as Graham got out and moved to the back to unload the gear. Before setting the case onto the dolly, Graham opened the backpack and removed a camera.

"Here you go, Iris."

"What?" Iris made a perplexed frown as she stared at the camera without moving to take it. "I can't do that. I'll wait in the car."

"No, no, no," Don Arturo said quickly. "You are coming with us."

An incredulous swirl of shame and gratitude twitched her face as her eyes filled with tears. She dropped her face into her hands, breathing quickly.

"You are a part of this team, Iris," Don Arturo continued. "You are our photographer."

Iris slowed her breathing and looked up, her hand wiping away tears, then moving down to cover her heart. She moved her mouth soundlessly before it caught, breaking as she spoke. "I don't know what to say. I don't deserve any of this."

"No one does." Don Arturo smiled knowingly.

"That's what makes the gospel good news," Graham added. "It can't be earned."

Her cheeks billowed as she blew out a long breath, then took the camera. "Right. Let's see what we have here."

"I carry a backup in case the main camera gets damaged during travel. It's actually a duplicate of what I use. Unfortunately, I don't have all the lenses you're probably used to."

"This'll do the job just fine," she said, inspecting it. She looked up, locking eyes with Graham. "Are you sure you trust me?"

Graham held her gaze for a moment before answering. "I trust the Iris who entered the Cámara Santa seeking truth. Is she still there?"

Iris sniffled and nodded emphatically. "I am. Absolutely."

# FIFTY-TWO

After ascending a flight of stairs, they filed through a door into a long, formal corridor with ceilings Graham guessed were twenty feet high. Iris studied the camera as they walked, familiarizing herself with it and taking test shots of Graham pulling the case.

They followed Monsignor Roberto around a right turn, then through a door on the left, into what appeared at first to be a small chapel with five rows of simple pews and a side altar beneath a gilded ceiling. Although the left side of the space was a chapel, it occupied the southern transept of the cathedral, opposite the chancel. Next to the door they had just passed through, a monumental black door stood at the top of a small flight of black marble steps, framed with black marble pillars.

"That leads to the Cappella della Sacra Sindone, Chapel of the Holy Shroud," Don Arturo said, his voice hushed with reverence. "The Shroud used to be kept in a silver chest stored in that structure in the center of the apse, though you cannot see it well from here. The architect wanted the chapel the create the experience of rising from dark to light. That's why the entrance is black. Inside, the walls go from dark gray at the bottom to white at the top. The farther up you look in the dome, the lighter it gets."

Graham pictured images of the enormous stone edifice rising like a stalagmite toward the ornate, geometrically patterned dome.

"How long was it kept there?"

"Three hundred years," Monsignor Roberto said. "Until 1993. That is when the chapel became unstable, and a new home for the Shroud was built directly behind the high altar. A bulletproof glass case allowed the silver chest to remain in full view at all times. But the case was damaged beyond repair in the 1997 fire."

Monsignor Roberto turned away from the apse and moved toward the nave.

"There was a fire in 1997?" Graham asked.

Monsignor Roberto turned right at the end of the chancel and glanced back at Graham, brow raised in surprise, as he crossed in front of the high altar.

"That was when the chapel was being renovated. During the night, a fire broke out. The corridor we entered the cathedral from was completely destroyed. And there was much damage behind the altar where the Shroud was. Just over there." Monsignor Roberto pointed vaguely to his right.

"What caused the fire?"

"It was never decided. However, there is evidence the fire was deliberately set."

"Arson? That's terrible," Graham exclaimed, louder than he intended, the words reverberating through the church.

"As if the enemies of Christ tried to burn Him in effigy," Don Arturo said. "Since they could not defeat His body, maybe they thought they could defeat His grave clothes."

"And yet they could not even do that," Monsignor Roberto said. "One of the firemen saw the danger the flames posed to the Shroud. He chopped through the glass with an axe to reach the silver chest. It took a very great deal of effort to break through, and he risked his life to rescue the Shroud."

Don Arturo motioned to the same area behind the altar as it came more fully into view as they turned right again and moved along the north side of the chancel. "A cameraman from the news videoed the whole thing. It is very dramatic."

Graham looked into the empty space where the case had stood. Even without the fixture, the majestic appointments of the cathedral created a cumulative effect of otherworldly grandeur, a holy ambiance. Another imposing black door loomed before them—the second of the pair of entrances to the old chapel—but as he turned to the left, it was the north transept that commanded his attention.

The alcove was supported by ornate, corbeled marble pillars, and heavy red curtains had been pulled back to reveal what was inside. A wide table spanned the width of the space, part reception desk, part banquet table, and part altar, though it was none of those things. The rectangular box was encased in a fitted golden cloth and festooned with twisted strands of thorns.

A red altar scarf bisected the display, embroidered with a white cross, three nails, a crown of thorns, and a sign inscribed with INRI—an abbreviation of the Latin mockery Pilate ordered fixed on the cross: *Jesus of Nazareth, King of the Jews.*

Beneath the symbols, the word *Domine* was embroidered, part of a larger message across the edge of the golden cloth. *Tuam Sindonem veneramur, Domine, et Tuam recolimus Passionem.* Graham's quick, rough translation read: *We revere Your Holy Shroud Oh Lord and We Meditate on Your Passion.* As if there was any question about what was housed in the transept, a negative close-up of the face on the Shroud was displayed on the wall behind the case.

"This has been the home of the Shroud since 2000," Monsignor Roberto said, proprietorially. "Long enough for it to have already been renovated once."

"Is it in the same silver box that was rescued in the fire?" Graham asked.

"No. For the exposition of 1998, a modern conservation chamber was designed and constructed by a laboratory here in Turin that specializes in pressurized modules for use in the International Space Station. It enables the Shroud to be permanently stored flat. It was rolled when it was kept in the silver box. The new reliquary is sealed hermetically and filled with argon to create an inert atmosphere that will not damage the cloth. Temperature, air pressure, and humidity are precisely monitored and controlled. And the reliquary is, of course, fireproof. Even the cloth covering the reliquary is flame-resistant."

Graham studied the reliquary's display with new appreciation. "Is there a way to tilt it for expositions?"

"There is a second reliquary used for that. It is designed to be elevated above the altar." Monsignor Roberto motioned back toward the chancel. "There is far less strain on the cloth now that it is stored flat. And that suits our purpose for photography. Shall we begin?"

# FIFTY-THREE

Graham moved with practiced efficiency, extracting the copy stand from the case and assembling it in ten minutes. He did a quick test, verifying that without the black mat laid across the cradle frame, the camera could shoot through to the surface below.

As in the Cámara Santa, Iris worked discreetly as she documented the preparations, focusing more on the reliquary than Graham.

Don Arturo helped Monsignor Roberto reposition a prayer rail that sat across the opening of the transept, then removed the decorative thorns from the top of the reliquary. After Monsignor Roberto folded the altar scarf over the prayer rail, the two reverently lifted the gold cloth, revealing the massive box.

The cold, sharp lines of the aluminum shell mounted on a framework of angled struts had a utilitarian aesthetic that stood in stark contrast to the extravagant splendor of the cathedral. From where Graham stood, the glass pane looked like a rectangular pool of calm, black water.

"Impressive, is it not?" Monsignor Roberto said appreciatively.

"Incredibly impressive." Graham had already paused his preparations to get a first look at the reliquary even before the comment. "It's amazing that it takes something so high tech to store a two-thousand-year-old burial cloth of a carpenter."

"That is what the Catholic Church does that you Prot-estants fail to appreciate," Don Arturo teased. "We preserve tradition. I think of it as an ancient future."

"You should read more Calvin," Graham said. "You may be surprised how often he appealed to the early church fathers." He reached toward the table and made a smoothing motion. "If we lay the Shroud on top of the table, that should work fine."

"Unfortunately, that is not possible, Dr. Eliot," Monsi-gnor Roberto said. "We will not be opening the reliquary."

"Forgive me, Monsignor Roberto." Graham worked to keep his voice non-confrontational and free of the desperation he felt ballooning. "I'm afraid the glass will cause distortion. Photographing the Shroud through it may not give us the most accurate image to work with. Especially since it is so thick."

"Six centimeters," Monsignor Roberto said. "But it is of the highest quality. There will be very little distortion, if any. I understand your concerns, Dr. Eliot. However, we have only enough time to do the limited work Don Gustavo spoke to me about. It is not worth the effort or risk of removing the cloth from its environment. Although the Shroud rests on a removable table, it requires technicians to restore the argon, which requires more time than we have and would make more people aware of an examination we mean to keep secret. If your images are helpful, then we can begin to plan more photographs made under less urgent conditions. I hope you understand."

Graham struggled to keep the disappointment from his expression. Shooting the image through glass would hand skeptics a reason to dismiss whatever work that might be accomplished that night. He could hear Ben Steele's voice explain that the images matching meant nothing since one of them had been distorted by the glass that protected it. To Steele, it wouldn't prove a thing regardless of the claims about the quality of the glass.

Graham suppressed the thoughts, instead thanking the priest. "Monsignor Roberto, we have already tested your hospitality far too much. We are grateful you have allowed us here at all."

The monsignor tipped his head in a gracious bow.

Graham looked again at the reliquary, reevaluating his plan for setting up. "I'll have to set the copy stand directly on the glass and shoot down into the case. Do you have anything I can put under the base of the stand to protect the glass surface?"

"I have just the thing." Monsignor Roberto retrieved the altar scarf from the prayer rail. "Will this work?"

"Yes, good thinking," Graham said. "I think our only issue now is making sure we don't get any reflection or glare off the glass."

He stepped to the reliquary and peered into the case, as if at a viewing before a funeral. But when he saw the image on the cloth and stared into the faint face, it occurred to him he had it backward. He wasn't looking at death; he was staring into the very source of life itself. He scanned the front of the image and focused on the wound on the side, or rather the stains issuing from it. His insight from the previous day came back to him: that was the actual blood shed for the forgiveness of his sins. Right there in front of him.

"There are two areas with the most likely correspondence."

Don Arturo's voice cut through his musings, forcing Graham to blink himself present.

"One is here, on the dorsal side, with the back of the head. See this pattern of stains?"

Graham's eyes followed Don Arturo's finger to a series of dark drops and splotches. "Right. I see them."

"The butterfly stain on the Sudarium appears to correspond to this darker patch here," Don Arturo said, indicating a spot farther from the center. "It is easier for me to see if I squint."

Graham squinted, focusing on the area. "I think I see it. Not quite sure. It's hard to believe how much more detail is revealed when we look at a negative image of what we're seeing now."

"Imagine the first photographer's reaction when he was developing the negative," Iris said. "He must have been awestruck in the purest sense of the word."

Don Arturo's hand glided to the area around the face, stopping over a teardrop-shaped stain near a double curl of blood shaped like the numeral three.

"The other location that appears to correspond is here, on this blood stain. It is very similar to what is on the Sudarium and corresponds to the way it would be wrapped around the head."

"That one I see," Graham said.

Iris lowered her camera and moved next to Graham. She brought a hand to her heart as if making a pledge. An air of reverence descended on all three. This time it was Monsignor Roberto who broke the silent contemplation.

"We really should begin."

"Yes, sorry," Graham apologized. "I didn't think I would be so captivated by it."

"It's like Easter in November," Iris said.

Graham bent to make final adjustments on the stand. "Interesting, though, that the women who discovered the empty tomb didn't seem to have cared about either cloth, and now millions of people have stood in line for hours for just a glimpse of them."

Iris constantly repositioned herself, finding new angles for her photographs as Graham and Don Arturo lifted the copy stand and carefully set it onto the altar scarf in the middle of the reliquary. Graham spread out two lens cloths on the reliquary glass as a pad for the laptop.

He stared intently at the screen showing what the camera saw as he fine-tuned the position of the stand under Don Arturo's guidance. Once they were satisfied, he adjusted the lights, searching for a sweet spot that didn't cast a film of glare across the glass. The straw-colored cloth almost glowed on the computer screen in the dim transept.

"Señorita Elizondo," Monsignor Roberto said, "please no direct images of the Holy Shroud."

Iris looked puzzled before realizing she was pointing her lens at the Shroud. "Oh, yes. Sorry. I wasn't actually taking pictures of it. I was zooming in to see how well the image could be seen from close-up. It seems the closer you get, the less visible it is."

Monsignor Roberto nodded. "That is very true."

Graham placed a ruler and color bar beneath the camera, creating a partial frame to the image. "This will allow me to match the scale and the color with the photographs of the Sudarium," he explained to Monsignor Roberto.

He used the laser to focus on the cloth, then set the lens the exact same distance from the cloth as it had been from the Sudarium. Once he was satisfied, he followed the same steps as with the Sudarium, taking images with identical light settings, and working through them in the same order. Despite the small window of time, he worked more carefully than he ever had before, knowing it would be his only chance to do the work.

As he adjusted the lights for his final shots, Monsignor Roberto's phone rang. Graham ignored the sound but looked up as the monsignor turned rigid in wide-eyed alarm and scanned the cathedral.

"Fire!"

# FIFTY-FOUR

"Fire!" Monsignor Roberto repeated.

Graham's gaze darted around the sanctuary as if following Monsignor Roberto's echo. Beneath his instant panic, he registered Iris and Don Arturo also searching frantically as he pivoted around.

"Where?" Don Arturo barked. "I do not see any flames or smoke."

"I do not know where exactly," the monsignor said, urgently. "Security reported that a detector was triggered. The fire department is on the way. We do not have time to investigate. Let us go. Now! Quickly out the front door!"

Don Arturo scrambled for the golden cloth, whipping it to unfold it.

"*Cosa stai facendo?*" Monsignor Roberto called sharply, falling back into Italian before catching himself. "What are you doing?"

"Putting the cover back on. You said it was flame-resistant."

"Leave it! The reliquary will protect the Shroud. The cover is merely one less thing that will quickly spread the fire." Monsignor Roberto started to turn to leave but caught himself and spun back around. "Dr. Eliot, there is no time for that. We really must leave. *Immediatamente!*"

Graham had his arms wrapped around the base of the copy stand, preparing to carry it to the case. At the monsignor's words, he abandoned the stand, yanked the cables from the laptop, and stowed it in his backpack as he started to follow Don Arturo and Iris toward the nave.

Iris trotted in stutters, pausing to photograph the cathedral from new perspectives, apparently preserving the church in its last minutes before the latest conflagration damaged it.

Monsignor Roberto pushed forcefully through the doors at the back of the nave and led them through the narthex, then out the front door. The train scurried down the dozen steps into Piazza San Giovanni to be greeted by a flurry of red and blue emergency lights from fire engines and police cars. The vehicles formed a wall, lining the street bisecting the piazza. Graham flinched as he transitioned from the contemplative to the chaotic, an imbroglio of noise and light.

Graham clustered with the others near the bottom of the stairs, unsure what to do or where to go. An officer with the fire department sliced through the scene, locked on Monsignor Roberto.

"It's the fire chief," Don Arturo said, translating the rapid Italian for Graham. "He asked where the fire is. The monsignor said he was not sure because we never saw it."

Monsignor Roberto gestured to the rest of the group as he explained.

"He said someone from security called to report it to him. The guard knew we were there, in the sanctuary, and wanted to warn us immediately."

The chief lifted a palm, cutting off the monsignor, and motioned for several firefighters to follow him into the cathedral. Graham watched them disappear into the doors, then turned around to look deeper into the piazza. The commotion had already collected some onlookers on the fringe of the first responders. On the far side of the emergency vehicles, people stood on the stone benches, most with their phones out to record the scene.

Graham turned back to the facade of the cathedral, looking for smoke or flames. He realized that not only was he too close to have a good perspective on the building, but he felt in the way. "Let's move back and let these guys work." He placed a hand on Iris's shoulder as she looked up at the roof. "We'll see more from back there, anyway."

After moving deeper in the piazza to the fringe of spectators, Iris lifted the camera and scanned the area.

"I'm zoomed all the way in, but I don't see fire. There's no glow or flicker or anything."

Graham pointed to their right, toward the buildings bordering the south side of the piazza. "Let's move over there to get a better angle. I can't see the side windows from here."

As they picked their way through the increasing crowd, Graham frequently craned his head to the left, looking at the church until they had a good view of the southern wall.

Iris swept the scene again with her camera. "Still no fire. Maybe they—"

A violent shove from behind thrust Graham forward as his backpack was wrenched from his shoulder. He twisted around and spotted a man moving quickly through the crowd.

"Hey! That guy stole my backpack!"

"*Il ladro!*" Iris yelled.

Graham had instinctively used English, rather than the Italian word for thief.

"*Il ladro!*"

He pushed his way past the few bystanders who had noticed the scene, zigzagging through oblivious onlookers, following glimpses of the thief. The man cut between two fire engines and broke into a full run along the south wall of the piazza where only a few spectators stood.

"There he goes," Iris called from behind.

Graham shot through the same gap between trucks in time to spy the thief sprint into the arch of a vaulted passage at the southwest corner of the piazza. He slowed to a jog as he reached the opening, glancing behind columns for the backpack as he moved.

Another piazza opened on the other side. A sign identified the building encompassing the expanse as the Royal Palace. He looked to the right at the open end of the piazza and spotted the thief about a hundred yards away, running along the outside of the wrought-iron gate to the palace.

Graham broke into a sprint as the man passed into a colonnade along the wing of the palace, disappearing from view. He bolted out of the gate in time to glimpse the man duck to his left into another vaulted passage. Graham suddenly realized he was at the underpass they had driven through earlier, the same one leading to the Royal Gardens on the other side.

Seconds later, he emerged and stopped under a pool of light at the gate to the garage they had parked in. He held his head up, looking into the park as he hunched over, struggling to catch his breath. Beyond the perimeter of light, the park was cloaked in the shadows of a starless four a.m. He peered into the darkness for any sign of movement, listening for footsteps. Directly in front of him, headlights exploded to life and lunged forward.

Graham reflexively stepped back toward the gate, surprised by how quiet the car was as it sped up. He bent to see into the car, pivoting as it passed him, and saw the driver was holding up a phone to video him.

As the car entered the underpass, Iris rounded the corner, taking it too wide, running into the street. The driver swerved hard to the left, but there was no room to maneuver. The car slammed into a pillar dividing the lanes at the same time he saw a red beret fly into the air.

"Iris!"

Graham ran into the tunnel and was instantly bathed in light. And just as quickly, it vanished. Along with his consciousness.

# FIFTY-FIVE

Oblivion loosened its grip like a cognitive tourniquet slowly allowing sensory signals to reconnect. Information began to arrive in Graham's mind before he had regained his ability to process it, reducing it to impressions. The words he heard seemed to have had their letters jumbled, mere accidents of sound. The activity surrounding him was nothing more than motion without purpose. Vivid blue and red lights pulsed and whipped across the scene in manic psychedelia. Something was happening, something urgent. What that something was, however, eluded him, just beyond his reach.

It occurred to him he was on his back. On pavement. The hard surface felt more real than anything he was seeing or hearing—a sensation that gave him comfort. The discovery of a sense he could trust felt like progress. But toward what? The answer floated to the top of his muddled thoughts, coined from confusion: unmeaningless. The solid foundation and his awareness of it was unmeaningless.

He rocked forward, trying to sit up, but was immediately pushed back to the ground. The strong hands on his shoulders were useless to struggle against, and he abandoned his struggle almost instantly. The face above the hands came into focus and shook as it began speaking unintelligibly. A second face slid into view, next to the first. Familiar. A priest. Monsignor

Roberto.

"Dr. Eliot. Praise be to God. You are okay."

Graham's relief at understanding the words was almost as strong as the relief at the news he was okay. He moved his lips to ask what happened, but it came out as a moan, distant to his own ears. On the other side of the words, a tide of pain quickly rose in his head, almost blinding him.

"*Sai dove sei?*"

Graham stared back at the first face uncomprehendingly.

"Do you know where you are?" Monsignor Roberto asked.

*Italian.* First-face was speaking Italian. "Turin," Graham croaked. "My head is killing me."

"*Hai le vertigini?*"

Graham realized the first face belonged to a paramedic, only then noticing the uniform.

"Do you feel dizzy?" Monsignor Roberto translated.

"Yes," Graham said, trying not to nod.

"*La luce ti fa male agli occhi?*"

Graham thought he understood a few of the words and confirmed it through Monsignor Roberto's translation.

"Does the light hurt your eyes?"

"No. What happened?"

"You were struck by a car."

A gale of understanding followed the news, blowing away the thick mental fog. Impulsively, he tried to sit up again, and again was held down.

"You were knocked unconscious," the monsignor continued. "It is important to remain calm. You may have a concussion. But you have no broken bones."

"That was Iris," Graham said as if the others were the ones who were confused. "Not me. She was hit by the car. It swerved, but it was too close. Crashed into a column." He paused, frustrated that the explanation came out in unnatural clumps of words. "I ran to help. And then—I don't know what happened." He paused again as though the meaning of his words arrived after they had been spoken. "Where's Iris? Is she okay?"

The priest opened his mouth but found no words.

"Where's Iris?" Graham demanded.

Monsignor Roberto and the paramedic exchanged looks, then glanced past Graham, into the distance behind him. Graham took advantage of the distraction and sat up, twisting his body to look behind him.

The underpass was a surreal cavern of rescue workers and police illuminated by frenetic emergency lights. An ambulance waited ready just outside the tunnel, and another sat on the far side of the passage. A small, dark gray Renault blocked the tunnel at an odd angle, its left front badly damaged. Graham fixed detachedly on the name of the model—*Zoe*, the Greek word for life.

"The driver was trying to leave the scene after striking Signorina Elizondo." Monsignor Roberto spoke cautiously as Graham took in the scene. "When you ran to help her, the car must have backed into you. You are fortunate no bones were broken."

"What about Iris?"

"I am afraid she suffered much worse. She was thrown several feet. The emergency technicians are loading her into the ambulance now to get her the help she needs."

A figure in black cut through the unblocked side of the tunnel and jogged toward them. As he moved out of the shadows, Graham recognized Don Arturo.

"Graham! How are you feeling?"

"How bad is Iris?" Graham asked, ignoring the question.

Don Arturo glanced at Monsignor Roberto, then sighed. "She was running ahead of me. I saw her...I saw the accident." He lifted his hand, covering his mouth as if trying to prevent the words.

Tears welled in his eyes as he slid his hand to the back of his neck. "When I reached her, she was trying to speak, but she was barely breathing. It sounded like she kept saying papi, papi. She was staring past me, over my shoulder, as if someone was behind me. I immediately began to administer last rites. I was still praying when the ambulance arrived. By then, she had stopped trying to speak. She was lying there with her eyes open. The paramedics found no pulse and began CPR. I prayed while they worked to revive her. And by the grace of God, they were able to bring her back."

Cold liquid shock flooded through Graham, fear and relief warring on his face.

"A moment ago, as she was being placed in the ambulance, she locked her eyes on mine. There was something… different in them. And then it almost looked like she nodded. Very slightly. Just enough. I do not know how aware she was. But she is alive, my friend. She is alive."

"You need to go to the hospital as well, my friend," Monsignor Roberto said. "We must make certain your concussion is not more severe than it seems."

Graham's whole body began to shiver, releasing a veil of tears. He grasped Don Arturo's hand, letting go only when he was lifted into the ambulance.

# FIFTY-SIX

The chime announcing a text message sounded especially cheerful in the sterile monotony of the hospital room. He opened the app to see Alexander had sent a photo without an explanation. The image of people sitting at an airport gate had no apparent subject or importance, possibly taken accidentally. As he puzzled over the text, Alexander called, triggering Peter Gabriel's "Digging in the Dirt" ringtone.

He hit answer to hear the chorus of "Leaving on a Jet Plane" already in progress.

"'Jailhouse Rock'" would have been more Nashville," Graham said by way of greeting.

"I had 'Free Bird' ready to go," Alexander said, "but I just couldn't bring myself to do it. Some songs just don't need to ever be heard again."

"Agreed."

"Speaking of Nashville and planes, did you see the picture I sent?"

"I was looking at it just now trying to figure out why you sent it."

"Dr. E., you're losing your touch. Look again. Check out who's sitting at my gate."

Graham took the phone from his ear and studied the photo again. "The lady with the gray hair?"

"Not just any lady," Alexander said confidentially. "Emmylou Harris."

"Very Nashville," Graham chuckled.

"Now look who's on the other side of the chairs."

Again, Graham scrutinized the picture, focusing on a balding man with a guitar case resting against his body, smiling as he chatted to someone. "Is that Adrian Belew?"

"None other," Alexander affirmed admiringly. "Stunt guitarist extraordinaire. I'm tempted to go say hi to him. You know that guy's got a jillion stories. Zappa, Bowie, King Crimson."

"Talking Heads," Graham added. "And his own records are pretty great as well."

"Turns out he lives in Nashville," Alexander said. "I looked it up. It's where Frank Zappa discovered him."

"Between Adrian Belew and Emmylou Harris, it's like you have musical bookends—traditional on one side and avant-garde on the other."

"That's better than a rock and a hard place, which is where I was," Alexander deadpanned. "I'm glad to get out of here."

"Me too. I'm sorry I got you into this."

"None of this is your fault, Dr. E. It's not really anyone's fault. But I am still trying to get used to the idea that I was the last person to see Christopher King alive. I really liked the guy, the little I got to know him. Incredibly smart."

"I had the same impression," Graham said. "What happened was a tragedy."

"That's one of the things I feel guilty about," Alexander confessed. "I feel happier about going home after being suspected of murder than I feel bad about his death."

"You said it yourself, Alexander. It's not anyone's fault. But what happened to you was not right. Pure character assassination."

"They think *they're* free-thinking?" Alexander asked

rhetorically. "I've been thinking about nothing else but being free."

Graham laughed, as much from relief as amusement.

"Seriously, though," Alexander continued, "I know I didn't know King very long, but I suspect he would not have been cool with how I was treated. But I didn't call for any of that. How are you?"

"The CT scan didn't show anything, but they're keeping me in the hospital for now in case there is some brain swelling."

"A swelling, itching brain?" Alexander said. "Sounds like you're being diagnosed by Devo."

Graham barked a laugh in surprise. "Totally forgot about that song. Nice. Anyway, I told the doctor I could use a bigger brain because mine is so full of useless rock trivia like that. I wish I could clear my cache like on a computer to make room for more important things. But apparently brain swelling is not the same as getting a bigger brain. Hopefully, I'll be able to get home in a few days, although I doubt my airport gate will be as interesting as yours."

"I still don't know what happened exactly, Dr. E."

Graham shut his eyes, blocking out the hospital room, and retraced the train of events that led him here. So much had happened it was hard to know where to start.

"Still there?" Alexander asked.

"Yeah, sorry," Graham said. "Still trying to process it all."

"What was it like being that close to the Shroud of Turin?"

"Profound. I'm more and more convinced it's authentic. I'll tell you all about it when I get back. But we scanned it in the transept where it's kept in the cathedral. And we weren't allowed to take it out of its case."

"You shot the images through glass?" Alexander asked.

"Unfortunately. Best we could do. I was almost finished

when a security guard called the monsignor and told him there was a fire and we had to get out immediately."

"And you didn't see any smoke or anything?"

"Nothing. None of us did. But we left as fast as we could. The Monsignor made me leave the copy stand. He was hurrying us out so quickly that he wanted me to leave the laptop as well, but I grabbed it anyway. When we got outside, fire trucks and police were already in the piazza in front of the church.

"It was still dark, but people were starting to come and watch what was happening. We stood there looking for the fire or smoke. But still, there was nothing. No glow or anything. While we were standing with the rest of the crowd, someone stole my backpack with the laptop. Snatched it right off my back and took off running."

"What?" Alexander exclaimed. "Just some random dude in the crowd?"

"I didn't know who it was. I just started running after him. I chased him through the crowd, but by the time I got a clear view of him, he was pretty far ahead. I couldn't keep up. The guy ran into another piazza, in front of the old palace, then went around the building, through a big underpass, and into the Royal Gardens. That's where I lost him."

"What about the priest you were with? Did he chase the guy as well?"

"Don Arturo? Yeah, both he and Iris—you know, the art historian-translator I told you about—they were behind me. They tried to get someone from the police to follow them, but they couldn't be distracted from the fire by a petty thief. I was standing there catching my breath, trying to figure out what to do. Suddenly, this car came zooming out of nowhere, one of those electric ones that's almost silent. But as it passed, I could see the driver was videoing me with his phone."

"Videoing you? Why would he do that?"

"I wondered the same thing. Turns out it was Paco. The guy who made the SIFT videos of me."

"Wait, you're saying Paco was the guy who stole your backpack?" Alexander asked. "What did he think was in it?"

"He knew I carried my laptop in it. We talked about the equipment at one point. And he was obviously waiting for me outside the cathedral. He must've known the images from the Shroud were on it."

"Did you get it back?"

"Hold on, you haven't heard the rest yet," Graham said. "Paco videoed me as he went past. But as he was about to exit the other side of the underpass, Iris ran around the corner and stepped into the street." Graham choked on the memory and had to pause.

"Oh no," Alexander groaned, drawing out the syllables.

"Paco swerved to miss her, but there was no room. The car hit her and then plowed into a column in the underpass. I tried to run to her, but Paco tried to back out. He ran into me and threw me backward. I hit my head and got knocked out. Don Arturo said he saw Iris get hit. When he got to her, she was still alive, but when the EMTs arrived they couldn't find a pulse. They did CPR and resuscitated her. Don Arturo told me she's awake now and doing great for having so much internal bleeding. Ruptured spleen and some other things."

"What about Paco? Did they catch him?"

"He was gone when the police and EMTs arrived. The police searched the park and found him collapsed on the edge of a fountain behind the palace."

"What was he even doing in Turin in the first place?"

"Following us. Long story. But he wanted to get some more footage he thought could be embarrassing. It wasn't very hard to guess we were going to Turin when he saw Don Arturo pick me up at the hotel. When we got to Turin, we took backstreets to the cathedral and parked in an underground lot reserved for the cathedral employees in case he was watching for us. Not only was he watching, but he was parked by the back entrance, so he knew we were inside. The police found a burner phone in his car, and it's the one used to call in the fire."

"Paco was in the piazza waiting for you to come out?" Alexander asked.

"I guess he figured we'd take the closest exit in an emergency."

"But there was never any fire, right?"

"Right. Just the call. Again, I'm just guessing, but he probably counted on everyone at the cathedral being overly cautious because of the fire in the nineties. I doubt he was scheming to get the backpack. I think that was more of a crime of opportunity. Police said his phone had a video of us hustling out of the cathedral. That's probably all he was trying to get, just video footage.

"When I came out with the backpack, he grabbed it and made it to his car before I could catch him. And his car was dark gray, so I couldn't see it very well. When he drove past while shooting a video out of the passenger window, he was so distracted focusing on me, he couldn't react fast enough to avoid Iris when she came running around the corner. The best police can tell, after I got knocked out, Paco panicked and ran into the park to hide."

"That guy's going to jail for a long time," Alexander said.

"He's not going to jail at all," Graham said. "Paco didn't just pass out. He bled to death internally."

# FIFTY-SEVEN

"Dr. Eliot. What a lovely surprise."

Iris's normally hoarse voice had a more pronounced rasp, like a coarser grit of sandpaper, but was surprisingly strong. Her hair splayed across the pillow, becomingly unkempt. Graham cranked his wheelchair through the door and maneuvered to the side of her bed.

"I don't know how you do it, but somehow you make hospital garb look fashionable."

Iris raised her brow playfully. "It's Vivienne Westwood's latest line. Her *Fall* line."

Graham waited for the punchline under Iris's expectant gaze.

"Her *Fall* line," she repeated. "As in *It's a Knockout*. Come on, now, keep up. I'm the one with the *real* brain injury here."

Graham laughed, wincing through his headache. "Truthfully, how are you feeling?"

Iris sighed, and lifted her left arm, displaying it. "Truthfully, I can't say I'm going to miss the IV."

"I don't blame you," Graham said. "What do they have you on?"

"Something to help with brain swelling. Or rather to keep it *from* swelling." Iris flinched a smile, then raised her right elbow, revealing a thick bandage. "But what's really irritating is the gravel rash. It's mainly on my back. How about you?"

"I can't top you." Graham raised his hands in surrender, acknowledging her more severe injuries. "Nasty headache is the main thing. The CT scan was clear, but they want me to stay overnight just in case. I'm so glad you're okay. The world needs more Irises. Actually, there's only one of you. The world needs *this* Iris."

"You're sweet." Iris's smile melted into a pensive stare. "Graham, can I tell you something? Something that sounds crazy?"

"Of course."

"After I—" She abandoned the sentence, closing her eyes tight as if shutting off the words.

Graham waited a beat, then tried to help her ease into what he thought—what he hoped—was coming. "Don Arturo said you—"

Iris held up a hand for silence, then continued.

"When I was on the ground, I...I saw my father." She studied Graham's reaction while he processed the words.

He nodded understandingly, remembering his experience in the cistern beneath the Temple Mount after a bomb had exploded. He had told very few people how he seemed to have left his body, drifted above the surface of the pavement, and could accurately describe the scene in front of the al-Aqsa Mosque.

"Go on."

Iris squinted, cocking her head appraisingly. Graham was certain she wanted to ask what was behind his expression, but she continued her story.

"Papi looked...he looked just as he did when I was a little girl. And yet, there was something different. It was like he was unveiled somehow. As if all the worries and cares and disappointments were washed from him and he was perfectly at peace. I felt like I was seeing him—the real him—for the first time. I knew everything would be all right. And I just…let go." She composed an apologetic face, raised her hands a few inches off the bed, and let them drop in futility.

"I don't think that sounds crazy at all," Graham said, once again hearing Don Arturo's delivery in his own.

"I…it was like— Never mind." Iris shook her head. "I don't know what I'm saying."

Graham suspected there was more to the story but didn't press her.

"All I know is that when I woke, nothing was the same."

"What do you mean?"

Iris thought a moment, her eyes blindly searching the room. "I guess the best way to say it is that the door opened. The one in the dark. Somehow God isn't on the other side anymore. I feel Him with me, here. And He isn't just part of the room. He's transformed everything in it. Renewed it."

"That's incredible." Despite explaining the faith and answering objections to it thousands of times, Graham had never seen anyone come to faith. Many had, but he only learned about them after the fact. He had come to understand his role as a seed planter, not a harvester. Hearing Iris articulate her nascent faith was a rare privilege for him.

"You know the funny thing is that the Shroud had nothing to do with it. I mean, in my wildest dreams I never would have imagined I would get to see it up close in a private viewing and get to spend so much time with it. And now it doesn't seem nearly as important to me as it used to. I'm still fascinated by it, but whether or not it is authentic doesn't seem to have anything to do with faith."

Graham took her hand, squeezing it gently. "That is a wonderful place to be."

"Don't get me wrong," Iris said, "I'm still glad we have the pictures. It's so exciting to even play a small part in advancing research into the Shroud."

"Unfortunately, there's not much we contributed to in the end," Graham said.

"What do you mean? You have all those new pictures of the Shroud now, and they can be compared to the ones of the Sudarium."

Graham shook his head. "We didn't have Wi-Fi in the cathedral, so the images from the camera weren't uploaded to a cloud backup. They were only on the local drive of the laptop, but that's all."

"But you grabbed your laptop as we left. I saw you. And then Paco ran off with it. Surely it must be in his car."

"He took it with him when he left the crash. Police found it at the fountain near his body, but it was in the water. Completely destroyed it. The images can't be recovered."

Iris contorted her face. "It was all for nothing?"

Graham shrugged philosophically. "We did take the best images of the Sudarium ever made, if that's any consolation."

"I should have warned you sooner about Paco. I feel so guilty. About everything. I let myself be used. I'm so stupid."

"Please don't get trapped in those thoughts, Iris. Whatever wrong was done is forgiven and behind us. You and I are good."

"Thank you, Graham. But I have a confession to make."

"Don't say anything you don't want to. You don't owe me anything."

"I need to say it. I wasn't straight with you before. Paco— he stayed with me that night after the café. I never do that. But I thought we had this instant connection."

Graham leaned forward and took her hand again. "Iris, listen to me. You are in a safe place. Whatever mistakes were made, those are on the other side of your door now. You are forgiven. Now forgive yourself."

Tears brimmed in her eyes, and she placed her other hand over Graham's, enveloping it. "Thank you." The words came out in a quavering whisper. She took a big breath as she re-composed herself. "I have something else to confess."

Graham tried to protest but was cut off.

"Remember Monsignor Roberto telling me not to take pictures directly of the Shroud? Well, I kept my word. But I did find a loophole. I took some pictures of your laptop monitor. When you took that first shot, I watched you pull up the image of the Sudarium and do a test placement to make sure the scale and registration would work. And I zoomed in and got pictures of that."

A broad smile dawned on Graham's face. "You did?"

"I did the same for the dorsal side as well."

"Iris, you're a genius! But the camera was probably destroyed when you got hit."

"But the images were on the SD card. That should still work if we can pull it out."

"I'll get right on that," Graham said. "The test images *did* show remarkable correspondence. But you do know they could never be used as scientific proof because of the inherently low resolution of the image. It is a picture of a screen. The evidence could and would be called into question by skeptics."

"But it does affirm everything believers and advocates already believe," Iris said.

"In other words," Graham said, "we developed better evidence, but it doesn't change a thing."

# FIFTY-EIGHT

"Hey, guys, Ben Steele in Nashville with an update on the Christopher King situation. Police just announced King's death has been ruled an accident. During their investigation, they learned that one of the illusions he was performing utilized a chemical method that relied on cyanide. Police concluded that King was poisoned by contact while cleaning the device used to activate the cyanide.

"Police also announced that the person from Calbi University who had been the focus of the investigation has been cleared. According to our sources, it was this man's eyewitness account, as well as his knowledge of magic and King's methods, that enabled police to understand why cyanide was found in King's equipment.

"SIFT condemns in the strongest possible terms the threatening actions made against this man. Although the substance used to threaten him was harmless powdered sugar, the threat itself was reprehensible.

"Threats go against every principle the Scientific Inquiry of Free Thinkers stands for. SIFT is an organization devoted to critical thinking, the scientific worldview, and an evolutionary approach to ideas where the best ideas survive and thrive, and the weak ideas are abandoned.

"In a related incident, it was in pursuit of this ideal that we lost another one of our own last night, Paco Escarrà. Paco was the reporter who broke the story in Oviedo, Spain, a few days ago. He is the one who talked with Dr. Graham Eliot, the scholar who was there to view the alleged face cloth of Jesus. Paco was in Turin, Italy, developing a follow-up video for the story when he was killed in a single car accident.

"He was at the cathedral when a fire was reported in the church holding the medieval cloth many revere as the burial Shroud of Jesus. The emergency call came in just after four a.m. This was the scene he documented outside the front of the cathedral."

The video cut to handheld phone footage of the facade of the Saint John the Baptist Cathedral. First responders moved through the scene, tinted by the unnatural emergency lights, preparing for action once more was known about the fire. The sirens of the last vehicles to arrive added urgency to the atmosphere in lieu of smoke or flame.

"As you can see," Steele narrated, "the situation quickly turned chaotic. Now watch what happens right here. You can see the cathedral doors between these two fire trucks."

A graphic circle encompassed the spot for a moment, then disappeared.

"Notice this group of four figures quickly walking away from the entrance into the crowd. Then they turn around and just stop, blending in with the scene. Now, check out what you can see when the camera zooms in."

The enlarged view centered on a profile of Graham talking with Iris as she pointed her camera at the roof of the cathedral. As he turned to look back over his shoulder, the video froze on a clear shot of his face.

"Look who he found coming out of the cathedral. None other than Dr. Graham Eliot. It's almost a replay of what happened in Oviedo just a few days ago. What was Dr. Eliot doing at the home of the Shroud of Turin in the middle of the night? I'm not suggesting he had anything to do with the incident—which turned out to be a false alarm, by the way—but it does raise a number of other questions. Is the church hiding a secret investigation of the Shroud? Is that why Dr. Eliot was in Oviedo? If there is an examination underway, why is it secret? And if it's secret, will the church announce the findings? And if they do, how can the results be independently verified? So many questions."

Don Arturo reached across the hospital tray and paused the video on the laptop. "This is precisely the kind of publicity the church wanted to avoid. So many questions."

"Makes it easier to hit the target when you have conveniently loaded questions," Graham said, hitting the *play* button.

"As he left the cathedral, Paco shot another video from his car showing Graham Eliot again. What was he doing alone in the park behind the church at four a.m.? And it looks like he's out of breath. What was he running from? Or was he running *to* something? Again, so many questions. Take a look."

The interior of a car appeared, the view joggling as the phone extended toward the windshield. Graham spotted himself hunched over, hands on knees, looking into the park. He locked onto the headlights as they appeared, then stepped back when the car lurched forward. He grew larger in the frame as the car grew closer, the vantage point changing to the passenger window. The video froze to show Graham directly to the side of the car.

"I know the image is blurry, but it seems to me that Dr. Eliot looks a little defeated, almost like he'd been pursuing Paco for some reason. The rest of the video is too graphic to post, so I've stopped it here. It shows the car enter an underpass where Paco unfortunately lost control of the car. He suffered internal injuries and succumbed to them at the scene. Dr. Eliot and another person were injured.

"Our understanding is that Dr. Eliot was not seriously injured, and that the other person is recovering well. On behalf of SIFT and myself, we wish both a full recovery."

A slide show of images of Paco began to play as Ben Steele continued.

"In addition to his talents as a videographer, Paco Escarrà was also a painter, and had planned on submitting an entry to the Hocus Pocus Challenge. In light of the tragedy, SIFT has decided to end the Hocus Pocus Challenge and award the prize money to Paco's family. We still encourage everyone who planned to submit an entry to do so. We still want to collect as much information as we can about the Shroud so the truth can be known. That is, after all, the goal of SIFT. Now and always, be lovers of truth."

"How long do you think it will take the nurse to run in here to see what's going on with my blood pressure?" Graham asked, closing the laptop.

"When Iris recovers, maybe she can help you with a response," Don Arturo said.

Graham flinched a shrug. "Doubt it's worth it."

"I will arrange for the diocese to make a matching donation to Paco's family as well."

"That's very generous," Graham said. "Probably the last thing SIFT would expect."

"What better witness does the church have but to act charitably when it is painted as an enemy?" Don Arturo asked. "I do not want to assume Paco's family shared his views. But even if they did, this is the right thing to do."

"I agree. And I've told you before that I actually liked Paco very much. That's what makes everything that's happened so hard for me. I feel guilty for looking deceptive in his eyes. I think if we could have talked again, he would have understood."

Don Arturo put a hand on Graham's shoulder. "It is a

tragedy that never should have happened."

"I hope Iris does not watch it any time soon," Graham said. "I'm having some PTSD watching that. And I especially hope the unedited video doesn't get leaked online. It would devastate her. I am sure it's hard enough for her as it is."

"How do you think SIFT obtained the video?" Don Arturo asked.

"Paco's phone must back up his pictures and videos to the cloud. As long as the phone wasn't damaged in the crash and still had power, it would back up automatically. I guess SIFT had access to that. Maybe Paco's family gave them access."

Don Arturo nodded, considering it. "Makes me wonder what the first man to photograph the Shroud, Secundo Pia, would think if he saw this technology. Just over a hundred years ago, his camera was the size of a small refrigerator. It's hard to imagine what technology will be available a hundred years from now. Pia wouldn't have been able to predict having any of your equipment. Speaking of that, Monsignor Roberto is having your camera stand sent over."

"You know there is still time to pick up where we left off and take a few more images," Graham said, hopefully.

"I mentioned that to the monsignor, but the circumstances are no longer right. Especially after this video was posted. He fears there may be other journalists now, watching for signs of another secret examination. He doesn't want to risk anything that can embarrass the church or even be misrepresented. It is his way of protecting the Holy Shroud."

"That's very disappointing, but I do understand," Graham said.

Don Arturo's gaze caught on the table on the other side of the bed. "Is that the camera Iris was holding when she was struck?"

"The police returned it just before you came in."

"Surely, it is too damaged to be of any use."

"You're probably right. But I wanted the memory card out of it. If it's unharmed, then we might at least have Iris's images of our work last night. Want to take a look?"

Don Arturo scowled, as if offended he had to be asked. "Very much."

Graham ejected the SD card from the camera and inserted it in a USB adapter before plugging it into his laptop.

"Hey, it mounted. We might get lucky."

Several dozen images opened into a digital lightbox grid. The first few documented the route through the palace corridor and their entrance to the cathedral. Iris had also captured Graham's preparations and the unveiling of the reliquary. But the majority of the images were devoted to Graham's work.

"It is good to have a record of this," Don Arturo said, "however, I am not sure what value these are, other than proving that we were there."

Graham selected two images and opened them.

"Check these out. I did a quick overlay test of both the front and back of the Shroud image to see if our theory had any chance of working. I didn't know it, but Iris was behind me when I made the composite, and she took shots of the screen. Look at how well the two match."

Don Arturo pointed to the screen. "The teardrop shape under the three-shape on the Shroud appears to sync perfectly."

"And you can even see the contours of the three-shape in the main stain of the Sudarium when you know what to look for and where to look."

"Very compelling," Don Arturo said. "There is certainly correspondence to me. Look at the back. The pattern of blood on the two cloths is very similar. They could come from the same wounds. I think when Monsignor Roberto sees these, it will have a strong impact on him."

"I hope so," Graham said with a note of caveat. "They're

not high enough resolution to have the technical precision we wanted, but they are definitely enough to be a proof of concept. It's evidence that there's more evidence that can be developed. *If* the church would allow it."

Don Arturo bowed his head in acknowledgment. "At the very least, I pray it is enough to convince the monsignor and archbishop not to abandon the project entirely. We may not have done what we wanted to, but we did not fail."

He sat up suddenly, straightened by an epiphany. "It occurs to me that your medical treatment at the scene of the accident is an argument for the authenticity of the Sudarium."

"How could it possibly do that?"

A knowing smile lit Don Arturo's face. "The paramedic who treated you at the scene used a cloth of some kind to sop the blood in your hair so he could examine the wound."

"Okay, so how is that connected to the Sudarium?"

"It is a cloth used to collect blood." Don Arturo paused, meaningfully.

"I get that."

Don Arturo raised a finger. "And where is that cloth now?"

"I have no idea," Graham said. "He probably just threw it away."

"Exactly. But for some reason, the Sudarium of Oviedo was kept. What reason would there be to keep it if it was not authentic?"

"I see what you're saying, but it's not exactly compelling."

"Think about this, then," Don Arturo said, motioning to the cabinets by the door. "See that trash bin with the red biohazard bag by the sink?"

Graham looked across the room.

"Would you rummage through it looking for a used, bloody rag? Especially if it was another person's blood?"

Graham chuckled, seeing where the argument was going.

"No way."

"Exactly." Don Arturo nodded. "You would not even think about it. So why would anyone keep that filthy, bloody rag you saw? And why would they defend it with their own blood, and found a city to give it home, and a cathedral where it could be kept and honored? There is only one reason to make people do that. Authenticity."

"Or at least the belief in its authenticity," Graham qualified, "which is something different entirely. But I get your point."

"And I see yours as well," Don Arturo said. "I will miss our conversations, my friend."

"Are you kicking me out?"

"In a way. I have arranged for you to fly home from Turin tomorrow evening."

"If you were really my friend, you wouldn't consign me to one more day eating hospital food," Graham said. "It's like purgatory."

Don Arturo barked a laugh that seemed to surprise himself. "Well, if you want to test your theology and buy an indulgence, I'm sure that can be arranged."

Graham returned the laugh. "Even Luther would pay an indulgence to get out of the hospital early."

# FIFTY-NINE

"I know most of you here are familiar with the story of how Christopher King got his name. But since I was actually here at the Magic Castle that fateful night when he was christened with that stately moniker, I think it's only fitting to tell the story at his celebration of life service."

"Who is the guy making the speech?" Graham whispered to Alexander. "Never heard of him."

"A consultant for a lot of illusionists as well as TV shows and movies. He doesn't do much performing himself." Alexander kept his eyes forward, focusing on the story as the man continued.

"This was—oh—about thirty-five years ago. The magician formerly known as Josh Smith and I were sitting on the red velvet settees inside the entrance of the grand salon. And as we were sitting there trading tricks, Dai Vernon—the Professor himself—sat down with us. We were just kids, barely old enough to get in this place, and we started trying to impress him, which was of course nearly impossible.

"Josh had been working on a sleight he had come up with on his own, and he demonstrated it for the Professor. He showed all four kings spread in a fan. Then he collapsed the fan, turned the packet facedown, and tapped the back. When he turned the packet faceup, there was only one card: a king with the pips of all four suits on it. Spades, hearts, clubs and diamonds; one in each corner.

"The Professor watched the whole thing while puffing on one of his Partagas. He pulled his cigar out of his mouth and said, 'Hey, kid, that's pretty good. What do you call that?'

"Josh said, 'I don't know. I'm still trying to think of a name.'

"The Professor said, 'What do you call yourself?'

"And Josh flashed that charming smile of his and said, 'I'm still coming up with that name, too.'

"The Professor glanced at me to see if it was a joke. I shrugged, and he turned back to Josh and said, 'You don't know your own name?'

"And Josh said, 'Well, right now it's Josh Smith.'

"And the Professor said, 'You're right. You need a new name. Sounds like you're rinsing your mouth out at the dentist.' He leaned back, stared into the ceiling, took a couple of puffs on his cigar, and suddenly snapped his fingers. 'I got it. How about King? You could even use the king with the four suits as a calling card.'

"Josh thought about it for a moment, then said, 'I like how that sounds. And I like how it looks.'

"The Professor said, 'The most important thing is that it has meaning. You're the king. Tells people you have mastered the art. The spade tells people you're a fighter. You defend the art and all that you believe in. The heart says you love what you do, and you love sharing it with other people. The clubs are clovers, grown from the earth, signifying perseverance, hard work, and that you reap what you sow. And the diamond stands for purity and excellence.'

"Josh sat nodding slowly as the Professor explained the idea. Then he said, 'I don't know. Josh King? Sounds like a cash register.'

"The Professor said, 'Let's include the suits in your first

name. Put them in *Chased* order like a magician stacks a deck. *C.H.S.D.* Clubs, hearts, spades, diamonds. The name *Chase* doesn't work because you want to be a leader, not a follower.'

"Josh said, 'Not to mention it sounds too much like *chaste*.'

"The Professor actually laughed at that one. Then he looked up into the ceiling again as he sounded it out a few times. Started out sounding like *kissed*. Finally, he said, 'How about Christopher? Christopher King.'

"And that, ladies and gentlemen, is how the Castle gave birth to the king."

Thirty minutes later, Graham was once again in The Dante Dining room, this time with Alexander.

"So how much of that story about King's name do you think is true?"

"No idea," Alexander said. "I do know Dai Vernon did mentor King, though. Other than that, who knows?" He poked the air with his fork in the general direction of the theater. "The magician who told that story is probably the only one who knows at this point. Or there may be some obscure letter or notebook with the whole story in the library here."

Graham paused, "There's a library here?"

"Oh yeah." Alexander drew out the words for emphasis. "Several thousand books on magic, many of them quite rare. I keep hoping they want to digitize them so I can get in on that action." His smile disappeared as he saw Graham's expression. "What's wrong, Dr. E.?"

"Ben Steele just walked in." Graham concentrated on his food, acting unaware. Almost immediately he had to drop the pretense as Steele approached the table.

"Dr. Eliot, I'm Ben Steele. So nice to meet you."

Graham shook his hand, awkwardly swallowing his food to speak. "Good to meet you in person finally. This is Alexander Pearl."

"Of course." Steele renewed his smile, shaking hands again. "Alexander, I owe you an apology. When I broke the news about the cyanide, it was supposed to be a scoop. Nothing more. It never crossed my mind someone would threaten you because of it. Please forgive me for being reckless and naive."

"I appreciate that," Alexander said. "I really do. I'm sure every cause has been misrepresented by people claiming to be true believers."

"You're too gracious." Steele bowed his head as he pressed his palms together in front of his chest. "It is a shame you did not get to develop your friendship with Christopher. He was a good man."

"I feel the same," Alexander sighed. "And thanks for inviting us to attend the memorial."

"I hope no one makes you feel uncomfortable. I was hoping that by inviting you it would go a long way to heal all the confusion and misperceptions that got exaggerated online. A good faith gesture like the donation you made, Dr. Eliot, to Paco's family. Very generous. I know they were grateful."

"It was the least I could do. But I *do* have a request."

"Certainly," Steele said. "What's that?"

"Watch the video from Turin you posted again and pay attention to my backpack."

"Okay." Steele bent the word into a question. "What am I looking for?"

"In the footage of me in front of the cathedral, it's on my back. But in the footage Paco shot from his car, you'll see it's not there."

Steele frowned, apparently replaying the scenes in his mind. "Where did it go?"

"Paco stole it off my back while we were looking for the fire. That's why I followed him. I was trying to get it back. I didn't even know it was Paco until after I regained consciousness. He wanted the laptop with the images of the Shroud we'd just taken."

"I hope you were able to recover it."

"That depends on what you mean. The police found it near his body, but he had dropped it into a fountain. Completely underwater, so it was destroyed."

Shame and embarrassment clouded Steele's face, flickering in micro-expressions. "I don't know what to say, Dr. Eliot. That certainly changes things. And it does make sense of the questions I had. I wasn't trying to— It appears I may owe you an apology as well. I am so sorry. I will issue a retraction as soon as I can."

"I'd appreciate that. I'd make a rebuttal video, but yours are so much better than anything I do."

Steele nodded a melancholy half-smile. "May I ask if your examination of both cloths added to the evidence for or against authenticity? Off the record, now."

"I don't mind going on the record." Graham pushed himself back from the table. "I suppose it depends on your philosophical presuppositions. Everyone who believes in the authenticity of the Shroud and the Sudarium will interpret what little data we were able to come away with as corroboration. And yet, that same data can be used to confirm doubt in the Shroud. It's a wash. At best, what we did may have sown the seed for future work, but that's all."

"Thank you for sharing that." Steele spoke as he completed typing the comments into a note file on his phone. "On or off the record, I promise to give you a heads-up if we publish it."

Graham playfully pointed an accusatory finger. "I'll hold you to it. Or you'll feel the wrath of my social media powers."

Steele chuckled. "Duly warned. I may not be a Christian, but I can't deny the Gospel was the first message to go viral. A dozen poorly educated guys from the sticks spreading their message all over the Roman Empire? C'mon."

"That's funny. Iris said something similar about Martin Luther's Ninety-Five Theses."

"And how is your friend?"

"Considering that her heart stopped for a few minutes, she's doing incredibly well. Her only real injuries are abrasions and bruises along with the concussion."

Steele let out an incredulous puff of air. "Miraculous."

"Careful there," Graham admonished. "Don't say that too loud around this crowd."

"Listen," Steele said after the laughs died out, "I know that we disagree on almost everything in our worldviews, but I want you to know I've been impressed by how you comported yourselves. Both of you. You are credits your faith, and I wish there were more like you."

Graham smiled modestly. "If you're ever up for making your case in front of one of my classes, you're welcome anytime. I'll give you the floor. No debate. But be warned: they have some pretty sharp critical thinking skills. You may be surprised."

"Thanks for the offer, Dr. Eliot. I may just take you up on that sometime soon."

"I like Ben Steele way better when he's not in front of a camera," Alexander said.

"I've heard some people have a completely different personality when they get on stage or in front of a camera," Graham said.

As he spoke, a server carrying a tray of desserts passed the table. A tube of cannoli dusted in powdered sugar caught Graham's eye. He decided against pointing it out as a joke but turned back to the table to meet a comically pained expression on Alexander.

"Don't even go there," Alexander deadpanned. "Not to change the subject, but do you think you'll ever get to go back and finish the job in Turin?"

"I don't know. I don't even care if it's me. I just hope someone gets to do it right."

"Me too. Especially, if that someone is me." Alexander flashed a wry smile. "I'll tell you what frustrates me the most is to have the technology and ability to study the Shroud in more depth, but not have access to it. It's like the Shroud is a lock and the Sudarium is a key to understanding it in a whole new way. And yet the key can't be used because it's hundreds of miles away."

"You have to keep it in perspective." Graham planted his elbows on the table and knitted his hands together. "Let's say the key does unlock the mystery, and that we can somehow conclusively prove the Shroud is the burial cloth of Jesus. It doesn't prove that what Jesus taught was true. There will always be a reason for unbelief because reasons are always reasons of the heart. Anything can be twisted to say something it doesn't. Jesus was betrayed with a kiss, after all."

"Just like Houdini's Rosabelle code," Alexander said. "That code Houdini's widow hoped to hear at the seances to see if he could make contact from the other side."

"What was the code again?"

"It actually fits our research perfectly. *Answer. Tell, pray, answer. Look. Tell. Answer, answer. Tell.*"

"And what's that spell?"

Alexander opened his palms as if the answer was obvious. "Believe."

# AFTERWORD

Despite the best efforts of scientists—whether true believer or skeptic—the origin of the image of the man on the Shroud of Turin remains a mystery. And although there is a mountain of evidence supporting its authenticity, there is just enough room for doubters to feel justified. Add to that the controversy surrounding the radiocarbon dating results, and you have a recipe for intrigue.

Enter the Sudarium of Oviedo. For 1,300 years its stains have offered silent corroboration. Silent because the two cloths have never been in the same location. But with the advent of photography and the possibility of multispectral light revealing areas of congruence invisible to the naked eye, it seems like the Sudarium could contain compelling evidence for a date of the Shroud that is at least 500 years earlier than the radiocarbon result. The prerequisite for any scientifically rigorous comparison, however, is a set of images of each artifact taken with the same photographic equipment under the same conditions. The existing images do show correspondence, but the different methods and equipment open the door for the results of any comparison to be questioned.

My interest in the Shroud of Turin goes back decades. But with the vast and ever-growing body of material on the topic, it is an overwhelming task to stay current on the research (a task I am admittedly not equal to). And when it comes to sources of information on the Shroud, it's not always evident how to discern the credible from the crackpot. I needed a guide through the jungle of data—or at least someone to point me in the right direction—and I found one in Dr. Gary Habermas.

I had the privilege of studying the historical evidence for the Resurrection under him, and one of the topics he unpacked was the Shroud of Turin. This was my introduction to the credible scientific and historical evidence I had always wanted to know. And it left me wanting to know more.

Fortunately, Dr. Habermas has co-authored two books on the Shroud with Kenneth Stevenson, the man who served as the public relations liaison for the 1978 STURP team. *Verdict on the Shroud* and *The Shroud and the Controversy* are essential reading for anyone interested in the Shroud.

On Gary's recommendation, I contacted Barrie Schwortz, the documentary photographer of the STURP team. He also is the webmaster of Shroud.com, the most comprehensive repository of credible Shroud research anywhere. He graciously helped me by providing images as well as taking the time to tell me about the STURP expedition.

Essential to my research was *The Shroud of Turin—A Critical Summary of Observations, Data, and Hypotheses* by Dr. John Jackson, leader of the STURP team and founder of the Turin Shroud Center of Colorado in Colorado Springs. The systematic organization and straightforward presentation of the scientific and historical data is both scythe and sieve for separating the wheat from the chaff. He also provides a classification system for each piece of evidence, distinguishing between data that is firmly supported, generally supported, and disputed. It is Jackson's radiation fall-through hypothesis that is to date the best explanation for the image on the Shroud.

Thomas J. Phillips of Harvard's High Energy Physics Lab proposed the neutron flux phenomenon as the reason the radiocarbon dating came back with an unexpected date.

Phillips's proposal is part of Marc Antonacci's alternate fall-through hypothesis detailed in his book, *Test the Shroud*.

In the world of Shroud research of the last fifty years, all roads eventually lead back to British historian Ian Wilson. Beginning in the early 1970s, his work has contributed significantly to the pre-European history of the Shroud, while also popularizing the scholarship devoted to it. In particular, his development of the iconographic theory (which did not originate with him) is one of the most fascinating lines of evidence to me.

It was in the course of wading through material on the Shroud that I stumbled across the Sudarium of Oviedo. The relic was completely unknown to me, and I was immediately fascinated by it. However, I quickly discovered there is very little information available about it. And that makes me all the more grateful to the work of Dr. Mark Guscin.

Guscin's book, *The History of the Sudarium of Oviedo*, is the definitive work on the cloth, and includes the first translations of Pelayo's history of the Sudarium into English. He, too, personally answered many of my questions. *The Invisible Thread* would not exist without his research.

These were the primary resources that led to additional trustworthy sources and warned me off others. So armed, I was equipped to wade into the scads of theories, historical documents, and conflicting traditions.

The scientific and historical evidence in the book has been presented accurately to the best of my understanding. Any mistakes are mine, not the researchers associated with them. The suggested techniques proposed in the book for recreating the image on the Shroud have all been attempted. However, no result has ever replicated all of the features of the image. Jackson's *Critical Summary of Observations, Data, and Hypotheses* includes a helpful chart enumerating the features on the Shroud along with a checklist indicating which features are accounted for in each method.

As for critics of the Shroud, the most prominent is Dr. Walter McCrone, a world-class microscopist. With Jackson's permission, he was given access to samples collected from the cloth, including areas containing blood. Surprisingly, he reported not finding any blood, but rather ocher pigment. His work contradicted the evidence collected by blood experts and has been a source of confusion. McCrone's claim is a minority report but is heavily relied on by Shroud skeptics.

One of the surprising discoveries I made in my research is that several Shroud critics have careers or backgrounds in magic. Although I have far more interest in magic than talent, I am a member of the International Brotherhood of Magicians, so this was a fantastic twist that allowed me to incorporate another passion of mine into the story. The best-known magician-skeptic was James Randi, better known as the Amazing Randi.

Randi carried on Houdini's mission of exposing frauds who used the methods of stage magic to claim to have real powers in order to exploit people. That noble goal expanded its scope to become a complete skeptical worldview leading to the creation of the Committee for Scientific Inquiry and the James Randi Educational Foundation, an organization devoted to scientific inquiry and critical thinking. Superstitions, legends, ghost stories, paranormal activity, and religious phenomenon all were targets of his criticism—most with good reason. Shortly before his death, Randi traveled to Turin to the Shroud exposition.

It was Randi who famously exposed televangelist Peter Popoff on *The Tonight Show*. One of the members of his team, Banachek became one of the top mentalists in the world, as well as consultant to other magicians. A few years before Randi's death in 2020, Banachek became the president of the James Randi Educational Foundation. His podcast, *Banachek's Brain*, is a fantastic introduction to the world of skepticism.

One of the most vocal skeptics of the Shroud is Joe Nickel, a decorated paranormal investigator who has written a book against the authenticity of the Shroud as well as a book at taking a critical look at all relics related to Jesus, including chapters on the Shroud and the Sudarium. He, too, has a background in magic, and was encouraged in his current work by Randi.

The trick of making an image appear on an apparently blank piece of cloth by misting cyanide on it is a real trick—one I hope I never see performed.

Houdini's Rosabelle code is also real, and his widow, Bess, did hold seances every Halloween—the day of his death—hoping to hear the medium spell the code word *Believe*. When she did hear it, the explanation was simple. The code had been published the year before in a biography, and the medium befriended Bess beforehand and learned the code word.

The sources for the Shroud's existence and history in Constantinople and Edessa, as well as the possible involvement of the Templars, are all given in the context of the story, so they won't be repeated here. All are real claims, though the histories they tell often contradict each other at points. Also, some of the elements—the letter from Jesus, for example—are clearly legendary.

Magician Kevin King shared the detail of Dai Vernon's preferred cigar. He also let me peek behind the curtains to see the backstage area of the Carter the Great theater at the House of Cards.

Lastly, thank you to Alan Parsons for graciously granting permission to quote lyrics from "Eye in the Sky." Incidentally, my research trip to the Magic Castle was done after spending the day at a recording session in Hollywood watching Alan record strings for a song I wrote with him and Todd Cooper called "Fare Thee Well." That was a day to remember. You can hear the result on his album, *From the New World.*

# ACKNOWLEDGMENTS

I am indebted to Cyndy McRae, Jamie Brandenburg, Jay Hollis, Eric Smith, and Boh Cooper for reading early drafts and offering helpful feedback. Thank you for still speaking to me after letting me experiment on you with a mixture of the Shroud of Turin and magic tricks with a little bit of Rock trivia sprinkled on top.

I am thankful every day for WhiteFire Publishing's David and Roseanna White's belief that Graham should continue to stumble into new adventures. They are pictures of graciousness and integrity.

Lastly, thank you to Alan Parsons for graciously granting permission to quote lyrics from "Eye in the Sky." Incidentally, my research trip to the Magic Castle was done after spending the day at a recording session in Hollywood watching Alan record strings for a song I wrote with him and Todd Cooper called "Fare Thee Well." That was a day to remember. You can hear the result on his album, *From the New World*.

# PICTURE GUIDE

The Magic Castle, and its secret entrance. (Photos: Doug Powell)

Cafe Gijon, Madrid, Spain. (Photo: Doug Powell)

Oviedo Cathedral, Oviedo, Spain. (Photo: Doug Powell)

Outside and inside the Camara Santa, Oviedo Cathedral.
(Photos: Doug Powell)

Cathedral of St. John the Baptist, Turin, Italy,
home of the Shroud since 1578.

The side chapel with the reliquary containing the Shroud.

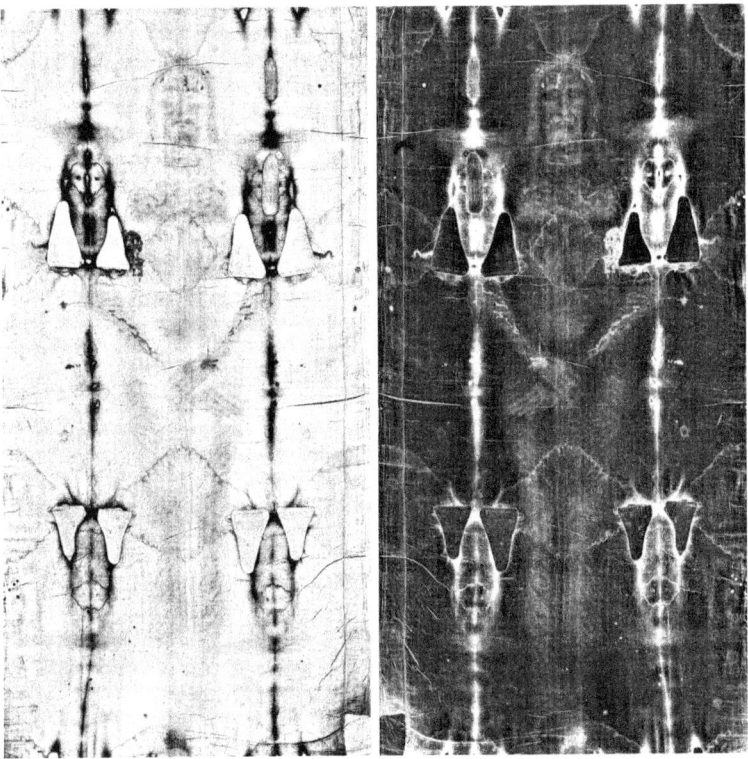

Positive and Negative images of the front side of the body on the Shroud taken by Guiseppe Enri in 1931. The contrast has been increased to emphasize the body image.

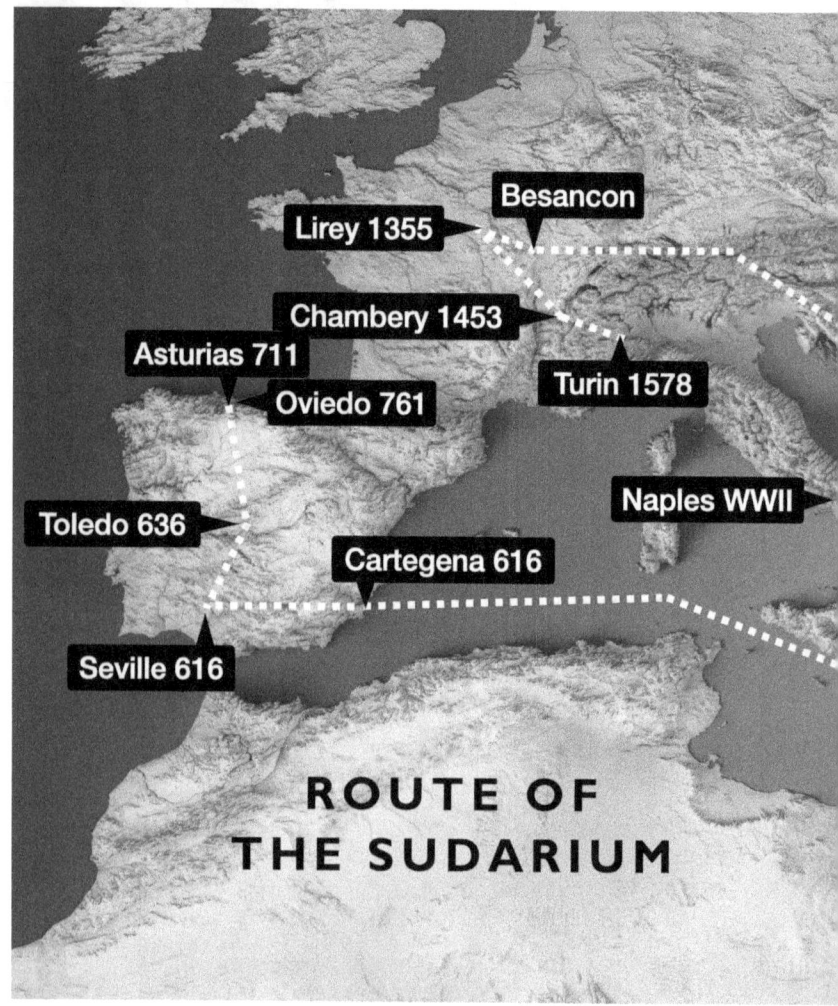

Besancon

Lirey 1355

Chambery 1453

Asturias 711

Oviedo 761

Turin 1578

Naples WWII

Toledo 636

Cartegena 616

Seville 616

ROUTE OF
THE SUDARIUM

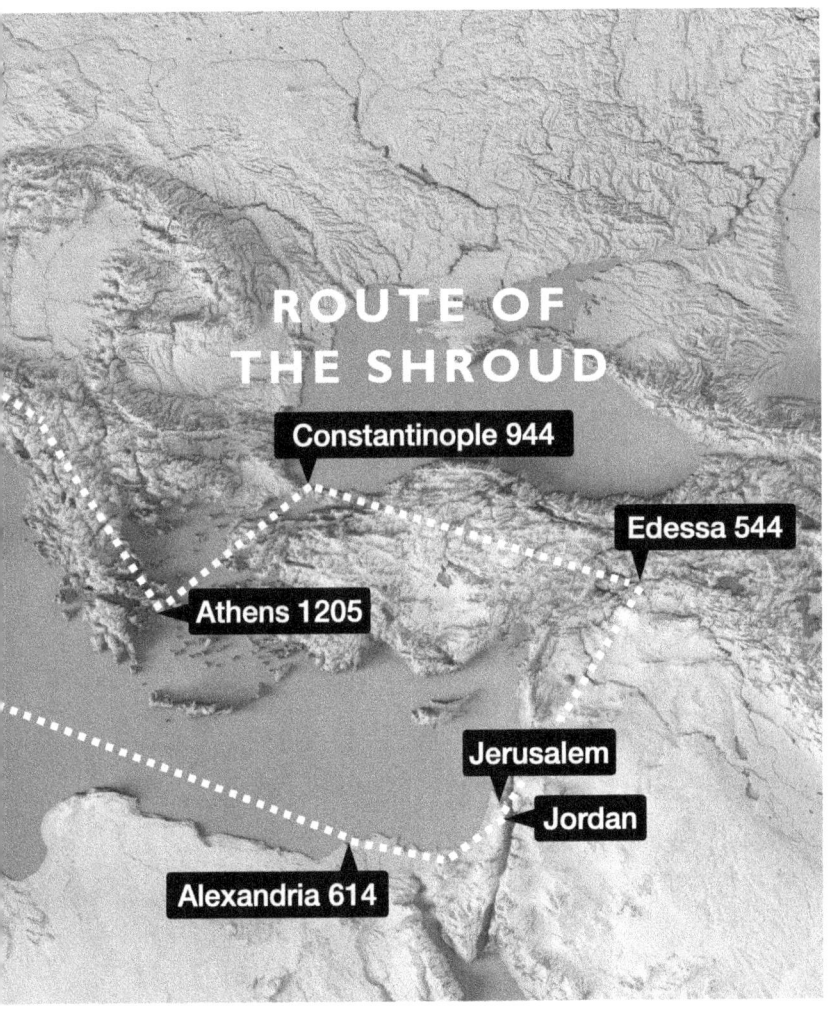

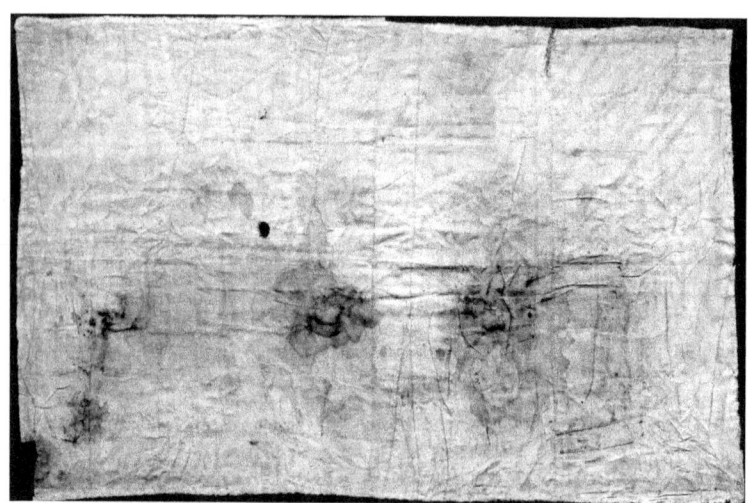

Above: The Sudarium of Oviedo.
Below: Negative image of the face on the Shroud of Turin.

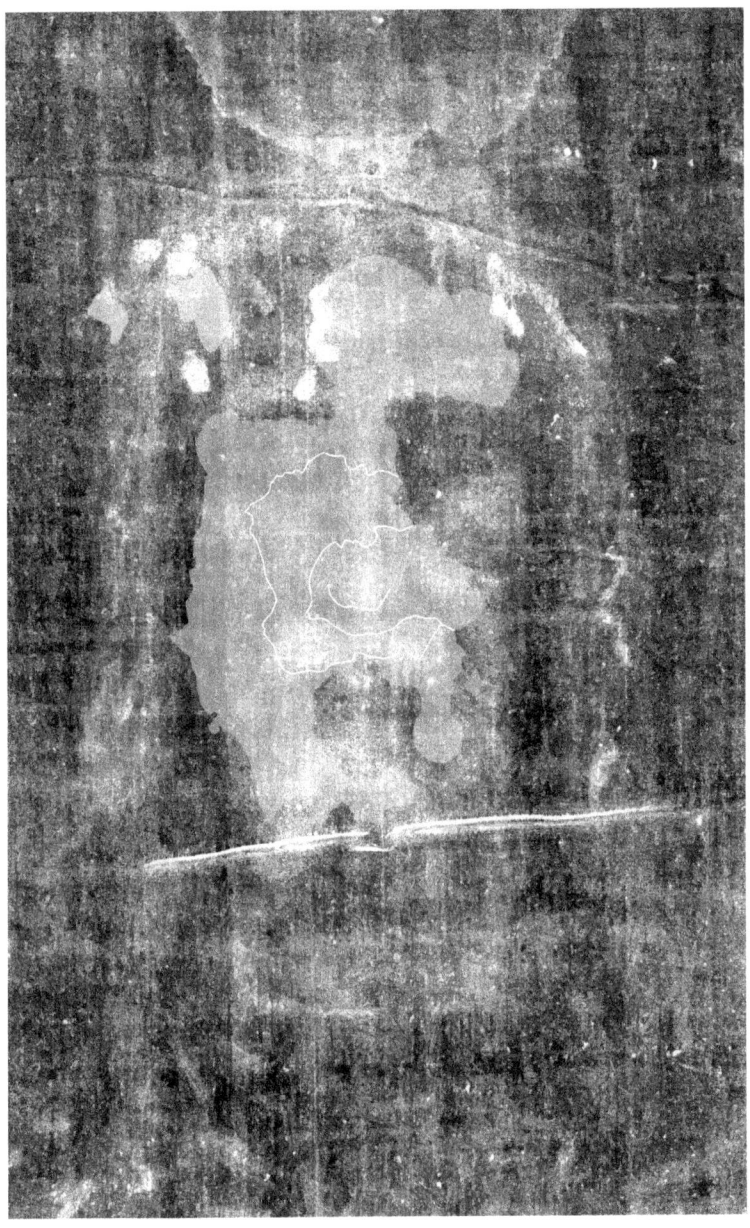

The main stain of the Sudarium overlayed on the face on the Shroud, demonstrating a striking correspondence.

Above: Some of the earliest images of Jesus, ranging
from the 2nd century to the early 6th century.

Below: Byzantine icons beginning in the mid 6th-century.
At least 15 unusual features (such as the "v" shape betweenthe eyes and the
cleft in the beard) are shared by the images.

Above right: Christ Pantocrator icon c.550. Above left: The Shroud face.
Below: Shroud face overlayed on the Christ Pantocrator icon.

See these and more images in the online photoguide at:

grahameliotseries.com

Follow the latest Doug Powell news at:

dougpowell.com